WHITE-OUT

Also by the Author

Walkabout

*A River Ran
Out of Eden*

*My Boy John That
Went to Sea*

WHITE-OUT

James Vance Marshall

Copyright © 1999 by Donald Payne

First published 1999 by
Souvenir Press Ltd,
43 Great Russell Street, London WC1B 3PA

First published in 2000 in the United States by
Soho Press, Inc.
853 Broadway
New York, NY 10003

Library of Congress Cataloging-in-Publication Data

Marshall, James Vance, 1924–
       White-out / James Vance Marshall.
            p.   cm.
        ISBN 1-56947-224-6 (alk. paper)
        1. Combat survival—Fiction.   2. World War, 1939–1945—
Antarctica—Fiction.   3. British—Antarctica—Fiction.
4. Antarctica—Fiction.   I. Title.

PR6066.A9 W47 2000
823'.914—dc21

                                                        00-034423

10   9   8   7   6   5   4   3   2   1

'White-out (i) a dense blizzard, especially in polar regions; (ii) condition in which features are confused and indistinguishable' (*Concise Oxford Dictionary*).

Contents

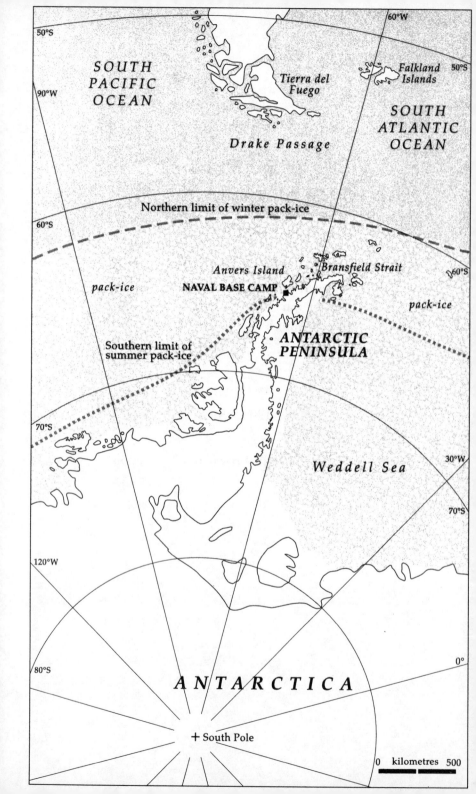

ANOTHER COUNTRY

'The past is another country'

The sealed envelope was brought to my consulting rooms in the Royal Naval Hospital, Haslar, by special messenger. I had no premonition as I opened it that this would be my introduction to one of the most difficult cases I ever had to handle. Inside the envelope were medical records and a memo from a colleague at the Admiralty. The memo read:

Admiralty, S.W.1
2nd April, 1944

Hugh

We have a case to refer to you as a matter of urgency.
Lt James Lockwood, RNVR, is the sole survivor from a Naval detachment recently deployed in the Antarctic. His survival was little short of a miracle, and he is still suffering considerable physical disability as a result of his privations. He also appears to be suffering from amnesia.
His duties in the Antarctic were classified 'Most Secret', and were of considerable, repeat considerable, importance. Their Lordships are therefore anxious to ascertain:

(i) Whether his amnesia is genuine.
(ii) Whether he is likely to recover from it and be able to recall all that took place during his time on the Antarctic Peninsula.

Your judgement on these points would be much appreciated.
Lt Lockwood's medical records and basic information about his

assignment are enclosed. May I remind you that the latter is classified 'Most Secret'.

Yours ever

Jim
(Surgeon Commander J.S. Sinclair, RN.)

I was intrigued. I was too busy that day during working hours to give the matter much thought; but after my last consultation I stayed on in my rooms to have a look at Lockwood's medical records and the file on his assignment—I would have preferred to take them home and read them at leisure, but classified information was not allowed out of the hospital. So I told the duty sickbay attendant I was working late, asked him to bring me a cup of the canteen's notorious *ersatz* coffee, switched on my reading lamp, and settled down to find out why this Lt Lockwood and his 'Most Secret' duties merited a special messenger and so much fuss.

It turned out to be quite a story.

Young Lockwood had been part of a ten-man Naval detachment who had been landed on the Antarctic Peninsula in January, 1942. Their orders had been to set up a base from which they could transmit daily weather reports and forecasts; these, it was believed, would facilitate operations (and in particular the passage of convoys) in the southern hemisphere. Unfortunately, after they had been operating successfully for about a year a German U-boat must have picked up their transmissions, homed in on their base-camp and totally destroyed it. There were three survivors: the commanding officer who was so seriously injured he died shortly afterwards, and Lt Lockwood and Petty Officer Ramsden, both of whom had been out of camp on a sledging trip at the time of the attack. Ramsden also subsequently died, leaving young Lockwood alone, with winter approaching, virtually no food, and no way of reaching or communicating with the outside world. He was the only living human being on an entire continent and it seemed impossible for him to survive. However, he apparently built himself a shelter, and somehow and against all the odds managed to live through the terrible Antarctic winter. Eventually, when the ice melted in the spring and a ship was able to get through to him, he was rescued. Not surprisingly, his experiences had left him physically and mentally shattered. He seemed also to have partially lost his memory; for according to his medical records he could recall little of what happened during his winter ordeal, and virtually nothing of what happened prior to the destruction of the detachment's base-camp.

There were things about this that I found a bit puzzling: not least why the Admiralty should regard it as so urgent. However, I told myself to put it out of my mind until Lockwood himself arrived at the hospital. This turned out to be sooner than I anticipated. For first thing next morning I got a phone call to say that my afternoon consultations had been cancelled, and the young lieutenant was to see me at 2 p.m.

*   *   *

He was a tall man: six foot exactly according to his records, but looking more because he was so pitiably thin. I could see that he had probably been good-looking once, and would, in time, probably be good-looking again; but right now he was a physical disaster. He moved stiffly, with a limp; his muscles had wasted away; his teeth were loose, his skin was blotched and discoloured by the aftermath of scurvy; his hair was snow-white, and he had the haunted eyes of a man who has seen things he would prefer to forget. My instinct warned me he was not likely to be an easy patient. We shook hands.

'Please take a seat, Lt Lockwood,' I said, adding, as soon

as he had got settled, 'now what have you been up to, in the Antarctic?'

'I'm afraid,' he said, 'I can't remember.'

'But you can surely remember *something*! The cold? The ice? Your friends? The hut you lived in?'

He shook his head. 'Sorry.'

I got the impression he wasn't telling me the truth: or at least not the whole truth. 'I do understand,' I said gently, 'that opening old wounds must be painful for you. I really do regret that. But believe me, in the long run it helps.'

'But I don't,' he said, 'want help.'

And that was the *leitmotiv* of our consultation. Lockwood was perfectly coherent, unfailingly polite and totally adamant. Psychiatric treatment was the Admiralty's idea, not his. All *he* wanted was to be left alone. To forget.

I was surprised. Amnesia isn't the easiest of afflictions to live with. Most people who suffer from it find it disquieting to have blank moments in their lives that they can't account for. They *want* to be cured. So why wasn't this Lt Lockwood conforming to type? Could it be, I asked myself, that he had something to hide? I decided, for the moment, to steer clear of the Antarctic, which he obviously didn't want to talk about, and discover something of his background.

I gathered he was the only child of middle-class parents. His father, it seemed, was a draughtsman, working for a firm of consulting engineers in the city: too old to be called up, but doing his bit as an air raid warden. His mother, before her marriage, had been a nurse, and was now helping out at a local hospital. Their marriage had been a happy one, and young Lockwood appeared to have had a perfectly normal home-life in the south London suburb of Norwood, and a perfectly normal school-life, first at Dulwich College Preparatory School then at the College itself. He appeared to have kept reasonably well and fit, and been reasonably successful academically, reasonably good at games and reasonably happy: in fact he came across as almost the archetypal young Mr Normal. It is true that, like a lot of only children who went to a public school, he had had little contact during his teens with the opposite sex; but this lack appeared to have been to some extent redressed when he left home and joined the Navy. On gaining his commission, he was sent to the Royal Naval College, Greenwich for a three-month course in meteorology, at the end of which he was appointed junior met officer to the aircraft carrier HMS *Eagle*. While serving with *Eagle* in the Mediterranean, he learned that the Admiralty were wanting met officers for 'most secret duties in the far south'. He volunteered. And was accepted.

This didn't sound to me like the sort of childhood and adolescence in which a psychiatrist might expect to unearth skeletons.

So long as I confined myself to asking Lockwood about his early life, he answered my questions spontaneously and, I felt sure, honestly. But as soon as I began to question him about what had happened in the Antarctic, his attitude changed. He shut up like a clam. 'I don't know,' he kept on saying, or 'I can't remember'; and when he did vouchsafe an answer, it was with guarded reluctance, as though he was fearful of digging a pit for himself to fall into. I sensed a mystery. And a problem. And, greatly to my annoyance, I sensed something else: that this was going to be one of those rare cases in which I became personally involved.

For more than 30 years, first in the backstreets of Preston, then in the fashionable precincts of Harley Street, people had been coming to me with problems they couldn't cope with on their own; I did my best to help them when they couldn't help themselves. Most of the time I was able to distance myself from my patients. I had to. I needed to preserve a clinical detachment to prevent myself being emotionally drained, and left as weak and vulnerable as those I was trying to counsel. But every now and then I found myself dealing with a case that tugged at my heartstrings. And it was happening now. I looked at Lockwood's emaciated body and haunted eyes; I listened to his careful and evasive answers; and both my instinct and my professional judgement cried out that something was wrong. I longed to help him: perhaps, perversely, all the more because he apparently didn't want to be helped.

So all that April afternoon I went on questioning, probing, prompting, cajoling. And eventually—though it was like squeezing blood from a stone—I got him to admit there were one or two isolated incidents that he *could* remember.

What helped me in this were the notes of his debriefing, which had taken place soon after his rescue. These had been attached to his medical records, and I now laid them out in front of me on my desk, so that he could see I was referring to them. 'It says here,' I told him, 'that in spite of all the terrible things you went through, you fell in love with Antarctica. Is that right?'

For a long time he was silent; then he said simply, 'Yes.'

'So how did this love affair begin?'

He said that he couldn't remember.

'Come off it!' I chided him. 'Lovers always know what got them going!'

There was an even longer silence, and I formed the impression that Lt Lockwood was weighing up the pros and cons of telling me the truth.

'Was it,' I prompted, 'a case of love at first sight?'

I could see he was in a dilemma. He wasn't by nature secretive and evasive; but for reasons known only to himself he felt that he had to be secretive and evasive about what had happened on the Antarctic Peninsula. And he felt guilty about this. It would come almost as a relief to him if we could find some aspect of his time there that he felt able to talk about.

'Please,' I said. 'What possible harm can come of your telling me how you feel about the Antarctic?'

'I can't see the point of all this,' he said at last. 'But OK, I'll tell you. It *was* a case of love at first sight.' He shut his eyes; and it was as though a dam had been broken, and the words so long held back came pouring out in a tumultuous flood . . . 'I'll never forget that first morning. You see, ever since we left Port Stanley we'd had nothing but rain and sleet and fog and great seas and a wind so strong we'd had to lean into it to stay upright. But when I woke that morning the ship was so still and quiet I thought something must be wrong. I went on deck. And it was like . . . well, like finding myself on another planet. There was no cloud. No wind. Hardly a ripple on the sea. And *Scoresby* was heading down a narrow channel. It was,' he hesitated, 'like a street hemmed in by skyscrapers, except the skyscrapers on one side were icebergs and on the other side mountains. The icebergs were *huge*. I reckon some were a couple of miles long and five or six hundred feet high. Most were flat-topped and slab-sided. But every now and then one would be sculpted into amazing shapes: like a castle, all keeps and battlements and turrets. Some had caves hollowed out along the waterline, with the sea rushing in and out, all emerald-green and sapphire-blue. And the sun was so hot, I remember, it was melting the ice, and great waterfalls were streaming down the sides of the bergs. Every now and then one of them would calve, and thousands of tons of ice would come crashing into the sea. The mountains were pretty amazing too. Covered with snow of course, and thousands of feet high. They stretched away to the north and south as far as we could see—and the air was so clear that morning I reckon we could see a good hundred miles. But that was only half of it.' He paused. 'What *really* amazed me was the wildlife. You see, when the weather had been bad we hadn't seen a living thing. In fact it didn't seem possible there *were* living things in such a terrible environment. But now the weather had cleared, there was life everywhere. Hundreds of thousands of seabirds—cormorants, gulls, petrels and terns—wheeling about the cliffs. Tens of thousands of penguins nesting along the shore and leaping on and off the ice. And the water was alive: with krill, fish, seals. There was even the odd pair of whales. And everything,' again he hesitated, 'was clean and new and fresh. Sort of primordial. As though the world had just been born.'

If only, I thought, I could get him to talk like this about his other experiences! I cast round for another aspect of Antarctica that he might be happy to tell me about. 'That must have been quite something,' I said. 'Do you suppose the others felt the same as you? About the Antarctic?'

'I don't know.'

'But a wonderful experience like that . . . You must have talked about it? With your friends?'

He said he couldn't remember.

I decided to try a shot in the dark. I'd noticed during my earlier questioning that he seemed to have a particularly high regard for his commanding officer, a Lt Cdr John Ede. 'What about the CO?' I asked. 'Do you think he fell in love with Antarctica too?'

His eyes went suddenly frightened. His hands, I noticed, had started to tremble.

I glanced again at the notes on his debriefing. 'You got on well with John Ede, didn't you?' I asked him.

It seemed a harmless question. But its effect was catastrophic.

Lockwood shivered. The first shiver was only a little one; but it was followed in rapid succession by another and another and another, each more violent than the one before. The shivering turned to shuddering. I could see he was trying desperately to control himself; but it was a losing battle. And suddenly he started to cry. He cried without hysteria, without self-pity and without embarrassment, the tears cascading out of him in a seemingly endless flood.

I was unnerved. I am no stranger to human suffering, and in the last couple of years I thought I had become inured to dealing with the casualties of war; for I had treated men who would never walk again, men who would never see again, and men who would never make love again. But not in 30 years of psychiatric practice had I met anything quite like this, the more frightening for being so totally unexpected.

'I'm sorry,' I said, aware of how inadequate my words must sound to him. 'Truly, I didn't mean to distress you.'

He managed, at last and with obvious difficulty, to bring himself under control. 'It's me who ought to apologise,' he said, 'you'd better send for a bucket and mop!'

I chose my words carefully: 'I want you to know,' I said, 'I'm only asking you all these questions because in the long run I believe it will help you.'

He stared at me, his eyes more pleading than angry. 'But I've told you. I don't *want* help.'

'I've been in this business of counselling,' I said slowly, 'for a very long time. And it's my experience that always—always and without exception—things are best brought into the open. The past isn't something you can bury. And forget.'

He winced, as though I had kicked him in the stomach. He gripped the top of my desk so tightly his knuckles were white. 'The past is another country,' he said. 'I don't live there any more. I don't want to remember it. And I won't remember it.'

And that was the end of our first consultation.

*   *   *

When he had gone I lit a cigarette and sat down to think things over. It seemed to me there was a conflict of interests here. The Admiralty wanted Lockwood to recall what had happened in the Antarctic. He wanted to forget. I decided that a chat with Jim Sinclair might clear the air.

It was late that evening by the time I got through to him, and I was relieved to find him still at his desk.

'I'm a bit worried,' I told him, 'about that case you referred to me.'

'Lt Lockwood?'

'Yes.'

'What are you worried about?'

'I can't help wondering,' I said, 'why he was referred to me at all. He says he doesn't want psychiatric counselling. Don't you think we ought to respect his wishes?'

There was a moment of silence, and I got the impression that Commander Sinclair was not pleased with me. 'This is an important case,' he said eventually. 'We have a high regard for your judgement. And we'd like to know what you make of young Lockwood.'

'To be honest,' I said, 'I'm not sure *what* to make of him. But he's obviously been through hell, and he wants to forget it. That strikes me as fair enough. Do we need to take things further?'

'The Admiralty think we need to.'

I realised this was going to be one of those cases when the Admiralty and I were on different wavelengths: they attuned to the needs of the war and the maintenance of Naval discipline, I to the needs of my patient and his mental well-being. In such a conflict of interests a career commander RN at the Admiralty was not likely to be a sympathetic ally. Nonetheless I stayed chatting for quite a while to Jim Sinclair, partly because I liked him and partly because I hoped he might put me in the picture about the background to young Lockwood's activities in the Antarctic. This latter hope was not fulfilled. As soon as I tried to question him about John Ede and his ill-fated team of meteorologists, he warned me off.

'Sorry, Hugh. This is a No Go Area.'

'Really?'

'You'd better take my word for it. There's *nobody* at the Admiralty who'll say a word about the Ede fiasco.'

'Why all the secrecy?' I asked him. 'I mean, they were only transmitting weather forecasts, weren't they?'

'Believe me, sir. The subject is taboo. *Verboten.*'

As soon as he started calling me 'sir' I knew I'd get nothing further out of him. We parted amicably enough; though I'm sure he felt I was being unduly inquisitive, and I certainly felt he was being unduly secretive. His parting shot made me think. 'You'll let us have your report right away, won't you, sir? We'd never have referred Lockwood to you in the first place if the matter hadn't been urgent.'

I told him I'd do my best.

I wasn't too happy about what I was being asked to do. However, there *was* a war on; I *was* in the king's uniform, and my superiors at the Admiralty had every right to expect me to carry out their orders. I arranged another consultation with Lt Lockwood for the following afternoon.

*   *   *

He was even more watchful this time, even more guarded, and even more unco-operative. He parried my every question with a stony 'I can't remember', and in next to no time we were at stalemate.

'Please,' I said, 'can't you be a bit more co-operative?'

He shrugged. 'How can I? When I can't remember anything?'

'But you *can* remember some things,' I told him. 'And I've formed the opinion that you can recall more than you let on.'

21

He said nothing.

I decided to put my cards on the table. 'I've been asked to make a report,' I said, 'to the Admiralty. They want to know exactly how much you can recollect. And unless we get this sorted out between us, these talks are going to drag on and on. We neither of us want that, do we?'

Again he was silent.

We talked—or perhaps it would be more realistic to say I talked—all that afternoon and some way into the evening. And slowly, hesitantly, and at times painfully, we managed to establish a sort of rapport: albeit the not very satisfactory rapport that sometimes binds warder to prisoner, or interrogator to detainee. I took my coat off and asked him to do the same—the Navy's way of indicating that things are on a person-to-person basis without constrictions of rank; and though I'm afraid he never really felt that I was on his side, he did, I think, come gradually to trust me. And in the end we managed to sort out if not everything he could remember, then at least everything he was prepared to admit he could remember.

It seemed that the key to his amnesia lay in the destruction of the detachment's base-camp. For the shock of coming back from a routine sledge patrol and finding the burnt and bullet-riddled bodies of his companions sprawled out in the snow was so traumatic it had blotted out all recollection of what had happened before. Or almost all recollection. The only things he could recall, he told me, of his first year in the Antarctic were a succession of disconnected images, like slides from a magic-lantern flashed fleetingly onto a screen.

On the face of it this struck me as fair enough. Yet I had the feeling that things were not as simple as Lt Lockwood would have me believe. For some of my questions seemed to make him unaccountably distressed, and altogether too vehement in his protests that these were things about which he knew nothing. And there were two subjects in particular that he was unwilling to talk about at all: how he and his companions had spent their leisure time, and his relationship with his commanding officer, John Ede.

It seemed to me that the detachment must have had a fair amount of leisure time. For there were ten of them, and once their hut had been built and their meteorological and radio equipment had been installed, there would have been few time-consuming jobs to occupy them. So what, I asked him, did they do? Did they read, play cards, listen to the gramophone, keep diaries, do exercises, take photographs, explore their surroundings? He said they did all of these things. And from a remark he inadvertently let slip, I gathered they did something else: geological research.

This interested me. But to my disappointment—and I have to say to my incredulity—Lockwood insisted he could remember almost nothing about their work as geologists. He had, he told me, a vague recollection of his companions boring holes in the ice, triggering off controlled explosions, and collecting the resultant fragments of rock. But when I pressed him for details, he screwed shut his eyes and clenched his hands. Little beads of sweat were standing out across his forehead.

'I can't remember,' he whispered. 'I can't remember. I can't remember. For God's sake leave it at that.'

I changed the subject. A repetition of yesterday's breakdown would do him no good at all.

It was some time before he regained his composure, and some time after that before I dared broach the other sensitive issue: his relationship with John Ede.

I could tell there was a problem here; but when I tried to identify its source it was like picking my way through a minefield. Lockwood was on edge and having obvious difficulty keeping his emotions under control. Hysteria, it seemed to me, was only a little way below the surface. My first thought was that perhaps Ede had been unpopular, and there had been discontent or even mutiny; but Lockwood's answers soon put paid to that idea. My second thought was that perhaps the two of them had been lovers; but this idea, too, I soon discarded; it didn't fit.

Eventually, it became clear that my questions were causing him so much distress it would be inadvisable to continue. I therefore changed the subject and turned to things he could remember more clearly and was happier to talk about: things that had happened *after* the death of his companions. We were on safer ground here, though Lockwood still seemed inexplicably cautious in his replies, as though he was not answering my questions spontaneously but was keeping to a premeditated script. Be that as it may, the longer we talked the more I came to realise just how much he had been through that winter in Antarctica; and my gut reaction was that he had suffered so terribly it was wrong to make him relive what he wanted to forget. However, because I had my brief from the Admiralty, I decided to make one last attempt to kick-start his memory.

Although the broad outline of how he had survived the winter was clear enough, there seemed to be one or two grey areas that he couldn't recollect all that clearly. 'If,' I said carefully, 'this is to be our last consultation, I'd like to end with an experiment.'

'What sort of experiment?'

'You know those old Hollywood movies. Where the wicked psychiatrist gets his patient on the couch. And dangles a watch-chain in front of him.'

'Don't tell me you want to hypnotise me!'

'No. But I *would* like you to lie on the couch. And close your eyes. And empty your mind of the present. And imagine you're back in Antarctica: in your survival shelter—what was it you called it? Your *behouden huis*. And answer a few last questions.'

'And that'll be it?'

I nodded. And he lay, almost thankfully, on the couch. Every word that passed between us in the next few minutes is etched into my memory. On nights when I can't sleep and my ghosts file past the end of my bed, I sometimes go over what was said and wonder what else I could have done.

As soon as he seemed to be comfortably settled, I said: 'Now I want you to imagine it's winter, and you're alone in your survival shelter.' I waited a long time—at least a couple of minutes—for it is my experience that nothing relieves anxiety more efficaciously than boredom; then I asked him, 'Where are you?'

He said he was in the *behouden huis*.

'What can you see?'

'Nothing.'

'Nothing at all?'

'No, it's too dark.'

'If it's so dark, how do you know you're in the *behouden huis*?'

'If I reach out,' he said, 'I can touch the walls.'

'That's fine. That's just the sort of answer I want. Now what can you feel?'

'Cold.'

'No pain?'

'No. I tell myself every morning there's no pain.'

'And what can you hear?'

'The silence.'

'And nothing else?'

'Sometimes I hear the wind.'

'The wind outside the *behouden huis*?'

'Sometimes that wind, sometimes another.'

'What's this other wind you can hear?'

A pause; then, unexpectedly: 'The wind on the heath.'

'You can hear the wind on the heath?'

'Sometimes.'

'What heath would that be?'

'It doesn't matter.'

'A heath you knew way back in England?'

'No.'

I made a note that this was something we ought to come back to. 'You're doing fine,' I told him. 'Now what can you smell?'

It seemed just another harmless question; but Lockwood went suddenly tense. There was a silence that went on and on, until I asked him again: 'What can you smell?'

'Seal blubber.'

I felt sure he was lying. 'OK. So you can smell seal blubber. And what else?'

'Nothing! Nothing! Nothing!'

I realised I had pushed him a question too far. 'Forget it,' I said quickly. 'Think of something else. The wind on the heath.'

But I was too late. Once again Lt Lockwood was shuddering in terrible, uncontrollable spasms. His mouth was opening and shutting, but not a sound came out. Suddenly he grabbed the blanket that covered the couch he was lying on, stuffed a corner into his mouth, and began to suck in great gulps of air as though he was choking. Then he was violently sick.

Like I've said, I am accustomed to dealing with life's flotsam and jetsam. Some psychiatrists say they get hardened to this; but for me compassion is always there—though I don't usually let it surface. But it surfaced now. It seemed to me that young Lockwood had obviously been through hell in Antarctica, and if he wanted to forget that hell he ought to be allowed to.

Jim, I wrote, when an apologetic young man had left and my consulting room had been cleaned up, *with reference to Lt James Lockwood RNVR, it is my firm opinion that further questioning of this patient would be detrimental to his condition. I believe his amnesia to be largely genuine. I am therefore discharg-*

ing him from my care, with the recommendation that he is sent on indefinite leave, and that as soon as his physical condition permits he is given a not-too-demanding posting in a not-too-demanding theatre of war.

Yours ever

Hugh Dempster, Surgeon Captain, RNVR.

* * *

I never saw James Lockwood in the flesh again, though from time to time I am reminded of him. I am reminded of him because he has joined my ghosts: those who, on nights when sleep is denied me, file phantomlike past the end of my bed—the men and women who came to me for help and whom I feel I have failed.

Lockwood is by no means the most tragic of these ghosts; but his case always struck me as particularly difficult and unsatisfactory: full of questions unanswered, mysteries unsolved and secrets undisclosed. And the more I think about our two consultations, the more I ask myself if I did the right thing. Didn't you, a voice keeps whispering, take the easy way out? Weren't you a bit like Pontius Pilate, simply to wash your hands of him? I know the reason for my anxiety. I am afraid that if Lockwood keeps his secrets (whatever they are) perpetually bottled up, they will become an incubus, like a dead albatross tied for the rest of his life round his neck.

If it had been peacetime I would have let a decent interval elapse, then suggested further consultation. But in wartime such a course of action wasn't on. However, that autumn I made it my business to find out what had happened to young Lockwood, and was told he had been posted as met officer to the remote little Fleet Air Arm airfield of Benbecula in the Outer Hebrides. I sent him a Christmas card, and rather to my surprise got one back. He thanked me for my concern and said he was happy enough on Benbecula. 'Its seabirds and silences,' he wrote on the bottom of his card, 'remind me of another and better world.'

As the war drags on, I find my sleepless nights are becoming more frequent—I dare say it is the strain of having to cope day after day with men whose lives have been shattered. I have therefore been seeing quite a lot of young Lockwood recently as he stands wraithlike by the end of my bed. Indeed, I have been seeing so much of him that I fear I am in some danger of becoming obsessed with his case. For I can't forget it: can't stop longing to know what *really* happened to him that winter in Antarctica.

SURVIVAL

Most secret duties in the far south

21.1.42, Lockwood wrote in his diary. *Huge seas, thick fog and never a glimpse of the sun. We are STILL heading south. And STILL have no idea where we are being taken to or why. It would be pathetic if we hit an iceberg and sank before we even knew what we were meant to be doing.*

And hitting an iceberg was now becoming a distinct possibility. For after four days standing south from the Falklands, the minesweeper *Scoresby* was sighting 'growlers'—cottage-sized blocks of ice which had broken free from the mainland of Antarctica and drifted into the Drake Passage. During these four days there had been no sign of land and no sign of life. But on the evening of 22nd January, the cries of seabirds echoing out of the fog were an indication to the more knowledgeable of the special detachment that they were about to make a landfall; and when *Scoresby*'s lookout reported the sound of breakers ahead, the minesweeper hove to for the night.

Next morning the fog had lifted sufficiently for them to make out, a couple of hundred yards on their port bow, a desolate-looking island, its ice-rimed cliffs rising sheer out of the sea. It seemed they had arrived if not at their destination, at least at the threshold to it; and as though to confirm this their CO, Lt Cdr Ede, mustered them in *Scoresby*'s wardroom for briefing.

Lockwood could remember this briefing with the clarity of a dream which for the rest of his life came back to him in moments of stress: the uneasy pitching of the minesweeper as she butted into a wide-spaced swell, the haze of tobacco smoke, the faces of his companions framed by the often none too hirsute beards they had started to grow in the Falklands, and the air of expectancy—a mix of anticipation, apprehension and excitement—as the CO came into the wardroom.

'Please sit. And if you want to, smoke.'

He could remember the noise of chairs scraping back on the steel-plated deck, then the moment of absolute silence as the ten-odd members of the special detachment waited, like boxers for the bell, to hear why, in the middle of the war, they had been brought with such secrecy to these farthest ends of the earth.

The CO was a man of few affectations and fewer words. 'I am now able,' he said, 'to tell you about the "most secret duties in the far south" for which we have all volunteered. We are going to push as far as we can towards the Pole. Land. And set up and man a weather station.'

Lockwood could remember his reaction—shared, it was evident, by the rest of the detachment: 'A weather station! What anticlimax! And why so much fuss and secrecy about setting up a weather station?'

The CO held up his hand. 'I can see what you're thinking: not very exciting, and not very important. But the truth is just the opposite. And I'll tell you why.'

Lt Cdr Ede had the academic's gift of lucid exposition—before the war he had been a lecturer in geology at the University of Durham—and Lockwood could recall how the special detachment had been first sceptical, then intrigued and finally hooked.

'What we're going to do,' Ede said, 'will help us win the war against the U-boats.'

Everything he told them that morning was perfectly logical, and—as far as it went—perfectly true. He explained that until recently merchant ships in the southern hemisphere had been sailing individually rather than in convoy. For some time this had worked well enough, but over the past few months losses had been mounting, and it had been decided that in future all ships in the southern oceans were to sail in convoy. The assembling, routing and safe passage of a convoy, as Ede pointed out, was a highly complex business, and one of the prerequisites of success was accurate weather forecasting. The weather of the southern hemisphere, he went on to explain, originated in the Antarctic—'that's where the fronts begin to build up'—yet the Allies had no weather station within 1,000 miles of Antarctica. Forecasts for the South Atlantic, South Pacific and Indian Oceans were therefore at present little more than guesswork, and as often as not the first a ship knew of a storm was when it hit them. 'We're going to alter that,' Ede told the detachment. 'We're going to set up a base on the Antarctic Peninsula. and we're going to transmit weather reports. Three times a day. Every day. For as long as it takes us to win the war.'

There were a lot of questions. What, Ede was asked, about equipment and stores? And he told them they were due that afternoon to rendezvous with the *Loch Tarbert*, a Falkland Islands Company supply ship which was carrying their prefabricated living-quarters and sufficient food and fuel for three years. Why were they going so far south? And he told them the farther they pushed towards the Pole the closer they would be to the area where the depressions originated, and the better they would be able to monitor them. Would they be allowed to keep diaries? And he said that would be OK, so long as they were circumspect in what they wrote and understood that their diaries were subject to censorship. And at the end of the briefing it seemed that every question had been answered and every loose end tied up. It certainly never occurred to Lockwood, at this juncture, that there might be more to their mission than met the eye.

The detachment were still mulling over what promised to be an interesting if not wildly exciting assignment, when

33

the blast of a fog-horn heralded their rendezvous with the supply ship.

The cloud was low; the fog was thick as a traditional pea-souper; the light was sepulchral; and those who hurried on deck to witness the rendezvous couldn't at first see another ship. Then they spotted her, the overladen merchant vessel emerging like some prehistoric monster out of the gloom. The *Loch Tarbert* was rolling scuppers-under, and the red and green of her navigation lights were one moment refracted into haloes in the cloud, next moment fragmented into spirals in the sea. She took up position a couple of hundred yards astern, and the two vessels headed south for the Antarctic Peninsula.

Lockwood and one of the detachment's leading seamen shared the first of the dog watches. As they scanned the sea for ice they had plenty of opportunity to talk, and one fragment of their conversation was to remain lodged in Lockwood's memory.

'There's one thing I don't understand, sir'—at eighteen Leading Seaman Burkenshaw was even younger than Lockwood and in need of reassurance. 'Why have they sent so many of us, just to set up a met station? And why are the Old Man and so many of the officers geologists?'

The same question had occurred to Lockwood, but unable to answer it he made light of it. 'Maybe,' he said, 'someone got contours mixed up with isobars . . . Look! Is that ice?'

Their binoculars focused on the water ahead. But the whiteness was no growler; only moonlight filtering for a moment through the fog to irradiate the sea.

That night the weather cleared. It was as though an artist had scrubbed his canvas clean, and come up with a totally different picture. As *Scoresby* and the *Loch Tarbert* stood south down Bransfield Strait (the narrow stretch of water which lies between the Antarctic Peninsula and its skein of offshore islands) there wasn't a cloud in the sky or a whisper of wind, and the sea had been ironed out to the consistency of a village pond. Around them mountains and icebergs glittered like piles of crystal, fractured here and there with cracks and crevices through which the blue ice glowed like imprisoned glow-worms. And everywhere there was life: seabirds wheeling over the cliffs, penguins nesting along the shore, and the water thick with krill. In the afternoon a pair of humpback whales kept pace with the ships for the better part of an hour; one of them tried to dislodge the barnacles from its back by rubbing itself against the hull of the *Loch Tarbert*.

John Ede spent much of the day getting to know his 'team', as he said he was going to call them. He was a quiet, unobtrusively efficient man: anxious, it seemed, to exercise his authority by consensus rather than rank. As he pointed out, the detachment was in many ways more like a peacetime expedition than a wartime operation. It was late evening by the time he got round to having a chat with Lockwood.

Young Lockwood had spent most of his off-duty hours wedged into the bow of the *Scoresby*, watching the fields of snow and ice unfold in a panorama of ever-increasing splendour. For a while the two men talked trivia, and it was soon apparent to both that they would probably end up liking one another. They were on the same wavelength: *en rapport*. Ede didn't need to be particularly perceptive to see that the most junior of his met officers was enchanted by his first glimpse of Antarctica. He gestured to the snow-covered mountains. 'Beautiful, aren't they?'

Lockwood nodded. Then hesitantly—for he was uncertain what his commanding officer's reaction would be—he said, 'It seems a bit like blasphemy, don't you think? To bring war to somewhere so beautiful.'

For quite a while Ede was silent, then he said: 'I hear you. And I understand you. But I'm going to ask you to remember something.'

35

'What's that, sir?'

'We can't draw a line on the map and say, "the war ends here". The Antarctic Peninsula is British territory. It and everything in it is ours: ours to do what we like with. You *will* remember that, won't you?'

Lockwood was surprised that someone who was usually so relaxed and unjingoistic as the CO should for no apparent reason be suddenly waving the flag and quoting king's regulations. However, he had the *nous* to say simply, 'I'll not forget, sir,' and for a while they talked of other things. But this was another conversation Lockwood was to remember.

Good weather seldom lasts long in the Antarctic, and that evening dark clouds came scudding out of the west, and little flurries of snow blotted out the mountains of the Peninsula. That night it was so cold a veneer of ice formed on the minesweeper's deck, and icicles, like beads of glass, coagulated in the rigging.

The farther south the two vessels stood the more problems they had with ice, and in particular sea-ice. *24.1.42*, Lockwood wrote in his diary. *Ice-floes thickening.* Scoresby *coping well, but* Loch Tarbert *starting to lag behind. With her wooden hull she's about as keen to enter the ice as a virgin to gatecrash a stag party! However, the Old Man seems determined to push as far south as we can: at least to the 65th parallel.*

Nosing aside floes that were becoming increasingly thick and more numerous, the minesweeper and the merchantman forced their way past Anvers Island and into a large horseshoe bay at the approaches to the Bismarck Strait. Here they dropped anchor, and it seemed that Ede was at last satisfied they had penetrated close enough to the Pole. Next morning they set about finding somewhere to land. This proved easier said than done. They needed a place where the water was deep enough for the *Loch Tarbert* to come close inshore to unload, yet was adjacent to the intended site of their base; for it would be difficult (if not impossible) for them to haul the prefabricated sections of their hut and three years' supply of fuel and food for any great distance over the ice.

It took them 24 hours to find such a place, and a further 48 hours of blood, sweat and toil to unload the *Loch Tarbert* and haul everything to the site of their hut—an apron of level ground some 100 yards from the sea, which was free from the danger of avalanches and sheltered from the prevailing wind. To reach this site they had to climb a gentle but slippery incline which soon became known as Slope Sodomy. It didn't take them long to realise that the best way to get their stores to the top of Slope Sodomy was to winch them up, and towards the end of this process there was an incident that gave Lockwood further food for thought.

It was late evening. For a day and a half the detachment had been working flat-out. Unloading is when a polar expedition is at its most vulnerable, the danger being that a change of weather will force the unloading vessel to run for the open sea, leaving members of the expedition marooned ashore with their hut not yet built and half their supplies still in the ship's hold. After 36 hours of manhauling and winching in sub-zero temperatures, feet were numb, backs were aching and fingers were bruised and clumsy. It was perhaps inevitable that one of the bundles being winched to the top of Slope Sodomy should be imperfectly secured. It slipped its lashings and, gathering speed, went slithering down the incline and into the water. Ede was not amused. Particularly when he saw that one of the items drifting out to sea was a tube containing the detachment's maps.

'Salvage that tube,' he shouted. 'At the double. Don't let the water get in.'

They could hardly have salvaged the tube more quickly if they had been competing in the Royal Tournament.

But one end *had* burst open, and the water had seeped in.

They clustered round Ede and his first lieutenant as the two senior officers carefully prised three or four sodden sheets of parchment out of the tube.

Ede motioned them away: 'Keep back.'

Lockwood didn't see why they were being told to keep back. The maps weren't people, were they, in need of air? Or bombs about to explode? He peered over Ede's shoulder, and saw on the largest of the maps the letters FIDS (which he subsequently learned stood for Falkland Islands Dependencies Survey), and embossed in big red letters in the margin of the map the date 2.4.33 and the latitude and longitude 65°01'S, 62°35'W—almost the exact position in which they were about to set up their met station.

'I said keep back.' Ede's voice was sharp.

The detachment recognised an order when they heard one. Surprised, they backed away. And Lockwood wasn't the only one to be left with the feeling that things were going on that they didn't as yet understand.

It took them a week to get their hut and their fuel store erected, their Esse stoves installed and operating, their radio-mast rigged against even the most frenetic gale, and their receiver and transmitter making trouble-free contact with Port Stanley. Their next step was to unpack their met instruments, soak them in Benzine and test and install them; and it wasn't long before they were transmitting weather reports three times a day, at 0800, 1400 and 2000 hours. *So far so good*, Lockwood wrote in his diary. *It looks as though our 'most secret' duties are going to be a piece of cake. Scoresby and* Loch Tarbert *anxious to be on their way home.*

There was no point in the warship and the supply ship hanging about. With the approach of autumn, the ice would soon be thickening and the weather worsening, and with every passing day there was increasing danger that the vessels might be damaged or even trapped. It was a time for goodbyes: a hurried writing of letters home, a final check on supplies, a last wild party in the minesweeper's wardroom. Then, in the early morning of 5th February, the two vessels stood north up the coast of the Antarctic Peninsula.

Ede and his team climbed a nunatak—an outcrop of rock rising out of the ice sheet—and watched the ships growing smaller and smaller and fainter and fainter, until no matter how hard they strained their eyes they could see no trace of them.

No one said much as they made their way back to their hut. Each was conscious of the fact that for a very long time indeed they would be the only human beings on the world's most inhospitable continent.

About a week after the ships disappeared below the horizon the detachment got their first intimation that there was going to be more to their duties than making weather forecasts.

On the morning of 11th February Lockwood had written in his diary: *There's not a lot for the ten of us to do. I reckon our main problem is going to be boredom.* However, that evening Ede got his team together and told them that the Admiralty had foreseen this very problem and had arranged 'a little something to keep us out of mischief'.

'I want to make it clear,' he said, 'that weather reporting is our number one priority. *Nothing* is to get in the way of that. But to keep us on our toes and stop us getting bored, their Lordships suggest we do a bit of research . . . Now I'll give you the background to this . . . In the early '30s scientists working for the Falkland Islands Dependencies started to make a geological survey of a cross-section of the Antarctic Peninsula. But they found they had bitten off more than they could chew. The weather was bad. The terrain was difficult. And to cut a long story short, they never got the survey finished. Now—ten years later—we've better equipment. We've time on our hands. So the idea is that we finish what they began.'

The detachment weren't at all sure what to make of this, and more than one of them wanted to know why they hadn't been told of this geological work in the first place. There were a lot of questions. Were they going to do their survey in the same spot as the scientists? Were they going to radio the results back to Port Stanley? Were they looking for something specific? Ede, however, proved unexpectedly evasive, and it wasn't long before he brought discussion to an abrupt stop. 'I know,' he said, 'all this secrecy makes things difficult for you. But I've been given sealed orders. These are for my eyes only. And I must ask you to accept that, and just get on with what we've been asked to do.'

And for more than a year this is what the detachment did. Lockwood's diary chronicled their growing preoccupation with their work as geologists.

14.2.42. Another lovely day. The sun low but still surprisingly hot. Made a start on our mystery survey. Ede meticulous about starting work at exactly $65°01S$—the latitude I saw marked on the FIDS map. So it looks as though we're going to follow the line of the scientists' survey as close as we can.

28.2.42. Survey has now reached the slopes of Mt McCumber. What we do is very simple. About every 25 yds we bore a hole in the ice, lower an explosive charge into the borehole, wire the charge up and trigger off an explosion by remote control. We then haul the bits of broken rock out of the borehole, and bring them back to the hut for analysis. Don't seem to have found anything so far to excite our interest.

11.4.42. Had yet another pow-wow to try and work out what it is we're after—for we're all agreed that we MUST be looking for something specific. But what? We've ruled out oil because we aren't drilling deep enough. We've ruled out gold because the rocks we're testing aren't auriferous. One of the geologists, Dave, suggested radium. He says radium is found in metamorphosed lavas, and these seem to be the rocks we're testing most carefully. But none of us can believe radium is rare enough or important enough to justify all this secrecy. So the mystery remains!

18.5.42. Farewell to the sun—a last tiny fragment of red, like a drop of blood, on the horizon. It'll be a couple of months before we see it again. What a prospect! 1500 hours of total darkness!

24.6.42. No more sun doesn't mean no more survey. On nights when it's fine we carry on by starlight or moonlight, helped sometimes by fantastic 'fireworks' from the aurora. We've all got the feeling that whatever it is we're searching for, it must be of real importance.

These and a few dozen similar entries in Lockwood's diary record the events that took place during the detachment's first year on the Peninsula. What such entries *don't* record is the camaraderie.

It didn't happen easily or without the members of the detachment often having to make a conscious effort; but slowly and hesitantly they became not only companions but friends. It might easily have been otherwise. Human beings forced to live cheek-by-jowl in cramped quarters and physically demanding conditions often get on one another's nerves. Heavy breathing, snoring, or picking one's nose or one's teeth are liable to cause outrage quite disproportionate to the offence. Even such minor *faux pas* as raising one's eyebrows or clearing one's throat can, by repetition, become near-unbearable. It says much for the good sense and adaptability of the detachment's geologists and meteorologists that they quickly learned to make a joke of one another's idiosyncrasies and were, before long, forming the sort of friendships that last for life. *I'm lucky*, Ede wrote on Christmas Day in the expedition log, *to have such a well-balanced lot of officers and men. We've knitted together into a wonderfully happy team.*

On 1st March they came to the ice-fall.

Their survey by this time had progressed almost two-thirds across the Peninsula, keeping meticulously to

65°01'South, with bore holes drilled and rock samples extracted every 25 yards. Some of the terrain they had worked their way through had been difficult; but the ice-fall struck them as not so much difficult as suicidal. It hung across the head of a glacial valley: a mosaic of white-ice and blue-ice, seracs and crevasses, that looked likely any moment to break away from the snowfields above it and start the sort of avalanche in which half a mountainside collapses. And the parallel 65°01'South ran directly beneath it.

Ede was determined that their survey shouldn't deviate, even by a few hundred yards, and should be 100 per cent continuous. So with many an apprehensive glance at the seracs above them, they descended into the valley.

It took them a week to drill boreholes, and almost as long to lay cables to a place from which they could detonate the explosive charges safely. When they did eventually detonate them, they wouldn't have been in the least surprised if the ice-fall had disintegrated. But it held. So with crossed fingers, and prayers to whatever gods they believed it, they set to work extracting fragmented rock from the boreholes. They trod warily, knowing that any small movement at the foot of the ice-fall might trigger a greater movement above it; and they spoke in whispers, knowing that sound too was a potential catalyst of disaster. They had cleared about half the boreholes when a mass of cloud came rolling up the glacier and it started to snow. One moment they were in brilliant sun, next moment in a near-blizzard. It was the last thing they needed: heavy, wet snowflakes piling up on unstable ice—a recipe for avalanche—and Ede very wisely decided to call it a day.

They left in a hurry. Under normal circumstances they would have loaded the rock samples onto their motor-sledge and made the return journey themselves on skis. However, conditions became so bad so quickly that Ede told them to leave the rock samples behind and all pile onto their motor sledge. The rocks were therefore stacked up at the side of the glacier, and their position triangulated and marked with flags. By 8 p.m. everyone was back in the hut.

That night, as usual, Ede wrote up the expedition log.

March 11. Have extracted rock samples from under the ice-fall. No avalanche! PM weather worsened, so left rocks by the glacier to be collected later.

Ede seldom used three words if two would do, and his entries for the next few days were minimal.

March 12. Blizzard. Confined to hut.

March 13. Blizzard continues.

March 14. Weather improving. Lockwood and Ramsden will go back to the glacier first thing tomorrow to pick up the rocks.

This was the last entry in the expedition's log.

The dogs of war

The special detachment were not the only people, that March, to seek shelter from the Antarctic blizzards. Less than a mile from where Ede and his team lay asleep in their hut, other men, in other uniform, were riding out the storm in the lee of an iceberg.

What brought about this unlikely coming together at the bottom of the world was an error of judgement by the commander of one of Germany's 'milch cows', the mother or depot submarines, which kept Hitler's far-ranging U-boats supplied with fuel. It happened in the South Atlantic, on 1st March, 1943—by coincidence the same day that Ede and his team arrived at the ice-fall.

The milch cow hadn't seen an Allied ship or plane since leaving Wilhelmshaven. In the last few days of February she had refuelled four U-boats in the lonely reaches of the South Atlantic. It had been unexpectedly easy, and the milch cow had grown over-confident. When one of her progeny had difficulty finding the rendezvous area, she had broken radio silence to guide her in. It was a mistake. Allied radar picked up the transmission and pinpointed her.

There were no warships in the vicinity; but American and British shore-based aircraft had a long range, and late that afternoon a Liberator of Coastal Command emerged from the gathering banks of nimbostratus to catch the two submarines at their most vulnerable: on the surface, stationary, and linked by their hose-pipes transferring fuel.

The odds were not in their favour.

The slow-moving milch cow stayed on the surface to

44

fight. Her ack-ack spat at the Liberator, defiantly but ineffectually; then she was smothered in a straddle of depth-changes that sent her spiralling down to lodge broken-backed in the mud of the Mid-Atlantic Ridge. Those of her crew who died instantly were lucky.

The quicker and quicker-witted U-102 cut the hose-pipes and dived.

She dived so fast that three of her crew were sluiced off her deck like tadpoles in a mill-race; but by the time the depth-charges detonated she was a hundred feet down and diving. Her alacrity saved her. In the pressure of the explosions her plates vibrated but didn't buckle; her lights flickered but didn't fuse; for a moment her steering-gear jammed but her crew had the expertise to free it, and the dive which might so easily have been her death dive flattened out, and she limped away like a wounded animal to seek refuge in the dark waters five or six hundred feet beneath the surface. There was no way, here, that an aircraft could detect her.

The Liberator circled, its crew scanning the sea for patches of oil. They felt certain they had put paid to the milch cow, but weren't sure of the smaller U-boat. She had vanished; but was she *kaput* or lying doggo? The Liberator radio-operator called for reinforcements.

All that evening and most of the night U-102 crept south at three knots. South because her *kapitanleutnant* reckoned this was the direction a hunter would least expect them to take; three knots because this was the optimum speed at which they could clear the area with their engines not easily detected. By the small hours of the following morning her crew were beginning to breathe more easily. But just as they were congratulating themselves on a lucky escape, they heard the sounds which for the last ten hours they had been dreading. Faint at first but growing gradually louder, the 'ping' of Asdic.

Hesitant at first but growing ever more purposeful, the churn of a warship's propellers.

The hunt was on.

Of all the deaths that men, down through the ages, have devised for one another, few are more terrible than that facing the submariner. This the crew of U-102 understood. Some swore, some crossed themselves, some tried to focus on the memory of a loved one, some tried to make their minds go blank, some urinated in terror. *Kapitanleutnant* Bungert took the U-boat down to 550 feet, and switched to emergency power. Then came the worst time of all. The waiting.

The 'ping' of Asdic increased in pitch and intensity; it rose to a high-pitched crescendo; then, as the warship came so close that the beam of her transmissions could no longer be lowered sufficiently to make contact with them, it cut out. There was a moment of silence. Then the pulse of propellers growing louder. And louder still. The noise of the propellers passed immediately overhead, and the crew of the U-boat waited for the thunder of depth-charges, but the thunder never came because the destroyer was uncertain of their depth and was only making a trial run, and this was bad news, because it meant that the captain of the destroyer was a hunter of experience.

But Bungert was experienced too. And cunning: cunning with the despair of a cornered animal that knows it hasn't the teeth to harm its adversary but can, by bluff, agility and luck, prolong its life. If only for a while.

The destroyer circled. Her Asdic rediscovered them. Soon she was coming in again. This time for the kill.

The moment the Asdic beam no longer bounced off their hull but passed above it, Bungert ordered 'Port 90', and U-102, her engines churning, slewed crablike out of the destroyer's path, so that the depth-charges burst not in a cluster round her but in a cluster 50 yards away. The

U-boat bucked and shuddered in the shock waves; her lights flickered; the door of a locker swung open and oilskins and a hammer went slithering across the deck; her plates creaked and groaned, like trees in a high wind; one buckled, and a jet of water, thin but potentially lethal as a lazer-beam, burst through the hull. There was a drill for this. The plate was battened down. Then, once again, they were waiting.

Silence, except for the throb of their engines idling. It was a respite. But only a temporary one. The crew knew what would happen next. And sure enough, after about ten minutes their hydrophone again picked up the ping of Asdic and the churn of propellers: growing louder, coming closer. Some of the crew stared straight ahead; some shut their eyes; some prayed; an *obersteurmann* tried to spit, but his mouth was so dry that all that came out was a hiss. And this time the depth-charges were closer. U-102 was jerked sideways like a struck fish; men were flung to the deck, and water came seeping through the plates of their hull and into the batteries. Little wisps of white—carbon monoxide—began to spiral out of their battery-casings like marsh gas out of a swamp. There was a drill for this too. The crew strapped on their breathing masks and sealed off the batteries. Then, once again, they were waiting: wondering if next time the depth charges would be closer, wondering how many runs the warship would have to make before she got them.

It seemed to Bungert that if they stayed where they were their chances of survival were nil. He ordered the U-boat down.

As U-102 slid into darker, 'heavier' water, the pressure built up on her hull. Six hundred feet, and little drops of moisture began to bead the inner surface of her plates as though she was sweating in agony. And still they went down. Six hundred and twenty feet, and a rivet gave way. Like the bolt from a crossbow it flew across the deck, narrowly missing one of the crew, and buried itself in the opposite bulkhead. Then another gave way. And another. And still they went down. Six hundred and forty feet, and their depth-recorder turned red as a tube of blood as they reached their safe-maximum depth. Reached it and, to the terror of the crew, sank below it. Not till they were at 660 feet did Bungert level off. Then they adjusted their trim, stopped their engines and hung suspended like a glass bottle floating in boiling water and liable any moment to disintegrate.

But even here the Asdic sought them out—though with less certainty now, because at the greater depth they were more difficult to pinpoint.

The destroyer made a hesitant run. Then, satisfied she had relocated them, she came in again, and again her depth-charges tore open the sea, this time some 50 feet above them. U-102 shook like a man with palsy. Water poured into her for'ard torpedo tubes; she porpoised, and teetered on the brink of the sort of dive from which there would be no levelling off. There was even a drill to combat this. But when some of the U-boat's compartments had been flooded and some had been battened down and she was back on an even keel and there was nothing for her ship's company to do except wait for the inevitable return of the Asdic and the propellers, these were times for which no drill could prepare them, and more than one man that morning prayed that the destroyer's next attack would give them the *coup de grace* before he cracked under the strain and beat his head screaming against the bulkhead.

Then, when they least expected it, came if not a reprieve at least a stay of execution. It seemed that the destroyer was having increasing difficulty locating them. Twice she broke off an attack, as though uncertain where they were. Once she made a run in the wrong direction, and her depth-charges heaved up the sea a couple of miles from where they were lying.

Bungert could think of only one possible explanation for this. They must have acquired an ally: the weather. He had noticed during their rendezvous with the milch cow that banks of cloud were building up in the west, the *tirailleurs* of an advancing storm. This storm, he told himself, must now have reached them, and the waves must have become so steep that they were playing havoc with the destroyer's Asdic. Perhaps, he thought, if we lie still enough, deep enough, long enough she'll lose contact and give up.

The destroyer captain, however, was not the sort to give up.

He had known a storm was in the offing—Allied weather forecasts for the southern hemisphere had been particularly accurate for the last year—and he had pressed home attack after attack in an effort to finish the U-boat off before conditions deteriorated. The U-boat, however, had proved elusive, and the destroyer captain now realised he was in danger of losing her. He was low on fuel, in heavy seas his Asdic was unreliable, and his vessel (an old Town Class destroyer) was about as easy to handle as a camel on ice. And the seas that morning were becoming heavier and heavier, until great rollers were sweeping endlessly out of the west like ranges of snow-capped hills. A little after mid-day one burst flush on the destroyer's bridge, crushing the supposedly unbreakable glass and killing one of the officers on watch. The warship began to have increasing difficulty keeping in contact with the U-boat. However, the destroyer captain felt certain she was still somewhere beneath them, lying motionless, playing possum. When the weather clears, he told himself, we'll get her. Hour after hour he circled the spot where they had last been in contact. Waiting.

So they waited. And waited. And waited. On the surface

49

the crew of the destroyer, battered by wind and wave, and numbed by cold, spray and squalls of sleet. Below the surface the crew of the U-boat, tight-packed in a claustrophobic cocoon, nauseated by the stench of sweat, diesel-oil, stale food and a lavatory they hadn't been able to flush for 36 hours, and becoming more and more disorientated through lack of oxygen. A couple of times Bungert tried, at 'dead slow', to slip away. But the destroyer, like a questing bloodhound, picked up the sound of their engines and followed them. They altered course, and the destroyer altered course. They stopped, and the destroyer stopped. And the waiting began all over again.

Bungert realised he had only one more card to play, and he needed to play it soon, before the storm blew itself out. In the small hours of the morning, when he hoped the crew of the destroyer would be least alert and preoccupied with keeping station, he made a dash for it. At maximum speed and depth he fled south: south because his U-boat had plenty of fuel and could stand deep into the Southern Ocean, whereas he hoped the destroyer might be short of fuel and reluctant to follow them into sea lanes far from her base.

In an instant the stealth of hide-and-seek gave way to the thunder of pursuit, with the destroyer able to follow the U-boat but not able, in the appalling weather, to mount an effective attack.

Aboard the U-boat conditions worsened. The vibration of their engines, hour after hour at maximum revs, made the crew quiver like epileptics. The heat made them sweat like pigs. The stench made them retch. Lack of oxygen made them torpid. They became more and more like punch-drunk boxers, bludgeoned to the brink of insensibility by discomfort and pain. And their ordeal seemed to have no foreseeable end, as hour after hour they fled south, like an animal running blind through the night, tracked by a pursuer it never sees but can never shake off.

Once they paused, to listen-out on their hydrophones. It was a mistake. For the destroyer was still in contact, and once again depth-charges heaved up the sea around them.

But this—though they had no way of knowing it—was the destroyer's final effort. Her captain's report said it all. *The U-boat was well handled and elusive. After a pursuit of 31 hours in grade C conditions, during which we made no fewer than 9 attacks—including two with the experimental Hedgehog—I was obliged by lack of fuel to break off the engagement and set course for Simonstown.*

The destroyer headed east for Africa. The U-boat, however, held course to the south; for Bungert had no way of knowing that the hunt had been called off. He had made the mistake of stopping once; he wasn't going to make the same mistake again. So at full speed U-102 continued to flee southward: south past the Tropic of Capricorn, south past the 50th parallel, south past the volcanic cones of Thule and Candlemas, and into the unfrequented reaches of the Scotia Sea. Not until they were farther south than a U-boat, in wartime, had ever been before, did Bungert give the order that for 48 hours his crew had been longing for: 'Stop engines.'

They lay motionless. And listened.

There was no roar of waves, no ping of Asdic, no churn of propellers. Nothing but silence. All the same Bungert waited. Only when he reckoned the sun would have set and U-102 as she surfaced would merge into the twilight, did he take the submarine to within a dozen feet of the surface. And only after another spell of seemingly endless waiting did he give the order 'Up periscope!'

He didn't *really* expect to see the destroyer thundering down on them; but the fear was still at the back of his mind, a nightmare too terrible to be discounted until it was disproved. As he rotated the viewfinder through 360° the nightmare was exorcised. There was no destroyer. There was, however, something else: something so totally unexpected that Bungert's first impulse was to down-periscope and dive.

To the north, east and west sea and sky were featureless. But to the south, filling his viewfinder, was a whiteness like the glare of distant arc-lamps, and strange spirals of green and purple gyrating in a *danse macabre* across the horizon. He was so conditioned to images of war his first thought was that he must be looking at a convoy being attacked. But even as the thought was forming he rejected it. It was impossible. Apart from the fact that no convoy would be sailing this far south, there were no ships, the light was nothing like the light of searchlights, and the spirals of green and purple nothing like tracer or vapour trails. Also the scene had an aura of tranquillity altogether different from the turmoil of war.

It was some moments before he realised that what he was looking at was the Antarctic pack-ice bathed in the light of the *aurora australis.*

He gave the order to surface, and U-102 heaved herself like a great whale out of the ocean, water cascading from her superstructure.

Not until the watch-keeping officers had scanned the horizon segment by segment with their binoculars, and then scanned it again, did Bungert give the other order his crew had been longing for: 'Off duty watch, on deck.'

They came out of the conning-tower like zombies out of their coffin. They were pale, weak and dizzy; filthy, sweaty and malodorous. But they were alive. They drew in great gulps of air, stared at the vastness of the ocean and the splendour of the aurora, and gave thanks to whatever god they believed in.

At first it was enough they had survived. They stood huddled on the deck in little groups, not doing much, not talking much, but feeling strength seep gradually back into their bodies as though they were being given a blood transfusion. Then they began to clean up, sluicing themselves down with sea water drawn up in buckets, and scrubbing clean their clothes, as though by erasing the dirt and the filth they could erase the memory of what they had been through. And as the fact that their ordeal was over sank home, they became increasingly aware of their surroundings.

It was one of those rare evenings in the Southern Ocean when there was no cloud and no wind, and the waves had been ironed out to a gentle, wide-spaced swell. About 50 miles to the south of where they had surfaced lay a vast expanse of pack-ice, glittering like white fire; while above the pack-ice shimmered the ever-changing patterns of the aurora, bands of purple, white and green interspersed with bursts of what looked like tumbling stars. It was not only the beauty of the scene that moved them, it was its sense of timelessness: the feeling that as the ice was glittering and the aurora was shimmering that evening, so they had glittered and shimmered a million years ago, and so they would still be glittering and shimmering a million years from now. They would have liked the night to be as by a miracle extended; but a little after 4 a.m. light came seeping into the sky, and Bungert gave the order to submerge. Although it struck him as highly improbable that Allied planes or warships would be patrolling this far south, even a thousand-to-one chance wasn't worth taking. So for the hours of daylight U-102 lay motionless beneath the surface while her crew slept.

For the first time in a week they slept soundly. And in their sleep several of them dreamed: dreamed they had been told that for the rest of the war they could stay beside the pack-ice; that there would be no more vibration, no more heat, no more choking for air, no more being flung from bulkhead to bulkhead, no more stench of excrement, no more slamming down their periscope so they couldn't see the men on the torpedoed merchantman burning to death in patches of oil, no more urinating in terror as the churn of propellers grew louder and the patterns of depth-charges closer; only the ice, the aurora, the wind, the sea, the sky and the stars, and the penguins and (some thought) the polar bears for company. And what gave their dream added poignancy was that even as they dreamed it they knew it was fantasy.

When it was dark U-102 resurfaced, and the other watch came up on deck. They checked the repairs that had been carried out; they recharged their batteries; they tried to swing their compasses, but soon got into difficulties because of the proximity of the magnetic pole; then they were told they could do whatever they liked. Some stood and talked; some stood and watched the aurora; some paced the deck, taking what exercise they could; and some put on survival suits and, attached to lifelines, were lowered over the side where they splashed about round the hull of the U-boat like pilot-fish round a whale, and when they had been hauled back aboard they boasted that they'd be able to tell their grandchildren they had swum in the Antarctic! It was a long time since they had known such happiness.

As the sky in the east grew lighter an *obersteurmann* came almost apologetically to Bungert: 'The men wonder if we could stay surfaced, sir? To watch the sunrise?'

His first reaction was that the idea was preposterous. There flashed through his mind the proceedings of a nightmare court martial ... 'And what, *Kapitanleutnant* Bungert, were you doing on the surface in broad daylight?' 'Well, sir, the crew wanted to watch the sunrise' ... Then he had second thoughts. The chances of their being attacked this far south were not, he told himself, a thousand-to-one, they were a million-to-one. And after all the crew had been through they could do with a morale-booster.

'Right. But one watch only on deck. The other at action stations. Ready to crash dive.'

The watch on deck never forgot what they saw that morning. Slowly a dull red glow suffused the eastern horizon. The glow deepened and brightened. The centre of it coagulated into a patch of crimson which gave the impression it was pulsating, until suddenly the upper rim of the sun burst over the horizon, and shafts of red and gold fanned out across the sky, like the coruscations of a gigantic catherine-wheel. Then, as the sun's rays hit the uneven surface of the ice, they were broken up by refraction into all the colours of the spectrum. For several minutes the pack-ice became a kaleidoscope of reds, yellows, greens and blues, as though a rainbow had tumbled from sky to earth. Then, as the sun lifted clear of the horizon, the colours gradually faded. Faded but didn't die. For in the aftermath of dawn the pack-ice went on glowing not brightly but softly: a melange of beryl and dove-grey, mother-of-pearl and lapis lazuli, amethyst and aquamarine. It was only the birth of another day. But as the submariners watched it, more than one felt something of the wonder he would have felt if he had been watching the birth of his child, and more than one remembered his dream of spending the rest of the war beside the pack-ice.

'Sir!' The radio operator came tumbling out of the conning tower. 'We've picked up a signal!'

The dream shrivelled, like paper held under glass in the rays of the sun. Bungert was catapulted from fantasy to reality. 'Bearing?'

'190°, sir. From the south.'

He couldn't believe it. To the south lay nothing but ice. No one could be transmitting from there. He looked at the radio operator without enthusiasm. 'You've joined the reciprocal club!' (It was an elementary but fairly common error for an operator taking a fix to make a 180° or reciprocal miscalculation—in other words, to pinpoint the source of the signal he was picking up as north rather than south, east rather than west.)

55

'No. I've checked.'

He stared at the pack-ice, the possibilities passing quickly through his mind, and being as quickly rejected. 'Is the signal in code?'

'No, sir. Plain language. In English. We think it's a weather report.'

He needed time to think. But if there was a warship in the offing, the surface was not the place to be caught thinking. He gave the order to dive.

Half an hour later U-102 lay motionless at 500 feet, while in the alcove which served as her captain's 'cabin' Bungert, his first lieutenant, his radio operator and a petty officer who was fluent in English pored over the signal they had so unexpectedly intercepted. They hadn't picked up the first few words, and the odd phrase had had to be guessed; but in essence it read:

. . . as usual are our 0600 hours observations. Pressure 998 falling. Temperature plus 2. Wind 40 to 45, gusting 60, south and backing. Cloud four-tenths at 1,000 feet, thickening. Intermittent fog. Forecast: a weak depression will move slowly east into the Weddell Sea. A bientôt.

The transmission undoubtedly came from the south. And, to judge by the strength of it, from not very far to the south.

"What do you make of it?' Bungert turned to his first lieutenant.

'I'd say it's a weather report from a warship, sir. She could be patrolling the edge of the ice.'

'Do you go along with that, Chief?'

The petty officer shook his head. In his opinion, he said, the Allies, who were known to be short of warships, weren't likely to have a vessel patrolling such a remote theatre of war as the Antarctic. He felt too that the language used in the signal wasn't the sort that a warship would use.

'You're the language expert. Tell us why.'

'Well, sir . . . The signal starts "as usual are our 0600 observations". That implies other observations are being sent out, at other times of the day. Then there's the way the signal ends: "*A bientôt*"—a sort of "I'll be seeing you" or "till we meet again": like between friends. I'd say these forecasts have been sent out before, and are going to be sent out again. On a regular basis. I can't see a warship doing that.'

'So what's *your* theory?'

'A weather-ship, sir. Anchored off the ice. Sending out reports two or three times a day.'

He nodded. It made sense. 'A weather-ship,' he said slowly, 'is too tempting a target to miss.'

In the next 48 hours U-102 picked up five more signals, all on the same bearing, which confirmed that their quarry was stationary and therefore more likely to be a weather-ship than a warship. Nevertheless they prepared their attack with the care of a predator who is uncertain if, at the end of the chase, he'll be faced by a tadpole or a tiger. They practised emergency surfacing and crash-diving; they rehearsed their 88mm gun-drill; and they worked out as best they could the exact position of their quarry. This wasn't easy, but by a combination of calculation and guesswork they decided the weather-ship must be anchored off the west coast of the Antarctic Peninsula at about 65° south.

'Maybe,' the chief engineer suggested, 'they're *not* on a ship. Maybe they're ashore.'

'You reckon they could survive ashore?'

This was one of many questions they asked but couldn't answer. For they knew so little about Antarctica. None of them had been anywhere near the continent: their charts didn't extend south of the 60th parallel, and their only source of reference was a single-page map in a not very up-to-date atlas. This they peered at, as astronauts might peer at the sketch of an unfamiliar planet, well aware that they were on the periphery of the unknown.

'Do you think,' a cautious *leutnant* muttered, 'the water's free of ice? That far south?'

Bungert snapped shut the atlas: 'There's only one way to find out.'

It was the start of another hunt. Only this time U-102 was the hunter.

They were lucky with their timing: a couple of months earlier or a couple of weeks later and the sea-ice would have been too thick for them. And they were lucky too with the weather. Early March that year was unusually free from blizzards, and their passage past the old sealing haunts of Livingston Island and Deception Island was less hazardous than might have been expected. They travelled by day. And cautiously, for there were still icebergs about whose edges could rip open their hull like a can-opener. But with light seas and good visibility they had no great difficulty reaching the maze of channels which *Scoresby* and the *Loch Tarbert* had passed through a year earlier. Here, like their predecessors, they were amazed by the abundance of life. They had always thought of Antarctica as a dead continent, but the sky above them was dark with birds massing for their annual migration north, and the sea around them alive with migrating penguins, dolphins and seals. And each day, three times a day, they listened to the voices of the men they were coming to kill. They almost got to know them: the Scot whose forecasts they had difficulty understanding, the man with the drawl who always ended *à bientôt*, and the man who rushed through his forecast as though afraid that time was running out for him—as indeed it was.

On 11th March they reached the end of the channels and saw ahead, bathed in the evening sunlight, a huge horseshoe bay, its southern reaches melding into a uniform expanse of ice. The weather-ship, they reckoned, was somewhere inside the bay. They now needed to change tactics: to stay submerged by day and locate their quarry by night. Bungert could see that patches of drifting ice were likely to be one hazard, and the worsening weather another.

Climatic changes in Antarctica are sudden and dramatic. An hour before sunset on the evening of 11th March there wasn't a cloud in the sky, the sea was calm and the wind a zephyr. An hour after sunset there was 10-tenths cloud, it was snowing, waves were pounding the shore, and a gale-force wind was driving rafts of drift-ice into the bay. U-102 was forced to retreat to the maze of channels. Here, in the lee of a 500-foot iceberg, she rode out the storm.

It was a strange situation. A bay in the middle of an uninhabited continent, with one group of men on one side of the bay and another group of men on the other. They were the only human beings within 1,000 miles. They didn't know one another, and had never seen or spoken to one another, yet they were about to try to kill one another. What made the situation even stranger was that three times a day one group could hear the other group talking, transmitting weather forecasts: forecasts which were a count-down to their requiem. So long as their forecasts remained bad they would live a few hours longer. When their forecasts improved they would die.

On the evening of 14th March the meteorologists forecast that the last remnants of a front would clear the Peninsula by midnight. The fifteenth of March—the Ides of March—would be a beautiful day.

That night the Chief Engineer asked to have a word with Bungert in private. He seemed embarrassed at what he was about to suggest: 'I suppose, sir, we couldn't take them prisoner?'

Bungert shook his head. 'I feel the same as you. I wish to God there was some other way. But think it out. If we give them the chance to surrender, they'll transmit an SOS. When we go back up the Peninsula, there'll be a warship waiting for us.'

'I know. The idea was crazy.'

He laid a hand on the Chief Engineer's shoulder: 'It's not your idea that's crazy. Just the war!'

A little before midnight he briefed his ship's company. 'We'll go in,' he told them, 'the moment the weather clears. We'll locate them. Stay submerged until dawn. Then surface. The 88mm will make short work of them. And we don't want any survivors.'

They saw the light almost as soon as they entered the bay: the bar of gold streaming out from a west-facing window of the hut. As the sky grew paler they could make out the outline of the hut itself: a slab-sided building less than 100 yards from the sea: the perfect target. They submerged, and kept watch through their periscope. There was no sign of life, but they could picture the men inside the hut asleep on their bunks, dreaming (as they so often dreamed themselves) of loved ones in a far country.

As soon as it was light enough for them to see clearly what they were doing, Bungert gave the order to surface.

The U-boat surfaced quietly, water cascading over her hull with hardly a sound. And with hardly a sound her crew assembled, loaded and aligned their 88mm gun. It could shoot down aircraft at a range of half-a-mile. To use it on a wooden hut at a range of 150 yards was like taking a sledgehammer to crack a nut.

When the gunner signalled that he was ready, Bungert raised his binoculars. 'Tell me the sequence.'

'First the radio mast. Then the hut. Then the building we think is a fuel store.'

'Do it.'

The first burst was about 20 feet low and a little to the right. The second a fraction high. The third spot on. The radio mast didn't so much fall as disintegrate; one second it was there, next second it wasn't. Then cannon-shells were scything into the hut, ripping open the walls, shattering bunks, tables and chairs, tossing bodies into the air like string-jerked marionettes. For a second the figure of a man was silhouetted in one of the gaps blasted out of the wall. He looked as though he was peering out to sea, shading his eyes, as though he couldn't believe what was happening. A shell cut him in half, the lower part of his body remaining for a moment incongruously upright while the upper part went flying in little pieces over the roof of the hut. The gunner, unnerved, lost his accuracy, and cannon-shell went streaking over and either side of the camp.

Out of the shattered building ran a man. In his hand was a rifle. He zig-zagged through the hail of shell and tracer against all the odds unharmed. He dropped to one knee. Their 88mm was making such a clatter they didn't hear the crack of the Lee Enfield. But one of the gun-crew doubled up and slid deadweight off the hull and into the water. He died as they were trying to haul him aboard.

That made things different. The pity which the crew of the U-boat had been feeling was metamorphosed to anger. It was as though the man by his hopeless gesture of defiance had provided them with justification for what they were doing. The 88mm swung onto him, and all that was left of what had once been a man was the snow incarnadined. Then cannon-shell and tracer were ripping once again into the hut. And the fuel store. For several seconds the shells passed clean through the fuel without igniting it; then came an explosion; a column of smoke rose out of the wreckage, and a shower of blazing diesel-fuel splattered over the encampment. Tongues of flame licked at the woodwork, hesitated, brightened, multiplied and began to devour whatever they came into contact with.

It seemed to Bungert that in such a holocaust nothing—

not even an insect let alone a human being—could live. 'Cease fire.'

One moment they were deafened by the crack of the 88mm; next moment there was a silence so absolute it hurt. No one spoke. There didn't seem to be anything to say.

They knew what they had to do next: make certain they had done the job properly. It would have been too risky to take the U-boat alongside the ice; but they had an inflatable rubber dinghy, and the shore was not much more than 50 yards away.

There were four of them in the landing party: Bungert, the Chief Engineer and two ratings. It seemed impossible that anyone could have survived, but the officers took their revolvers. Just in case.

As they moored the dinghy and clambered onto the ice a rating asked, 'What do we do, sir, if we find one of them still alive?'

'It would be kinder this way'—Bungert tapped his revolver.

They hadn't expected to find anyone alive. And they didn't.

The camp was not so much destroyed as obliterated. What the shells hadn't reduced to matchwood the flames had consumed. The bodies were barely recognisable as having once been men. It was not a place they wanted to linger in, and as soon as Bungert had satisfied himself that there were no survivors, he needed only to collect evidence of the attack to take back to Wilhelmshaven. He clambered into the debris. From one of the bodies he took an identity disc and the remains of a wallet, and from a pile of still-smouldering clothes a naval officer's cap.

'Sir!' A rating was combing through a jumble of debris which had been scattered by shell-fire. 'Looks like they were collecting rocks.'

It made him think. He remembered the surprise he

had felt when they had first picked up the transmissions: surprise that the British should have sent men deep into Antarctica to transmit weather reports. Could there, he asked himself, have been more to this weather station on the rim of the world than meteorology?

'What sort of rocks are they?'

They stood in a little circle, buffeted by the wind, passing the samples from hand to hand. None of them knew much about geology. The Chief Engineer thought they looked like granite. Bungert thought they looked like some sort of lava. 'Maybe,' one of the ratings suggested, 'they were looking for oil.'

There didn't seem to be anything of particular interest about the rocks; but if the British had bothered to collect and stockpile them, there might, Bungert told himself, be more to them than met the eye. 'We'll take a couple back,' he said. 'For analysis.'

As he bent down to pick up one of the rocks he thought, out of the corner of his eye, he saw movement; he thought one of the bodies twitched. It was what he had been dreading ever since they stepped ashore. He reached for his revolver. He had it still uncocked in his hand when there was a hail from the U-boat. 'Landing party! There's ice drifting into the bay.' The message couldn't have been plainer if the shout had been, 'We need to get out of here, fast.'

The echoes were still reverberating over the ice when a sudden explosion scattered the remains of the hut, ending in a series of staccato cracks and the whine of bullets. It was as though, as in some horror movie, one of the corpses had come to life and was firing at them. It was several seconds before they realised what was happening ... Parts of the hut were still smouldering, and the heat had touched off a belt of ammunition. They dropped to the ground as bullets went whining over the ice.

Bungert had already lost one man to an unlucky shot.

He had no intention of losing another. 'Keep down. And back to the dinghy.'

He remembered the body that he thought had moved. He stared at it. It lay motionless. But the wind, tugging at the bullet-torn cloth of the man's trousers, made it look as though one of his legs was twitching. That, he told himself, must have been what had caught his eye. With bullets still ricocheting over the ice and flames licking with renewed vigour at what was left of the hut, the landing party made for their dinghy.

A few minutes later U-102 was heading for open water; and a few minutes after that the sun came up like an oriflamme out of the ice.

Bungert never forgot the scene that morning. It disturbed him at the time; it still disturbed him some 50 years later as he lay in a hospital in Mannheim waiting to die . . . To starboard were the mountains of the Antarctic Peninsula, flamingo-pink in the light of the rising sun, their reflection mirrored with precision in the still water: a scene of beauty, tranquillity and peace. To port was an icefield wreathed in smoke, its snowdrifts bloodstained and littered with the remains of what had once been men: a scene of devastation and horror. He wasn't what you'd call a religious man; but he had the feeling, very strongly, that he was looking at God's handiwork defiled.

That night he wrote in his diary: *We are at war, and I don't see how we could have acted differently. Yet we all have a sense of guilt. For to bring war to a place like this*—he hesitated, then wrote the exact words used a year earlier by Lockwood—*seems a bit like blasphemy.*

The Ides of March

It was 2 a.m., and Lockwood was dreaming of a girl he had seen only fleetingly and spoken to only once, when he felt a tug at his shoulder. 'Wake up, sir.'

He opened his eyes and saw the familiar ice-rimed walls of the hut, and smelt the familiar smell of half-burned anthracite, and heard the petty officer's voice: 'Weather's cleared, sir.'

'Right.'

Half an hour and a mug of cocoa later Sub-lieutenant Lockwood and Petty Officer Ramsden were man-hauling their sledge over the crisp new-fallen snow. Above them the stars pulsated like globules of acetylene, and a crescent moon hung low over the mountains of the Peninsula. It was a perfect night for sledging.

It took them three hours to reach the ice-fall. They had no difficulty spotting the marker-flags, and no difficulty digging away the snow, finding the rock samples and loading them onto their sledge. The samples had been put into canvas bags—a different bag for each of the bore-holes from which they had been extracted, so that if the geologists were interested in a particular rock they could tell which borehole it had come from. The rocks from under the ice-fall looked no different from the thousand-and-one others which, over the last thirteen months, the survey teams had been bringing back to their hut for analysis. For more than a year they had been testing what seemed like endless mountainsides of rock, and not getting the slightest reaction from their instruments. They had run out of enthusiasm. So when Ramsden, out of habit, held his Geiger-counter over the bags he had no sense of expectation.

But to his very considerable surprise his Geiger-counter gave a succession of staccato clicks.

'Sir!'

Lockwood had heard the clicks. He came across and lowered *his* Geiger-counter over the bags. And this time the clicks were if anything louder: like muted machine-gun fire.

They stared at the bags with a mixture of suspicion and bewilderment. Two or three years later, they would have had no difficulty working it out. But early in 1943 not one person in a million knew anything about atomic research; and beyond the borders of Japan the names Hiroshima and Nagasaki didn't mean a thing. They were neither of them geologists; but for the past year they had been living with men who were, and they had acquired a smattering of geological knowledge.

'Exactly what,' Ramsden asked, 'do the clicks mean?'

'That the rocks are radioactive.'

'And what does *that* mean?'

'That they're rare. And valuable. And, I guess, what we've been looking for.'

'But why?'

Lockwood adjusted his skis. 'The sooner we get back, the sooner we can ask the Old Man.'

They checked that none of the bags were still hidden under the snow, then they were heading back for their hut.

They were sledging round the rim of a tadpole-shaped depression when there was a sudden succession of cracks. They slewed to a halt, staring this way and that, thinking for a moment that the ice was splitting and they were about to be catapulted into some bottomless crevasse. But there was no movement in the ice. They stared at the rocks on their sledge, not *really* expecting to see them erupting like a volcano, but suspicious of what they didn't understand. But the rocks were inanimate. It was several seconds before they realised that the noise, though loud, was coming from some way away. From the direction of their hut.

They stared at one another, and each saw his fear reflected in the other's eyes.

'Gunfire?'

The petty officer nodded.

'Come on. Quick!'

They left the sledge and set off with great lumbering strides on their skis. They were not expert skiers; they were half-a-dozen miles from the hut, and ahead lay a 500-foot snowslope which blocked their view of the coast. It would, they realised, be quite some time before they could see the hut, let alone reach it. The sound of gunfire had gone on intermittently for something like a minute, and was followed by a silence the more unnerving for being so absolute. They didn't speak. They concentrated on reaching the hut as quickly as they could, not daring to think what they'd find when they got there. It seemed a long time before they were nearing the top of the snowslope.

'Sir!' Ramsden came to a halt, panting for breath. 'Let me do a recce.'

He saw the sense of it. If a German warship *had* been shelling the hut, maybe German seamen had landed and taken it over. To go charging in blind would be fatal.

'You're right.' He pointed to a pressure-ridge near the top of the snowslope. 'That'll give us cover. We'll *both* do a recce.'

They hauled themselves to the top of the slope, pushed through the jumble of ice, and stood staring down at what was left of their hut. And of their companions.

*   *   *

He heard Ramsden, beside him, retching. He heard a voice that he didn't recognise as his own repeating over and over again, 'My God. My God. My God.' For a moment sea and sky, snowslope and icefield, seemed to waver out of focus, and he thought he was going to faint. Nothing he had imagined was anything like as terrible as what he saw: their hut reduced to ashes, the bodies of his friends sprawled lifeless in the snow, shattered by bullets and blackened by fire. For a moment, in his mind's eye, he saw them as they had been once but would never be again: Dave with his endless repertoire of jokes that everyone had heard before, John with his little acts of unobtrusive kindness, Ken forever rearranging the photographs of his wife and two young children. Then something seemed to snap inside his head, and the past which didn't bear thinking of disappeared as into the vortex of a whirlpool, and all that mattered was the present. He pushed off down the snowslope: 'Come on. Maybe someone's still alive.'

The flames by now had subsided—there was nothing much left for them to burn—but little spirals of smoke were still coiling up from charred timbers and the smouldering remains of blankets and clothes. As they moved from body to body it seemed no one had survived. Until Ramsden came to the CO.

He lay in the centre of a circle of blackened timber. There was blood from ricochet and splinter wounds all over his chest; bullets had ploughed a bloody furrow across the side of his head, and he looked as though he was badly burned. But the petty officer thought he detected a heartbeat. 'Here, sir.'

Ede's eyes were closed. Little beads of sweat were turning to ice on his forehead. His breathing was shallow.

They knelt beside him, not knowing whether to hope he regained consciousness or died in their arms. Either way, it looked as though he was going to die pretty soon. Then, unexpectedly, his eyes opened. For a moment they seemed to be staring at something a very long way away; then they focused on Lockwood. He tried to smile. And when Lockwood gently squeezed his hand, he felt the pressure of a squeeze in return.

'I'll stay with him. See what you can salvage.'

After about ten minutes Ramsden came back. His shoulders were slumped. 'There's nothing *to* salvage, sir.'

'Nothing?'

'A few tins of food. A few gallons of kerosene. And that's it.'

'Any hope of mending the radio?'

'No.'

'You stay with the Old Man. I'll have a look.'

It didn't take Lockwood long to realise that the petty officer was right. All he could find were a few dozen tins of food, most of them damaged; about ten gallons of kerosene, which was used by their motor-sledge and had been kept in a cache some way from the hut; a few half-burned blankets and clothes, and one or two metal objects such as met instruments and cooking utensils. The more they thought about their chances of survival, the more slender they seemed.

'We've had it.' Ramsden's voice was without hope.

'Well, *I've* no intention of dying!'

'You think we'll be rescued?'

'I think we'll have to rescue ourselves.'

'Aye aye, sir.'

He could tell what Ramsden was thinking: 'Bloody officers and their stiff upper lip.' He did his best to sound matter-of-fact. 'Will you stay with the Old Man? While I do something with the bodies?'

'Right, sir.'

He knew it would have been easier if the two of them had disposed of the bodies together; but he couldn't bear the thought of Ede dying alone with no one to hold him; so he steeled himself to cope with what was left of his

69

friends by himself. He realised he had neither the time nor the strength to dig graves; but it seemed to him that he and Ramsden would go quietly mad if they didn't get the bodies out of sight. So he dragged what was left of them one by one to the top of a little ridge about 50 yards from the hut, toppled them over the edge, then hacked away at the snow until he triggered off a mini-avalanche that covered them. It wasn't much of a burial, but he told himself his friends would understand and their loved ones never know.

When he got back to Ramsden, Ede was in a coma, but still alive.

They talked things over quietly and they hoped sensibly, although in the solitude and vastness of the Antarctic the decisions they arrived at seemed somehow inconsequential.

They decided there was no hope of rebuilding a shelter out of the debris of the hut; everything was too fragmented and charred. However, there was a tent in their sledge, together with survival packs, emergency rations and first aid kits. So their first priority must be to bring back the sledge, a job that Ramsden seemed to reckon was his. 'If you want to stay with the Old Man, I'll get it, sir.'

Well, Lockwood *did* want to stay with him; but he wasn't sure if it was fair on the petty officer to expect him to man-haul the sledge for five or six miles by himself.

Ramsden solved the problem for him. 'One of us ought to stay with him, sir,' he said. 'And rather you than me!'

Snow conditions and the weather were good, and Ramsden was confident he'd be back well before dark. It seemed a sensible arrangement. But as the petty officer disappeared over the crest of the snowslope, Lockwood was tempted to rush after him and beg him to stay. Never in all his life had he felt so utterly alone.

He draped what was left of one of the blankets over the CO, and sat beside him. Everything was very still and very quiet. At first it was frightening; but once he got used to it it was almost a relief to have no distractions, to be able to concentrate on the one thing that mattered. How were they going to survive?

He went over the options. First option, they could stay where they were. This was standard procedure for an expedition in trouble; but the more Lockwood thought about it the less he liked it; for he could see all too clearly what would happen. The authorities at Port Stanley would wonder why the detachment had suddenly stopped transmitting weather reports; their first assumption would be that their radio had gone on the blink, but as day followed day and there were no transmissions they would realise something more serious must have happened. But what could they do? They wouldn't be able to mount a rescue by air because the met station was well out of range of Allied aircraft. They wouldn't be able to mount a rescue by sea because with every passing day the ice was now thickening and extending farther to the north; by the time rescue operations were under way the approaches to their met station would almost certainly be impassable. So if they stayed where they were there would be no rescue. They might survive a month or even two months; then winter would close in, they would run out of food, and that would be that. Second option, they could sledge to the tip of the Antarctic Peninsula, and hope to be rescued from there. This was the emergency procedure, Ede had told them, which was to be followed in the event of some unexpected disaster—if, for example, their hut burned down or their food went bad—the thinking being that whereas their met station (at $65°$ south) was ice-free for only three or four weeks each year, the tip of the Peninsula (at $62°50'$ south) was ice-free for three or four months. If, therefore, they could get to this northernmost tip of the Peninsula any time between late December and early April a rescue ship would have a chance of getting through to them. As a corollary to this, Ede had been promised back-up. The sea lanes between Tierra del Fuego and Antarctica were patrolled at intervals by the minesweeper *Scoresby*; and if the expedition was thought to be in trouble *Scoresby* had orders to stand-in as close as she could to the tip of the Peninsula and keep an eye out for survivors. Ede had made it clear that getting to the tip of the Peninsula was no guarantee of rescue; it did, however, make rescue a possibility.

But how, Lockwood asked himself, could they get to the tip of the Peninsula in time? Already it was mid-March. By early April the whole of the Antarctic continent was likely to be surrounded by sea-ice: sealed off from the rest of the world by a barrier no human ingenuity could breach. It was over 200 miles to the tip of the Peninsula: 200 miles over some of the most difficult terrain on earth: a mosaic of snowfield and icefield, crisscrossed by precipitous mountains, bisected by pressure-ridges and colandered by crevasses. It seemed impossible that they could make the journey in three weeks. Yet what other chance did they have of survival?

He suddenly realised Ede's eyes were open, and he was trying to speak.

Lockwood bent closer. There had always been a rapport between them, and Lockwood now sensed as much as heard what the Old Man wanted. 'You'd like me to read the orders, sir?'

Ede wasn't able to nod, but his eyes were grateful.

In the last few hours Lockwood had had other things to think of than the detachment's most secret orders; but he was conscious now of a quickening of interest. They might have come to the end of the road, but at least in a few moments it seemed they were going to know why they had been brought with such secrecy to this remote corner of the Earth—provided, that is, the metal box which they knew contained their sealed orders and other 'sensitive' documents had survived the holocaust.

He found it lying beneath a pile of ash and charred rafters. An 88mm shell had blasted off one end of the box, and Ede's log and their carefully compiled geological maps, exposed to the heat, had shrivelled to cinders. But a waterproof packet, heavily sealed, had survived.

The mid-day sun was pleasantly warm as he sat in the snow beside Ede. 'I've got the orders, sir. If you'd like me to read them, blink.'

His eyelids flickered.

Lockwood unravelled the packet and broke the seal.

The orders consisted of two close-printed pages, and a further four pages of what appeared to be appendices.

Lt. Cdr. John Dickson Ede, RNVR. For your eyes only.

A Special Naval Detachment, under your command, will set up a base on the Antarctic Peninsula. From here you will transmit meteorological observations and carry out geological research.

Meteorological Directive. Your ostensible objective will be to transmit daily weather forecasts. These will facilitate Naval operations, in particular the passage of convoys, throughout the southern hemisphere.

Geological Directive. Your covert objective will be to make a geological survey of a cross-section of the Antarctic Peninsula in the hope of discovering uranium, traces of which were reported by Falkland Islands Dependencies Survey scientists in 1933. This is a Top Secret assignment. Its importance is demonstrated by a signal from the Prime Minister to President Roosevelt, the text of which has been authorised for your perusal.

Former Naval Person to President Roosevelt. 27 Nov.41

I concur with your view that US and British scientists engaged in the atomic research programme should exchange information freely and fully.

My scientific advisers tell me that the key to developing

an atomic bomb is plutonium, and that the key to plutonium is uranium. Unfortunately uranium is an extremely rare element about which little is known. Traces have been found in Australia and central Africa, and we are currently investigating a report that it exists in the mountains of the Antarctic Peninsula.

Rest assured I shall keep you fully informed of our efforts to locate and extract this key substance.

In the short term, the Chiefs of Staff regard it as imperative that we develop an atomic bomb; it is essential we do this before the Germans, and highly desirable we do it at the same time as the Americans. In the long term, harnessing atomic energy is likely to be of the greatest importance in the post-war world. Uranium appears to be the key, and a great deal therefore depends on your locating this little-known element.

In view of the fact that so much is at stake, the strictest secrecy is to be observed at all times. These orders are for your eyes only. Under no circumstances should personnel be told what they are searching for or why.

Attached as appendices are (a) An inventory of equipment and stores (b) Radio codes (c) Emergency procedures (d) FIDS maps and geological data.

He felt like a piece of wood in a millrace, an ordinary man caught up and swirled away by events that were anything but ordinary. He would dearly have liked to talk things over with Ede; but the Old Man's eyes were closed. He tried to work it out himself. He reckoned that he and Ramsden must have stumbled across the substance for which the detachment had been searching—uranium-bearing rocks—and that these rocks were likely to be a key factor in making an atomic bomb. However, he had not the faintest idea what an atomic bomb was. Phrases like 'nuclear fission', 'fall-out' and 'mushroom cloud' were not in his vocabulary: or, in 1943, in any ordinary

74

person's vocabulary. In the weeks ahead, emotions such as patriotism and loyalty were to influence the way that he felt about the uranium-bearing rocks; he was to see it as his duty to get them back to England. However, his gut reaction at the time was one of disquiet that man in his folly should have come to these farthest and most beautiful ends of the earth to search for the ultimate weapon of destruction.

He turned, as though for help, to Ede; but his commanding officer had lapsed into unconsciousness.

He got to his feet and began to scavenge through the debris of their hut. He hoped Ramsden might have been wrong to write off their radio; but he found that both transmitters had suffered direct hits; they hadn't so much disintegrated as disappeared. The same was true of their motor-sledge. However, to the pile of things already salvaged he was able to add a snow-shovel, a revolver, half a tarpaulin, a couple of first aid packs and, incongruously, a paraffin stove which had been tossed by blast some 20 yards from the hut and lay virtually undamaged in a snowdrift. At least, he thought, we'll be able to cook—provided, that is, there's anything *to* cook.

However, it quickly became apparent that food was going to be their Achilles heel. All that was left were 16 undamaged tins (most of them containing dehydrated vegetables, tea or powdered milk) and as many again that had been split, buckled and blackened by fire. Disaster had struck at a bad time. A month earlier and there would have been seals and penguins to be killed and eaten; but by mid-March the continent's migratory wildlife had fled the approaching winter. Lockwood estimated that their food would barely last them a month. So if they didn't reach the tip of the Peninsula and were rescued before the ice closed in ... well, that was something best not thought of.

He went back to Ede, and used one of the first aid packs

to dress the worst of the wounds in his chest—the great gash that ran from temple to ear to the back of his neck he didn't dare to touch. Then, in his efforts to make the Old Man comfortable, he ended up sitting in the snow, half-cradling him in his arms.

The sun streamed down on them. Lockwood hadn't slept for 16 hours. He knew there was nothing more he could do until Ramsden got back with the sledge. He shut his eyes. Everything was very still and very quiet; and although he kept telling himself he ought to stay awake, there came a time when sleep, like a benediction, blotted out both the terror of the past and the uncertainty of the future.

*   *   *

He felt, for the second time that day, a tug at his shoulder, and heard a voice saying over and over again, 'Wake up, sir!'

The sun was setting. He was stiff, cold and disorientated, and the Old Man lay deadweight in his arms. In a moment of panic he thought that Ede was dead; then sensed as much as heard the shallow rasp of his breathing. He sensed too the reproach in the petty officer's voice as he kept repeating, 'Wake up, sir!'

Reproach, he told himself, was what he deserved. It was inexcusable that for the last three hours he had slept, while Ramsden had been hauling back their sledge single-handed. 'Thank God you've made it. I'll brew some tea.'

He had already checked that the paraffin stove was working and there was tea in one of the tins. However, water in the sub-zero temperature was reluctant to boil, and by the time they were sipping their mugs of tea it was getting dark. Dark and cold.

'We need shelter. And hot food.'

Ramsden nodded; he was too exhausted to speak, let alone think.

76

'Help me put up the tent. Then I'll cook us a meal.'

Luckily for them it was one of those rare nights on the Peninsula when there was neither wind nor snow. It was numbingly cold—their one surviving thermometer read minus 26°—but the cold was a dry cold, and the sky was clear. Soon the moon lifted clear of the ice, and the gold and purple banners of the *aurora* began to weave in and out among the stars. It was a beautiful night. And the beauty helped. It made them feel that the earth was a place worth living in, and—quite illogically—that God had not forgotten them.

They did most things right that evening, and came to most of the right decisions, including the important one of heading as soon as possible for the tip of the Peninsula. But everything was much more difficult and took much longer than they anticipated. It was midnight before the tent had been erected, the meal had been cooked and eaten, and Ede's injuries had been disinfected with Acriflex and covered with sterile dressings. As they checked the guy-ropes, Ramsden said casually, 'Do you think he'll still be alive? In the morning?'

'It would be best if he wasn't.'

'I agree, sir.'

Their eyes met, each of them uncertain if the other was thinking what he was thinking.

By midnight they were asleep, the only human beings in 20 million square miles of snow and ice, as effectively cut off from the rest of the world as if they had been on the moon.

It was as well they were too exhausted to weigh up their chances of survival. Or to think about what they were going to do with Ede.

Alone

An injured man was going to be an incubus, extra weight to carry, another mouth to feed; at a time when their survival depended on speed, he would slow them down. Both Lockwood and Ramsden knew it would make things a great deal easier for them if Ede died in the night.

But next morning he was still alive. He was too weak to move or to speak; but his pulse was marginally stronger, and at odd moments he seemed aware of what was going on around him. They spoonfed him with biscuits soaked in hot tea and changed his dressings; then they set about loading the sledge.

As they sorted things into two piles—one to be taken, one to be left—Lockwood said matter-of-factly, 'We'll take him with us.'

'Right, sir.'

It was impossible to say whether Ramsden meant 'what else could we do?' or 'that will cost us our lives.'

'And we need room for the rocks.'

'With respect, sir. If we load too much on the sledge we'll never shift it.'

He realised they had been so preoccupied with surviving the night he hadn't yet told the petty officer why the rocks were so important.

He told him now, and let him read the sealed orders and the memo from Churchill. He wasn't sure if Ede would have approved, but to his way of thinking secrecy was a luxury they could no longer afford.

Ramsden was as mystified as Lockwood had been. 'Do you know what this atomic bomb is, sir?'

He shook his head.

'Or why it's so important?'

'No. But if the chiefs of staff say it's important, and Winnie says it's important, that's good enough for me . . . Now we don't need *all* the rocks. I suggest we test them. Take one or two that seem to have the most uranium in them. And ditch the rest.'

When the rock-samples were laid out ready for testing, Lockwood crawled into the tent. At least, he thought, we can give the Old Man the satisfaction of knowing his expedition has been a success.

He knelt beside him: 'Sir! I've the most wonderful news.'

Ede stared at him blankly, his eyes focused on something beyond Lockwood's comprehension.

'We've found uranium!'

For a moment Ede's eyes lit up; then all expression drained out of them.

'Do you understand?'

There was no reaction. And in a moment of intuition Lockwood guessed what the Old Man was thinking: he was thinking that Lockwood knew he was dying, and was spinning him a tall story to let him die happy.

'Chief! Lay out a groundsheet by the rocks.'

They propped him up on the groundsheet, then ran their geiger-counters over the rock-samples and let him listen to the clicks.

At first he couldn't understand what was happening. Then he couldn't believe what was happening. But when they raised him up and let him see what was happening, and held their geiger-counters to his ear, he realised that what Lockwood had told him was true.

He smiled: a smile that seemed to permeate his whole being. So, Lockwood thought, might Atlas have looked when the burden of the world was lifted from his shoulders. He realised that Ede was trying to say something.

His lips were moving, but not a sound came out. It was the ultimate test of the *rapport* between them.

He sat beside him. He took his hand. 'Don't worry, sir. We'll get the rocks back.'

The lips went on moving.

'I promise. I don't know how. But we'll get them back.'

Ede's lips were still moving. And this time Lockwood heard, very faintly, what he was saying. 'Leave me behind.'

'Chief!' His voice was loud and harsh, as though by shouting he could convince himself that what he was saying made sense. 'Give us a hand with him. Onto the sledge.'

They would have liked to make an early start while the weather was good; but finding out what weight they could man-haul, deciding what should be taken and what left behind, and loading everything so as to achieve the best balance, took far longer than they had anticipated. It was mid-day before they were ready to leave.

A couple of bone-bruising jerks on the harness and they were on their way.

It took them an hour's hard hauling, working in tandem, to reach the top of the snowslope which overlooked the site of their hut. From here they were able to look not only back to what had once been their home, but forward to the unknown country to the north: their escape route, God willing, to the outside world. They paused, panting for breath, their faces already tingling from sunglare, their clothes soaked in sweat.

As he looked down on the site of their hut, Lockwood felt suddenly loath to leave: like a swimmer who knows the boat he clings to is sinking, yet fears to let go. To his surprise he seemed able to remember only a few disconnected fragments of what had happened in the past 13 months: the warmth from their stoves when the temperature outside was minus 60, the strength of their walls when the wind was gusting 100, the odd moments of camaraderie. But even these memories, he told himself, he must put behind him. For what mattered now was not the past but the future. And getting the rocks back to England.

He turned to Ramsden. 'How many miles do you think we can do? Before dark?'

'Five. If we're lucky.'

'Let's try for ten.'

They headed north.

Everything was in their favour that first afternoon. The weather was benign. The snow was firm. Their route lay over a coastal plain that was free of the crevasses which so often make Antarctic sledging a nightmare. And they were fit and comparatively fresh. Yet they made slow progress.

One reason for this was the weight of their sledge. Heaped up on it were their tent, their sleeping-bags and their skis; what little food they had, their cooking stove and their fuel; also a handful of items too precious to be left behind—ice axe and snow shovel, instruments such as barometer and compass, first aid kits and survival packs, and a minimum of spare clothing. There was also Ede. He was slightly-built and weighed only a little over nine stone; but his weight brought their total payload to over 250 pounds. It was almost too much for a single person to pull. The ideal arrangement would have been if one of them could have gone ahead on skis to reconnoitre a route, while the other followed on snowshoes hauling the sledge. They soon found, however, that it often took their combined strength to keep the sledge moving. The result was that neither of them got a decent break from hauling, and they had to make frequent halts to be sure they were taking a safe route.

Another reason for slow progress was the terrain. Sledging on the Antarctic Peninsula is never easy. Amundsen may have averaged 30 miles a day on his dash to the

Pole, but that was over the central plateau with dogs. Manhauling a sledge through the mountains is another ball game. Even in good weather the labour is Herculean, the pitfalls multitudinous and progress snail-like. It was the sastrugi, that first afternoon, which were the bugbear. They ran diagonally across their line of advance: little snow-walls formed, like the dunes of a desert, by the prevailing wind, one slope a long gentle incline, the other an abrupt near-vertical ice-face. Sometimes they were half-a-dozen yards apart, sometimes half-a-mile. Sometimes they were less than a foot high, sometimes more than ten feet. And there was no way round then. They had to be crossed.

But what slowed them down most of all was Ede. When they came to an ice-wall they couldn't haul-up or lower-away the sledge vertically for fear of tipping him out; when they came to hummocked ice they couldn't sledge over it at speed because of the pain the jolting obviously caused him. He was an ever-present source of anxiety, a constantly-restraining factor; and Lockwood spent most of the afternoon wondering if he had been right to insist on bringing him. But the alternative didn't bear thinking of.

So they struggled on.

There was no wind, no cloud, and the sun metamorphosed the snowfields to a cauldron of brightness and heat. Soon their eyes were aching, the skin of their faces had the tightness which is a prelude to peeling, and they were suffering from the cracked lips and parched throats that are symptoms of polar thirst. They daubed their noses and cheeks with protective cream and sucked lime pastilles; but both cream and pastilles were in short supply, and the relief they brought was transient. About every quarter-of-an-hour they slewed to a halt, panting for breath. Eventually they sought the shade of a nunatak, a pyramid of volcanic rock jutting up like a mini-cathedral out of the ice. From here they studied the way ahead.

They were now approaching the end of the coastal plain. About a mile from where they were standing the level ground petered out and the mountains fell sheer to the sea in a succession of ice-falls. This was clearly a no-go area for sledges. However, it looked as though there was a good alternative route. A gentle arête, sweeping up into the main range, appeared to offer them not only a way north but, from its summit, the promise of a panoramic view of the terrain ahead. And a view of the terrain ahead was exactly what they wanted. For their maps had been destroyed in the hut, and they were having to pick a route by compass, by the line of the coast, and by the little they could remember of the layout of the Peninsula.

'Looks OK.' Ramsden, shading his eyes against the glare of the sun, was studying the arête section by section.

Lockwood nodded. He knew that distances in the Antarctic were easy to underestimate, and that the summit of an arête was no place to be caught by a blizzard; but he knew also that they needed to push on as far as they could and as fast as they could while the weather held.

'We'll give it a go.'

The weather that evening couldn't have been kinder or the snow easier. However, the arête proved longer than it looked. And steeper. By the time they heaved themselves onto the summit-ridge, the sun was already low on the horizon.

They got their panoramic view all right, breathtaking in its grandeur, but not as far-reaching as they had hoped, for their view to the north was blocked by a higher massif about a dozen miles ahead. What they *could* see, however, was the terrain immediately in front of them laid out as if on a map. And they could hardly believe their luck. Snaking northward between the mountains and the sea was a piedmont: a strip of comparatively level rocky ground, veneered in ice; a route—or at least the start of a route—to safety. The snag was that the only way onto the piedmont appeared to be via a small glacier, where they knew that sledging would be difficult if not impossible.

By this time they had been man-hauling the sledge for six hours. They longed to put up their tent, crawl into their sleeping-bags and topple headlong to oblivion. But they knew that to camp on the exposed arête would be to court disaster. They studied the glacier. It faced west, and the rays of the setting sun were transforming its seracs to battlements of fire and its crevasses to trenches of indigo. About a third of the way down it they spotted what looked like the ideal camp site: a level expanse of ice, sheltered from the wind yet free from the danger of avalanche. But could they get to it by dark?

One thing was in their favour. The setting of the sun in Antarctica is not so much a violent death as a gentle euthanasia. In many parts of the world the sun rises near-vertical out of the east, climbs to directly overhead, then plummets near-vertical into the west. In the polar regions it orbits to a different pattern. In summer it never sets; in winter it never rises; in spring and autumn it rolls around the horizon, never climbing all that far above it, never sinking all that far below it. So long after the sun had disappeared that evening it was still only a little way below the horizon and gave off a dull incandescence, as though the western skyline was being illuminated from below by flames thrown up from a subterranean furnace. Lockwood knew there would be sufficient light to sledge by right up to 9 p.m.

It was as well they had not only the afterglow of the sun to help them, but also, after a couple of hours, the moon and the aurora; for it was close to midnight before they staggered, punch-drunk with exhaustion, onto the level expanse of ice. It had been a nightmare journey. Twice the sledge had fallen onto its side; once it had toppled into a mini-crevasse. It seemed incredible that Ede should have survived. Yet as they set up their tent he was still

84

breathing, still clinging against all probability to life.

Too exhausted to cook a meal, they crawled into their sleeping-bags and within minutes were dead to the world.

In the small hours of the morning a mass of cumulus, dark as coal-dust, came drifting in from the sea. The stars were blotted out; the wind freshened, and little flurries of snow came pitting into the canvas of their tent, like the *tirailleurs* of an army massed beyond the horizon and testing the defences of an outpost soon to be obliterated.

They didn't hear the moan of the wind or the patter of the snow. Too tired even to dream, they lay insensate hour after hour until woken by the brightness of the sun. By morning the cloud had vanished as though it had never been, the wind had subsided, and the only trace of snow was a dusting of fine white powder on the surface of the ice.

It was another beautiful day.

And Ede was still with them: an albatross about their necks, a problem unresolved. More than once in the past 36 hours Lockwood and Ramsden had found themselves looking at him, looking at one another, then looking away as though ashamed of what they were thinking. They must, Lockwood told himself, bring things into the open. As they were loading the sledge he said to the petty officer, 'What on earth are we going to do with him?'

'That's up to you, sir.'

Ramsden wasn't being deliberately unhelpful, but according to his book officers gave the orders, other ranks carried them out. This was the creed he had lived by for half his life, and he wasn't now going to start marching to the beat of a different drum ... As ill-luck would have it, of all the members of the detachment Lockwood and Ramsden probably had least in common—the one a war-time officer from a middle class family, the other a career petty officer of the Royal Navy risen through the ranks. Their characters were different too: Lockwood tended to make spur-of-the-moment decisions dictated by his heart, Ramsden did everything 'by the book'. Certainly that morning they were on different wavelengths, and it took Lockwood some time to realise that his companion expected him to be displaying those qualities of leadership by which the senior service set such store. 'Let's try,' he said, 'to work this out together. As I see it, we've three choices. We can take him with us. We can leave him to die. Or we can kill him. I don't think I could kill him. Could you?'

It was a hypothetical question, but Ramsden took it literally. He looked at young Lockwood without enthusiasm. 'If you can't. And you order me to. Yes, I'll kill him.'

Lockwood was taken aback. But he told himself they had enough on their plate without falling out. 'Let's check the sledge,' he said.

As they greased the runners and tightened the lashings he tried to weigh up the alternatives.

If they took Ede with them, the odds were that he would so slow them down they would never reach the tip of the Peninsula in time to be rescued. They would get there after a journey of four or five weeks only to find the sea-ice had thickened to such an extent there was no hope of a ship getting through to them. As autumn gave way to winter they would die slowly of exposure and starvation. No one would ever know they had discovered uranium. Their mission would have failed.

If they left him to die, that would be a terrible thing to do, and a terrible thing (if they survived) to live with. They would have to off-load him from the sledge, dump him in the snow and simply drive off. And what would his thoughts be, Lockwood asked himself, as the rumble of the sledge faded to silence and he realised that would be the last thing he would ever hear apart from the moan of the wind? It was true he had whispered 'leave me'; but that would do little to mitigate the loneliness of his dying. There had to be a more merciful way.

If they decided to kill him, they had morphia and they had a revolver. The trouble with morphia was that he knew little about it and wasn't sure how much he would need to give him for an overdose to be lethal. So it would have to be the revolver: while he slept. It sounded easy, but he knew it wouldn't be. In his mind's eye he saw himself by the light of the aurora creeping up to where Ede was lying and holding the revolver to his temple, when suddenly the Old Man opened his eyes. He shuddered. But one thing he was sure of: he would never ask Ramsden to do it.

These were the facts, and the more he mulled them over the more obvious the answer became. Everything— logic, reason, self-preservation—all screamed the same message.

Kill him.

He stared at the tent where Ede was lying. And suddenly something snapped. To hell, he thought, with logic. To hell with reason. To hell with self-preservation. Weren't love and kindness and mercy the things they were supposed to be fighting for?

'We'll take him with us,' he said.

It was not the decision Ramsden had hoped for. But he had never refused an order in his life, and he wasn't going to refuse one now.

'Right, sir.' He helped carry Ede to the sledge.

An hour later they were again picking their way through the labyrinthine battlements of the glacier.

As they expected, the going was painfully slow. In a couple of hours they covered little more than a couple of hundred yards. However, as they pushed through a wall of unstable-looking seracs they spotted something that lifted their spirits. Branching off from the main glacier was a feeder-valley which looked as though it was filled not with broken ice but with hard-packed snow: a route that promised them unexpectedly easy access to the piedmont. By mid-day they were standing on the strip of level ground between the mountains and the sea.

Fifty million years ago the piedmont had been Antarctica's continental shelf, formed when Gondwanaland was drifting through more temperature seas. Now it was a desiccated terrace of rock, running parallel to the present-day line of the shore. Here and there it was split, riven and tilted by pressure into a succession of steps, faults and inclines; but long reaches of it were relatively flat; and all of it was covered in a veneer of ice that had been formed by spray flung onto it by the waves. It would be hard to imagine a better surface for sledging.

They set out, cautiously at first, then with growing confidence as they found that their sledge ran smoothly and was not too difficult to control.

It was the start of a halcyon few days in which they covered over 100 miles.

They soon fell into a routine. Knowing the ice would be best for sledging before the sun got to it, they struck camp early, brewing their tea and eating their biscuits by the light of the stars. Well before dawn they were on their way. The cold was beyond belief. If they had touched metal with their bare hands the skin would have been seared as by a flame; if they had left their faces uncovered they would have suffered the sort of frostbite that turns to gangrene. But after more than a year in the Antarctic they were experienced enough to take precautions. As the first rays of sunlight transformed the peaks from dove-grey to flamingo-pink they were heading north along the piedmont. Here again they couldn't afford a mistake. If the sledge had tipped over, that would probably have been the end of Ede; if it had slid off the piedmont and into the sea, that would probably have been the end of them all. About nine o'clock they usually stopped for a rest.

Since they were short of food, and cooking at 40° below is time-consuming, they had agreed to make do with only one hot meal a day. For lunch they relied on their emergency food packs. Several of these had survived the holocaust, and each contained enough concentrated food tablets and vitamin capsules to enable a man to survive for four days. The tablets were unappetising, but nutritious and easy to take; and after a rest of half an hour they were again heading down the piedmont.

As morning gave way to afternoon the coast of the Peninsula came under the full impact of the sun. At first the warmth was welcome; but after a while conditions began to deteriorate. The ice became first tacky, then slushy, and their sledge became increasingly difficult to shift. Ramsden saw the worsening conditions as a challenge to his very considerable strength; he thought of Antarctica as an adversary to be squared up to and conquered—he would have gone on till he dropped. Lockwood was more flexible: he thought of Antarctica as neither friend nor foe but as an alien environment to which they had to adapt—as soon as the ice became difficult, he started to look for somewhere to camp. They were careful always to choose a camp site where they would be safe if the weather worsened: well clear of the piedmont and protected by one of the many nunataks. It was a time Lockwood loved. He was dog-tired; but ahead lay the prospect of rest, a hot meal, the beauty of the sunset, and time to sit with Ede and try to bring him some sort of comfort after the ordeal of their journey. It was difficult to say if Ede was getting better or worse, but one thing was certain: he didn't want to die; he clung to life with the tenacity of a limpet to a wave-swept rock. They seemed, for the moment, to have kept gangrene at bay. But his head wound was a problem not resolved so easily. It was difficult to tell if he was brain-damaged. In his moments of consciousness he seemed perfectly lucid, but for most of the time he was in a coma, and his power of speech had been seriously impaired. The last thing they did each evening before they dossed down was check their barometer. And the barometer, night after night, read a steady 30.5. They could hardly believe their luck.

A little before mid-day on their fourth day on the piedmont they came to a horseshoe bay. It was a peaceful scene: a low, featureless shoreline, backed by an innocuous-looking flood plain, backed in turn by the great white snake of a glacier coiling down to the sea. The ice appeared to be firm, although this was something they couldn't be sure of because they were looking directly into the sun. The bay was like a mosaic of diamonds, a kaleidoscope of refracted haloes, arcs, parhelia and mocksuns too bright for their eyes to adjust to.

They headed cautiously into a whiteness so dazzling it was almost a white-out. Lockwood went first on skis; Ramsden followed about 20 yards behind, man-hauling the sledge. In most places the ice was firm; but every now and then, for no apparent reason, it seemed spongy.

Lockwood came to a halt. He felt that the petty officer had drawn the short straw. 'Do you want a hand?'

'I'm OK. You pick a route.'

He peered into the maelstrom of light. Immediately ahead was what looked like a depression. That, he told himself, was a place to avoid. A better route would be close to the glacier. He headed inland.

Everything was very still and very quiet. No wind moaned through the seracs. No waves pounded the shore. Yet there *was* a sound, so faint as to be almost imperceptible: the sound of running water. What puzzled him was that it seemed to be coming from somewhere below him. Another thing that puzzled him was the snow; it seemed to have become curiously springy, like a dance floor.

He stopped. He leaned on his ski-stick. And it disappeared. The hair pricked up on the nape of his neck and his mouth went dry and his knees limp. For he suddenly realised that all around him the snow was patterned with blue: blue that was pale mauve around the perimeter and deep sapphire at the centre. And he saw that he was standing on a snowbridge, surrounded by crevasses. A dozen yards to his left was a gaping void whose depth he could only guess at; a couple of dozen yards to his right the ice was split by a crevasse which looked as though it fell sheer to the innards of the earth.

'Get back!' His frightened shout echoed and re-echoed among the walls of ice.

But he was too late. There was a terrifying crack, a frightened curse, and as he spun round he saw the sledge, only a few yards behind him, teetering on the lip of a crevasse. Even as he stared at it, appalled, the lip of the crevasse crumbled, and great cornices of snow cascaded into the abyss.

Ramsden leapt clear.

It looked like the end of the sledge. And the end of Ede. And the end of their equipment and food. Then, at the last moment, the sledge struck solid ice and came to rest half hanging over the crevasse.

They didn't have time to think. They made a dash for it. Ramsden got there first. He grabbed the runners, dug in his feet, and tried to pull the sledge clear. Lockwood, arriving a second later, saw the danger. If the sledge was freed it was likely to topple headlong into the crevasse.

'No! Throw me the rope!'

The petty officer didn't hesitate. His obedience to an order—even one that put his life in jeopardy—was instinctive. He grabbed the rope that was coiled in the stern of the sledge and flung it to Lockwood.

'And your ice axe!'

It was like parting with a lifeline; but again he didn't hesitate. Lockwood drove the axe deep into the ice and belayed the rope to it and the sledge was held firm. They took up the slack, and inch by inch levered it away from the lip of the crevasse and onto ice that was solid. They went on heaving it back until all traces of blue had vanished, and the ice, when they stamped on it, no longer felt spongy. Then they collapsed in a heap in the snow, numb with shock.

Lockwood, to his annoyance, couldn't stop trembling. He knew he had been at fault; but offering an apology that didn't sound like making excuses wasn't easy. 'Sorry about that,' he muttered. 'I should have gone more carefully.'

'Like we agreed, sir. Better safe than sorry.'

There was an awkward silence; then Lockwood went to check that the Old Man hadn't been injured, while Ramsden retrieved the rope.

Ede, mercifully, was in a coma and seemed unaware of what had been happening. As for the rope, Ramsden saw it had been roughened up as they hauled back the sledge; but it was the only one they had, so there wasn't much he could do except recoil it and put it back on the sledge.

The flood plain was clearly no place to linger. However, it had to be either crossed or circumvented. It was Ramsden who suggested a way round it. 'How about the glacier?'

Lockwood studied it section by section. Glaciers were about the worst possible terrain for man-hauling a sledge, but in this case there didn't seem to be any alternative. 'Looks the best bet,' he said. 'You go first. I'll take the sledge.'

'Aye aye, sir.' Ramsden, visibly relieved, strapped on his skis.

Forewarned and forearmed, he did indeed pick a better route than Lockwood, avoiding the potholes and crevasses and arriving without mishap at the glacial moraine.

The glacier wasn't particularly wide or deeply crevassed, but they had a hard time crossing it. What made their traverse particularly difficult was the airlessness. It was mid-afternoon and the sun, blazing down on them, was reflected and refracted by the ice with a ferocity that seemed to suck the oxygen out of the air. Before they were half-way across they were suffering from glacier lassitude. The weather didn't help: there was no wind and no movement. They were the only living creatures in a world that seemed to be frozen, as in a time warp, to absolute stillness. On one of their halts Lockwood unearthed the barometer. It was not so much falling as plummeting.

By the time they emerged from the glacier and were standing once again on the piedmont, the sun was setting. And what a sunset it was!

The sky was turquoise. In the west the sun hung low over the sea like a great globule of blood. In the east the moon hung low over the mountains like a disc of copper, magnified by refraction and encircled by haloes. And even more spectacular was the sea. It was covered in frost-smoke—layers of foglike vapour formed by cold air passing over the sun-heated water. And the rays of the dying sun were transforming the frost-smoke to a kaleidoscope of scarlet and vermilion, so that it looked as though the sea was on fire.

The scene was beautiful. But beautiful with the menace of a tiger poised to spring. They took particular care, that evening, over choosing a site for their tent; for the indications were that the weather was about to break, and they knew that an ill-chosen camp site could cost them their lives. It was almost dark before they found what they were looking for: a nunatak in a north-facing snowfield, well away from the sea. Here they set up their tent in the shelter of a 40-foot outcrop of granite, hammering the ground-pegs deep into the ice, weighing down the periphery of the canvas with boulders, and securing an extra tarpaulin over the entrance-flap.

Before dossing down they again checked the barometer.

It read 29.2, falling. Away in the south the sky had an opaqueness they didn't like the look of. Nor did they like the look of the moon. Its haloes, huge and brilliant, seemed to be now expanding, now contracting, as though the night was panting for breath.

As they crawled into their sleeping-bags, they wondered how long it would be before the bad weather hit them.

It came out of the south not with the fury of a frenzied assault, but with the measured tread of a great army confident in its invincibility. First came little flurries of wind, hesitant, now from this direction now from that, scuffing up the snow and sending it scurrying over the piedmont. Then come little puffs of cumulus, like marauding impis sent ahead to test an adversary's defences. The puffs of cumulus grew darker and more numerous; they coalesced into a layer of unbroken cloud. But it wasn't until the arrival of the cumulo-nimbus that it started to snow. At first the snow was hesitant as the wind: a flurry from the south-east then a pause, a flurry from the south-west then another pause. But slowly the flakes became heavier and more closely packed, and the flurries coalesced into a continuous fall; by midnight snow was pouring out of the sky like a never-ending avalanche. And with the snow came the cold: cold given a cutting edge by a wind straight off the ice-cap. Down by the shore the sea-ice thickened and spread. On the walls of their tent the condensation from their breathing solidified to ice. Every now and then, as the tent shuddered in the wind, the ice was dislodged and splattered down on their sleeping-bags.

They stirred uneasily, vaguely aware of what was going on but reluctant to leave the dreamworld of their sleeping-bags for the reality of their tent.

But dreams are an insubstantial refuge. In the small hours of the morning the wind increased. It built up from a dull roar to a cacophony of booms and screams, punctuated by an occasional terrifying crack as the tarpaulin they

94

had secured to the entrance-flap broke free and began to slam this way and that like a jibbing sail.

Lockwood lit their pressure-lamp, and a pool of anaemic light crept as though frightened round the walls of the tent. He focused the light on the entrance-flap.

Ramsden guessed what he was thinking: 'I wouldn't!'

'No?'

'Too risky. And you'd let in too much snow.'

He realised the petty officer was right. A blow from the tarpaulin could break his arm or even his neck; and as he was crawling out through the open flap, the tent would become a maelstrom of snow.

So there was nothing they could do but lie in their sleeping-bags, listening and waiting, hoping the storm would abate.

But it didn't abate. If anything it increased in fury, jerking the tarpaulin this way and that until a particularly vicious gust wrenched it free and smashed it against the face of the nunatak. There was a staccato crack, like a burst of gunfire; the tarpaulin was shredded to fragments, and snow came hammering against the entrance to the tent. They stared at the canvas, steeling themselves not to flinch as it quivered and jerked. It was the hour of the blizzard. All they could do was sit it out. And hope it wouldn't last long.

Their hopes were not realised. The wind and the snow continued not merely hour after hour, but day after day. And they found themselves in the situation they had dreaded: incarcerated in their tent, like prisoners in a cell, while down by the shore the sea-ice thickened and spread northward towards the tip of the Peninsula.

To say they were uncomfortable would be an understatement. Their tent was a lightweight emergency tent for two. For three it was a crush. For three plus gear and cooking equipment it was purgatory. Their sleeping-bags were jam-packed, half on top of one another. Any movement created a major (and unpopular) upheaval. So each had his allotted space. Ede was on the inside, wedged up against the nunatak. In theory this was prime position, but in practice drift-snow piling up between the tent and the nunatak made the canvas bulge inwards, and so restricted his breathing-space that he was forever half-choking and fighting for air. Ramsden was in the middle. This was the warmest place but also the most uncomfortable; every time Ede or Lockwood moved they dug an arm or a leg into some part of the petty officer's body. Lockwood was on the outside. This was the coldest place. It was next to the entrance-flap, which meant it was draughty; it was also the lowest part of the tent, which meant that moisture tended to trickle down there and solidify. Sometimes when Lockwood woke he couldn't move his head; it was frozen solid to his sleeping-bag by a girdle of ice.

It wasn't long before they began to suffer all the ills that polar explorers in difficulties are heir to. Diarrhoea and heartburn—a result of their ill-cooked and unbalanced diet; cramp—a result of having to lie in the same position hour after hour; disorientation—a result of day and night being merged into a uniform limbo of near-total darkness; and above all cold. Cold may not be the most dramatic of afflictions, but Dante knew what he was doing when he made the innermost circle of his Inferno 'all frozen', and entombed the Judases of the world in pits of ice; for few things are harder to bear than the sort of continuous numbing cold which makes every pore of the body ache, yet never reaches the intensity that brings the relief of unconsciousness.

They began to deteriorate, both physically and mentally.

Physically, little jobs like brewing tea, chipping away the ice or tightening the guy-ropes became increasingly difficult; waking up became increasingly less inviting.

Mentally, they found themselves becoming more and more irritated by one another's personal idiosyncrasies—

the way they kept their diaries was a case in point. Lockwood made no secret of what he was writing in his, and often left it lying about in the tent. Ramsden, on the other hand, clearly regarded his as confidential; he always kept it with him—even when they were sledging, it was wedged into the survival pack on his back. And it now occurred to Lockwood that he ought perhaps to check what the petty officer had been writing.

'Have you,' he asked, 'mentioned the rocks in that diary of yours?'

Ramsden nodded.

'I hope you haven't said where we found them?'

The petty officer was puzzled. 'Why not?'

'In case the diary falls into the wrong hands.'

'You mean in case Jerry finds it?'

'I know it isn't likely. But it *is* possible.'

Ramsden thought about it. 'Right, sir,' he said eventually. 'That never occurred to me.' And over the next few days Lockwood noticed much tearing out of pages and rewriting.

Not that their diaries seemed all that important. A more pressing problem by far was what to do with their commanding officer. For as the blizzard continued without respite there were times when the Old Man's incoherent mumbling frayed their nerves, when his heavy breathing and fits of choking denied them sleep, and when he couldn't keep down the food they prepared for him and the stench in the tent became almost more than they could stomach.

At times like these Lockwood was tempted to reach for his revolver.

For five days they were prisoners in a six-foot by five-foot cell that they couldn't get out of. All they could do was lie in their sleeping-bags, knowing that with every moan of the wind their expectation of life was draining away. But at last, on the morning of the sixth day, the wind dropped and the snow subsided to the occasional flurry.

It was a new world they crawled into. Four feet of snow had fallen. Summer had gone. Autumn had come. And winter was all too obviously in the offing.

They set out for the piedmont, knowing their lives depended on what they found there. If the sea-ice had thickened to a solid sheet, their number was up.

The distance was less than a quarter-of-a-mile but it took them more than an hour. In the powder snow their skis were useless, and with every step they took they sank in up to their waists. Man-hauling the sledge didn't bear thinking of. When at last they stood staring at the ice, it was worse than they had hoped but not as bad as they had feared.

It was as though, during the week they had been incarcerated, a myriad seamstresses had woven an enormous patchwork quilt of brash-ice and fast-ice, raft-ice and pressure ice, ice-floes and icebergs to form a mosaic that was not yet solid but which had about it an air of depressing permanence.

Lockwood pointed to the occasional leads and pools. 'A minesweeper could get through that.'

Ramsden was silent.

'Well, couldn't it?'

'Like it is now. Not if it gets any thicker.'

'We can still make it.'

'Two of us, maybe. Three of us, not a chance.'

He chose his words carefully. 'You think we ought to kill him, don't you?'

'Yes.'

'You don't see that as murder?'

'As I see it, sir, gettin' the rocks back is what matters.'

'I'm with you there. I promised the Old Man we'd get them back. And if the *only* way of getting them back is to kill him, I'll do it.'

Ramsden said nothing.

'Don't you believe me?'

'Actions speak louder than words.'

He was wondering what to say to *that* when the petty officer launched into an unexpected tirade.

'You think all I care about is myself, don't you? Saving *my* neck. But it's not like that. I reckon we owe it to the blokes who died. They was good blokes. And if we *don't* get the rocks back, they'll have died for nothing, won't they? Better kill one man, I say, than bugger up the whole operation.'

He saw the sense of it; but something—and something other than squeamishness—made him unwilling, yet, to pull the trigger. 'If it has to be done,' he said slowly, 'I'll do it. But in my own time.'

Ramsden walked to the edge of the piedmont and started kicking powder snow onto the sea-ice. It was obvious he was thinking 'tomorrow never comes'.

When they got back to the tent they decided, more in hope than expectation, to try out the sledge.

It was like hauling a load of bricks through glue. Neither of them, by himself, could move it an inch. With both of them heaving for all they were worth, the sledge edged forward a couple of feet, then toppled over onto its side. And that was unloaded! It was obvious that by day they were immobile as a car without wheels. But by night, they told themselves, it could be another story. For as the temperature dropped, the surface-snow would freeze into a solid crust, a crust that might well become firm enough to bear the weight of their sledge. They knew that sledging by night would be risky, especially in bad weather. But with the sea-ice now thickening with every passing day, it was a risk they had to take.

They cooked a meal, then took it in turns to cat-nap, one of them sleeping while the other kept an eye on the weather and tested the snow. It was midnight before they reckoned it might be firm enough.

As they set out, it was very still and very clear and cold beyond belief. Down by the shore the sea-ice was cracking and groaning as the temperature dropped. Around them the glaciers glittered like rivers of quicksilver. Above them the moon hung like a silver dish over the mountains of the Peninsula. And the ice was surprisingly firm. As they hauled their sledge over it, the runners left hardly a mark.

Soon they were again heading north along the piedmont.

They were telling themselves that things could be a great deal worse, when a skein of cloud came scudding in from the sea, the light went out of the sky, and it started to snow.

It was an augury: the prelude to ten days of alternate hope and despair, with the periods of hope becoming shorter and less frequent and the periods of despair longer and more frequent. The problem was the weather. It was never the same for two hours running. They would be sledging along at a decent pace when the sky would darken and it would start to snow. They would grind to a halt, and wonder what to do next. It was then that sod's law came into operation. If they unloaded the sledge and set up camp—a job that took the better part of an hour—then the weather would clear. If they opted to go on sledging, the snow would get worse. It was a start-stop scenario that frayed their nerves. When the going and the weather were good and they were bowling along the piedmont at three or four miles an hour, the tip of the Peninsula seemed almost within reach; when the going and the weather were bad and they were confined to their tent, it seemed distant as a rainbow's end. What added to their frustration was that they could see the sea-ice gradually thickening. In Lockwood's darker moments he likened their situation to that of men in a condemned cell who, looking out through the bars, could see the gallows on which they were about to be hanged being constructed plank by plank. For a while the ice appeared each day to get only marginally more solid; but one morning when they made their way down to the shore after an exceptionally cold night, they found that the open pools and the zigzag leads had vanished. The ice extended in an unbroken sheet far out to sea.

Neither of them had much to say that morning.

After a while they began to run short of things. Not anything important—yet—but enough to remind them of the spectre of starvation to come. They became short of bandages for Ede—Lockwood had to wash and re-use the few that were left again and again. One morning they used up their last spoonful of sugar, a couple of evenings later their last few grains of coffee. They also began to lose things. Again nothing important; but in the hurly-burly of erecting and dismantling their tent, often in darkness and near-blizzard, they mislaid a pair of snow-goggles and a tent peg. Little things; but Lockwood couldn't help remembering the adage that a horse, a rider, a message, a battle, a war and a kingdom might be lost 'all through the loss of a horseshoe nail'.

They knew they were becoming weaker, and were falling seriously behind schedule.

There were only two things they could so about this: kill Ede, or try to push on even faster and even when conditions were bad. Lockwood still vetoed the first alternative. So they were reduced willy-nilly to the second. They began to take risks: to sledge over terrain where their survey teams would never have set foot, and to keep going in weather Ede would never have allowed them out in.

On the 25th day of their journey, the weather was difficult: neither so bad that they felt justified in crawling into their sleeping-bags, nor so good that they felt safe sledging. However, they had agreed to keep going so long as conditions were even remotely possible. And indeed there were times that evening, when the clouds broke and moonlight lacquered the snowfields in a veneer of silver, when the going was not too bad. But there were other times, when nine-tenths cloud hung low over the snowfields and the light was deceptive, when they could only grope forward, like mariners in uncharted seas, 'by guess and by God'. Earlier in the day they had been forced off the piedmont by a succession of ice-cliffs, and they were now crossing the foothills of the main range, an area of apparently featureless snowfields. These were in fact full of gentle rises and shallow depressions, but in the half-light they had the appearance of a uniform and virtually level plain. Ramsden, who was in the lead, never spotted the saucer-shaped depression. He skied straight into it.

And vanished.

'Ahhhh! Ahhhh! Ahhhh!' The petty officer's scream of terror echoed and re-echoed between the walls of the crevasse. He tried to slam his axe into the ice, but it didn't hold. He felt the jerk of the rope attaching him to the sledge; but the rope, roughed up and weakened, snapped. And still he was falling. Down and round. Round and down. Ricocheting from wall to wall until he crunched into a projecting ledge of ice. Pain knifed through his legs. Darkness like the maw of a great wave engulfed him. And he lay unconscious and broken as a rag doll, above him 100 feet of pale blue ice framing a slit of sky, below him 100 feet of ice of a darker blue, framing a little subterranean river on its way from glacier to sea.

For a long time he lay without movement. But eventually, after something like an hour, his eyes opened and, like a swimmer fighting through surf, he struggled back to consciousness. He felt the most terrible coldness and a dull ache at the base of his spine, but not much pain. However, when he tried to move his legs nothing happened, and it didn't take him long to work out that he was paralysed from the waist down. He started shouting for help.

'Help . . . Help me . . . I can't move.'

But no reassuring face was framed against the slit of sky. No rope came coiling down from the lip of the crevasse. And it came to him that he had been left to die.

It felt suddenly colder in the crevasse, colder and darker. He stared at the walls of ice, realised they were the last things on earth he was going to see, and shivered. What a way to go, he thought. His first emotion was bitterness, and because there was nothing else and nobody else he could focus his bitterness on, he focused it on Lockwood. Incompetent young bastard, he thought: falling asleep in the sun while I bring back the sledge, giving me the worst place in the tent to sleep in, not having the guts to kill the Old Man, and now this, walking away and leaving me to die. However, he was not by nature a vindictive man, and as the time of his death drew closer his thoughts turned to what mattered to him most: the creed by which he had lived. He had spent his life obeying orders, and it worried him that he was now about to die with his orders unfulfilled. Young Lockwood, he told himself, would never survive the winter; the rocks would never get back to England; this atomic bomb (whatever it was) would never be made; and all because they hadn't carried out their orders . . . With his legs paralysed and only minutes to live, there didn't seem to be much he could do about this. Then it occurred to him that maybe young Lockwood would die and his body would never be found, but that *he* would die and *his* body would one day be found. So I must make certain, he thought, that the people who find me realise my diary is important, because *that* will tell them about the uranium-bearing rocks.

Painfully—because some movements turned the ache at the base of his spine into spasms of agony—he opened his survival pack. Awkwardly—because his fingers were

103

numb and had no feeling in them—he extracted his diary. Holding it close to his chest, he told himself that he had now done everything possible to carry out his orders. So there was nothing more to live for.

After a while he noticed a solitary star—Canopus—silhouetted against the slit of the sky. He stared at it, thinking it looked as cold as he was, and so very far away. He was wondering what, if anything, lay beyond it, when he slid into the unconsciousness from which there is no awakening.

*   *   *

One moment the petty officer was there. Next moment all that was left of him was a scream. The sledge gave a momentary lurch as the rope tightened, then continued on its way, and Lockwood told himself the rope had parted and Ramsden was surely dead. He slewed to a halt, half-expecting to find himself surrounded by crevasses. But the snow ahead looked firm and white. Perhaps, he thought, there's only one crevasse and it's not too deep and he's still alive.

His instinct was to rush forward; but that, he knew, would be fatal. Slowly, testing each foothold, he followed the tracks of Ramsden's skis. He was within a dozen feet of the crevasse before he spotted it: a line of innocent-looking blue merging chameleonlike into the greyness of the snow. No wonder, he thought, the poor devil didn't see it. He made certain the sledge was on firm ice, extended his harness as far as it would go, crawled forward, and peered into the abyss.

When he saw how deep it was he felt certain Ramsden was dead. 'Chief! Chief! Are you there?'

'Chief, Chief, Chief . . . Are you there, there, there'. The echoes mocked him, ricocheting *diminuendo* from wall to wall. Little flurries of snow plastered his goggles, making it difficult to see. There's no way, he told himself, he could have survived.

Then he saw him. Far below. Squelched out like a fallen plum. Motionless.

I'd need 100 feet of rope, he thought, to get to him. And all I've got is a dozen feet of harness.

'Chief! Chief! Chief' . . . For a moment he couldn't think of his Christian name . . . 'Jim! Jim! Jim! Can you hear me?'

The wind moaned through the crevasse, carrying his voice to places where no sound from a living creature had ever been heard. I haven't a hope, he thought, of getting down to him.

He crawled back to the sledge. It struck him as ironic that Ramsden, not Ede, should have been the first of them to die. The Old Man was conscious, and aware something was wrong. He bent over him. 'The Chief's fallen into a crevasse.'

'Is he dead?'

'I think so.'

There was a silence that went on and on, as both of them adjusted to the fact that if, before the accident, the odds against them had been 100 to 1, they were now more like 1,000 to 1. Then Lockwood realised that Ede was trying to speak. He leaned closer.

'Leave us. Leave us both.'

He sat on the sledge, his head in his hands, and tried to work things out. Common sense told him the Old Man was right. It was the rocks that mattered. By himself he might still have a chance—albeit a slender one—of getting them back; with injured passengers he had no chance at all. Yet as, earlier, he had refused to leave Ede, so, now, he refused to leave Ramsden. He stayed by the sledge, and every few minutes crawled to the lip of the crevasse and stared at the splayed-out figure; but it never moved. He shouted; but there was never any response.

After something like an hour he told himself it was no good. There was nothing he could do.

He checked that Ede was strapped in, and began man-hauling the sledge away from the crevasse.

He had gone only a few yards when he could have sworn he heard Ramsden's voice. 'Help!' It sounded like. 'Help me. I can't move.'

He told himself he was imagining things, hallucinating. And if by some chance he *wasn't* hallucinating, if by some miracle the petty officer *was* alive, he might as well still keep going. Because there wasn't a thing he could do to help him.

He headed into the night.

And it wasn't long before the cries gave way to silence.

Lockwood recorded the events of the next nine days in his diary.

6 April. Weather fine. Should have made good progress. But without Ramsden everything is MUCH more difficult and takes MUCH longer. Covered 8 miles. Sea-ice thickening. It now looks impenetrable.

7 April. Weather poor. Confined p.m. to tent. Covered only 3 miles.

8 April. Blizzard. Confined to tent. Ede weaker.

9 April. Blizzard. Confined to tent. Don't like the look of Ede's head wound.

10 April. Weather better. Climbed ridge AND SAW TIP OF THE PENINSULA! Only another 30 miles to go. Sad to think Ramsden got so close and never saw it. Ede very weak.

11 April. Weather good. Ice good. Made good progress. Wonderful day till nightfall, when my worst fears were realised. Ede's head wound is turning septic.

12 April. Weather fair. Progress fair. Ede delirious.

13 April. Weather fair. Progress fair. Surprised Ede lasted the night.

14 April. Nearing tip of Peninsula. Terrain not too bad, and downhill all the way. But am afraid we're too late. There is now no break in the ice, and all round the tip of the Peninsula it extends far out to sea. But I keep telling the Old Man we still have a chance—what else is he hanging onto life for?

The tip of the Antarctic Peninsula consists of three granite headlands, bunched together like knuckles, thrust out into the Drake Passage. Lockwood wasn't sure which headland was the most northerly, but it was of no consequence: he could be spotted and rescued as easily from one as from another. Or rather, he could have been spotted and rescued if it hadn't been for the sea-ice.

Right up to the last moment he had hoped that by some miracle, by some freak combination of current, wind and tide, the northern extremity of the Peninsula might be free of ice. It wasn't. The pack was thick and solid—an icebreaker might perhaps have forced a way through, no other vessel would have a chance—and it extended far offshore. Only along the distant horizon was there a water sky: a band of dark green, caused by the reflection of the open sea on clouds. They had about as much chance of being rescued as if they had been on the moon.

He set up their tent like an automaton.

For the last 48 hours Ede had been alternating between spells of unconsciousness, delirium and lucidity. In one of the latter he asked Lockwood to let him see the pack-ice.

There was a limit to prevarication; and about the time the sun was setting he ran out of excuses and took the Old Man to the tip of the Peninsula.

They sat side by side on the sledge, staring at the limitless expanse of ice.

For a long time Ede said nothing, and Lockwood wondered if perhaps he was too far gone for the implication of what he saw to sink home. But when he did speak, that idea was very swiftly discounted.

'Remember your promise?'

'Yes.'

'*What* did you promise?'

'That I'd get the rocks back.'

'Then you'll have to survive the winter, won't you?'

'Yes, sir.'

For a moment Ede's eyes were very clear and very bright; his voice was stronger than it had been for weeks. 'You can do it. I *know* you can do it. Promise me you'll do it.'

'I'll do my best.'

'Not good enough. Promise me you'll survive.'

Why not? he thought, if it makes him happy: 'I promise,' he said, 'I'll survive.'

Ede's eyes clouded with pain. It was as though he had put everything into his sudden burst of speaking, and the effort had used up what little strength he had. But he still had one last message to get across. 'I'll help you,' he whispered. 'Remember that. Always remember that. I'll help you.'

Those were his last words. He closed his eyes and drifted into unconsciousness.

When they got back to the tent, Lockwood put all their remaining capsules of morphia together, and gave him an injection.

In the small hours of the night he dreamed that he was in the sitting-room of his parents' house in Norwood. A log fire was glowing in the hearth, and to keep in the warmth his mother got up and drew the curtains. The curtains were heavy, held in place by wooden rings which ran along the curtain-rail with a rattle. He stirred but didn't wake.

When he *did* wake, he found that Ede's body was already stiffening. What I heard in my dream, he thought, must have been his death rattle.

He carried the body out of the tent.

He sat on a ledge of rocks, the Old Man laid out beside him, while the sun came welling up through the ice. It wasn't the most spectacular of sunrises—there was too much cloud—but it had a quiet beauty for which he was thankful. There are worse places, he thought, to die in.

Rather to his surprise, he didn't feel all that afraid; but he did feel an almost unbearable loneliness. It would have been nice, he thought, to have someone to share the beauty of the sunrise with.

Along the north horizon the water sky was shimmering like a band of emerald. It reminded him of a distant forest: a line of fir trees shaken by the wind.

And suddenly she was there. The most beautiful girl he had ever seen: in a white fox coat and boots of ermine, standing beside a team of pure white dogs. She smiled at him. And walked into the forest.

He closed his eyes and counted up to ten, and when he opened them of course she was gone.

But his fantasy-girl left a legacy. He felt suddenly reluctant to die. And he remembered his promise to Ede.

Winter

He felt he hadn't much hope of keeping his promise.

His only shelter was a lightweight tent, so how could he survive the winter blizzards? He had virtually no fuel for heating, so how could he avoid being frozen to death? He had enough food for only eight or nine days, so how could he hope to stay alive for eight or nine months? A betting man wouldn't have given him a chance in a hundred thousand.

Yet even as he realised how heavily the odds were stacked against him, he felt welling up within him a determination to live. He was 22, and all the things he had never seen, all the words he had never heard whispered, and all the things he had never done became suddenly imbued with the bitter-sweet desirability of the unattainable. Life had never promised so much as now, when it seemed he was about to lose it.

In the north the water sky shimmered green as the trees of a forest, and he half expected to see her again, the girl with the snow-white dogs and the smiling eyes. There was no sign of her. But he told himself she was there, waiting for him, the epitome of fantasies unfulfilled.

He looked about him, desperately, as though hoping by some miracle to see the wherewithal of survival.

But all he could see was mile after thousand square mile of ice.

And the body of John Ede.

The idea was so terrible he tried to convince himself he had never *really* thought of it. But a voice inside him whispered: 'Be honest. You thought about it right from the start. Why else have you been carrying him round with you?'

He jumped to his feet, determined to put the unthinkable out of his mind. If I'm to have any sort of chance, he told himself, I need to build a survival shelter, and I need to build it soon and in the right place.

He scanned the headlands methodically, section by section, ruling out first one site then another—too near the sea, too exposed, too far from the stones he would need for building it. The most likely place, he decided, was near the centre of the east headland, where a cluster of nunataks rose like mini-pyramids out of the ice. That would be the area to reconnoitre first.

He told himself he'd think about burying the Old Man when he got back. In the meantime his body was dry and in the shade. It wouldn't deteriorate.

An hour later he was picking his way through the nunataks—granite outcrops which looked as though they had sprung up through the ice only to be fractured, compressed and pushed half-way back again by a giant's footstep. He ruled out the first he came to as too exposed. He was about to rule out the second as too precipitous when he saw the cave.

It was as though he had caught a fleeting glimpse of the first step in a long and perilous stairway which might, just possibly, lead to safety.

When he got to the 'cave' he found that in fact it was little more than an overhang: a hollow about forty feet long, ten or twelve feet high and eight or nine feet wide, scoured out of the rock by the river of some bygone age. In terms of actual shelter it provided no more than one wall and half a roof; but it *did* provide protection from the prevailing wind and the snow, and perhaps most important of all it lay close to an area of potential building material. For the seaward face of the nunatak had been split by volcanic pressure into a conglomeration of granite

boulders, some big as a car, some small as a marble—
ideal material for building dry-stone walls. And there was
another plus point. Within easy walking distance was a
beach, littered with kelp and shingle, both of which, Lockwood reckoned, would be useful for filling in cracks and
crevices between the stones.

He spent the rest of the day exploring the other headlands, but found nothing half as promising as his 'cave'.
So a little before sunset he made his way back there,
together with his sledge, his tent and the body of John
Ede. It was too late, he decided, to bury the Old Man—
that was something he'd think about tomorrow. He set
up his tent in the shelter of the overhang, crawled into
his sleeping-bag and tried to will himself to sleep.

He was dog-tired. But sleep wouldn't come. For he
couldn't get out of his mind the fact that he was the only
human being on an entire continent. One man surrounded by something like ten million square miles of
ice.

His promise seemed, that night, little more than a
chimera.

Next morning he woke to the howl of a 60-knot wind
and snow streaming near-horizontal over his nunatak. He
lay in his sleeping-bag hour after hour, working out what
sort of shelter to build and how to build it. The knowledge
that his life depended on getting it right concentrated his
mind wonderfully!

It was 36 hours before the wind and the snow eased off
and he was able to make a start.

He decided to build his survival shelter close to one
end of the 'cave' where the roof was low and the ground
comparatively level. The measurements he decided on
were 7 foot by 7 foot, an area big enough to set up his
tent in and small enough to conserve what little heat he
could generate. His first job was to clear this area of ice
and loose stones. Then came the difficult part: building

the three walls (the overhang provided the fourth wall and most of the roof). Every stone he used had to be prised out of the ice and carried into position. The larger stones, which he used for the base of the walls, were often so heavy he could hardly lift them; they had to be hacked out, levered onto his sledge, hauled back one at a time and offloaded beneath the overhang. The stones had then to be fitted together, like the pieces of a huge three-dimensional jigsaw puzzle, into walls which were thick and strong and contained as few cracks and crevices as possible. Where there *were* cracks and crevices, he could, he told himself, fill them with a mixture of shingle and kelp from the beach. He was tempted to start building as soon as he had collected a few dozen stones, but he quickly realised this wasn't the most efficient way of going about things. The best thing to do would be to gather together *all* the stones he was going to need, grade them according to size, arrange them in three heaps (one for each wall), and not start the actual building until all his material had been assembled. This way, when it came to fitting the stones together, he would have a wide variety of shapes and sizes to choose from.

So for a week he did nothing but quarry stones and carry them to the overhang.

It was work that sapped both his patience and his strength; and his strength was already at a low ebb because he was short of food.

Almost every hour of every day he asked himself if building a shelter was worth the effort. What was the use of protecting himself from the cold if he was going to die in any case from hunger? But he plodded on, restricting himself each day to two cups of tea, a biscuit at sunrise, and one small hot meal at sunset, and telling himself there was always the million-to-one chance that manna, as in a miracle, would descend from heaven.

And on the last day of April the miracle occurred.

He was down at the water's edge collecting seaweed when he saw the seals.

Most seals and penguins have left Antarctica by the end of March, let alone the end of April; but sometimes—due to injury or late breeding—the occasional pup or chick gets left behind when the others put to sea. These late-leavers never survive the winter, but in the autumn they can sometimes be found still clinging to life, wandering disconsolate about the Peninsula in search of food.

There were three of them, sunning themselves on the edge of the sea-ice. Truth to tell they were scrawny creatures, but to Lockwood they represented a cornucopia of succulent steaks, fatty blubber and warm pelts. He was determined to have them. But how? The obvious thing was to go back for his revolver, but his revolver was in the tent; it would take him all of five minutes to get there, and he was afraid in that time the seals might find a hole in the ice and disappear into a world where he couldn't follow. The knife that he had been using to cut seaweed was neither long enough nor sharp enough. But there were other weapons to hand. He picked up a rock, sharp-edged and heavy. And in an instant 20,000 years were sponged away, and he was a Stone Age hunter faced with a simple choice: kill or die.

He looked for and found another rock, sharper and heavier. Then, half-crawling, half-slithering, he began to work his way between his quarry and the sea. He had never killed an animal before; but he was going to kill three of them now, if need be with his bare hands.

The seals took not the slightest notice of him. Even when he rose to his feet from among the rocks only three or four yards from where they were lying, they made no effort to move, but stared at him with passive unconcern. He recognised them as Weddells: bulky, slow-moving creatures, about nine feet in length and 500 pounds in weight; by sea graceful, but by land clumsy. The nearest, a young female, showed no sign of fear as he walked up to her. Nor did she make the slightest effort to avoid the blow that cracked open her skull. As the rock thudded into her, her eyes opened wider and wider; she quivered once, keeled over onto the ice and lay stiller than she had ever lain before. The second was killed almost as swiftly. But the third, realising it was in danger, went slithering over the rocks. No way was he going to let it escape. He scrambled after it, striking it again and again, until it lay motionless in a pool of blood.

During the butchery Lockwood had felt neither pity nor repugnance. Every fibre of his being had been concentrated on the one thing that mattered: the kill. But when the last seal lay dead, and he stood with the blood-soaked stone in his hands, bathed in sweat and trembling, he reverted to the twentieth century; and, as he stared at the carnage for which he was responsible, he shuddered. So, he thought, must Cain have felt as he stared at the body of Abel: as though he had killed a part of himself. He felt physically sick, and it was some time before he was able to stop trembling.

It took him the rest of the day to drag the seals to the overhang, and the whole of the next day to skin and dismember them. They were pitiably thin and no more than half their normal weight. Nonetheless, by the time he finished work on them he had blubber for his lamp, pelts to sleep on, and sufficient meat to keep him alive for more than a month—although to his disappointment one of the seals had a skin disease and its flesh looked suspect.

There seemed to be more point now in building his survival shelter.

Over the next few weeks he worked at it slowly: deliberately slowly, so as to reduce the energy he expended and the possibility of injury. For he knew that a strained back or a crushed finger might be fatal—wasn't one of Scott's men supposed to have died because he hit his thumb with a hammer and the bruise turned gangrenous? So when he levered stones out of the ice he used a makeshift crowbar (fashioned from the runners of his sledge), when he built the walls he was careful not to so much as graze a finger, and when he lit his lamp or his stove he took painstaking precautions to make certain he never got burned. What was it poor old Ramsden had said? 'Better safe than sorry.'

Another thing that slowed him down was the light, or rather the lack of it. For the sun was dying. At mid-day it hung briefly above the horizon like a wizened orange; for the rest of the time it was nowhere to be seen. And its disappearance brought problems.

Only those who have wintered inside one of the polar circles can understand how Lockwood felt as darkness closed in. He felt that as light was draining out of the sky, so life was draining out of his body. As indeed it was. For in the polar winter darkness is synonymous with cold, and cold with death.

But not all was gloom and despondency; for he found an unexpected ally that autumn in the weather. April and May in 1943 were unusually calm, cold and dry on the Antarctic Peninsula, and the few blizzards that did occur came mainly at night. This enabled him to get on with his building without too many interruptions. And almost exactly a month after he reached the tip of the Peninsula he completed the basic structure of his shelter: his *behouden huis*, he had come to call it—the name given by Willem Barents to the shelter which enabled him and his crew to become the first explorers in history to survive a polar winter frozen into the ice. It consisted of three five-foot-thick stone walls (the fourth wall was the side of the cave), and a ceiling which consisted partly of the roof of the cave and partly of the battened-down frame of his sledge. He covered the floor with a carpet of dried seaweed, set up his tent in the middle of what was now in effect a man-made cave, and moved in.

He had few possessions, so settling in was hardly a problem. Everything he had, he took with him. Everything, that is, except the body of John Ede. This, now deep-frozen and still perfectly preserved, he laid out at the base of the nunatak not far from the entrance to his *behouden huis*. He told himself that now his shelter was built, he really *must* get round to burying the Old Man. But no sooner had the thought taken shape than he found an excuse to put it out of his mind. The ground, he told himself, was now too hard for him to dig a grave.

He found that his shelter was basically windproof and snowproof. It was also lightproof. And almost at once this lack of light became a problem.

So long as he kept his lamp burning, the inside of the *behouden huis* was almost cosy: lamplight, like firelight, illuminating the tent and its encircling walls in a comforting glow. But he only had enough blubber to keep the lamp burning for three or four hours a day, and when it was extinguished the *behouden huis* was about as cosy as a death cell.

Huddled inanimate in the dark, he could see nothing, hear nothing, smell nothing, do nothing. He felt like a chrysalis cocooned in concentric layers of canvas, stone and darkness—a darkness more absolute than he could have believed possible. It was like being buried alive. And it wasn't long before he felt welling up inside him a sensation he was powerless to control.

Claustrophobia.

He had felt twinges of it before, while he was fitting together the last few stones which effectively walled him up; but nothing like this. It was as though in some macabre nightmare he was tied down in a cell and the walls were closing in, were moving closer and closer, until he could almost feel the crunch of his bones as the stones pressed down on his body. He realised his eyes were screwed tight and he was gasping for breath.

God help me, he thought. How can I stay sane? How can I stop this shelter I've built becoming first a prison then a tomb?

He thought of praying. But when things were going well he hardly ever prayed, and he didn't like the idea of crawling to God as soon as things began to go badly. In any case, he told himself, God helps those who help themselves . . . He felt his way round the walls until he came to the entrance-stone. As he levered it aside, the night air on his face was like a benediction.

He crawled into the open.

The sun had set eleven hours ago and wouldn't rise for another eleven; the sky was a canopy of cumulus; there was neither moonlight nor starlight, and the cold struck him like a physical blow. But he told himself he was better off outside. He sat huddled against the nunatak, hoping that eventually his eyes would adjust to the dark and he would begin to see things. But it didn't happen. All that happened was that he got colder and colder. Common sense told him to go back. But he didn't. And he knew why. He was afraid that once he was back in the *behouden huis* his claustrophobia would return and play with him as a cat with an injured mouse.

He knew what had to be done. The difficult bit was screwing up the courage to do it. It wasn't until he began to lose all sensation in his hands and feet, and realised he was in danger of freezing to death, that he steeled himself to crawl back inside. He pulled the entrance-stone into position behind him, sat in the middle of the floor, threw away the matches that were the only means of lighting his lamp, shut his eyes and said firmly, 'I won't open my eyes for an hour.'

But almost at once he felt it coming: like a flood-tide creeping towards him over the mud-flats of an estuary: at first no more than distant ripples, then waves advancing with slow but dreadful certainty, then swirling over him in a flood from which he was powerless to escape. He felt as though he was pegged out in the sand unable to move, and the waves were rising higher and higher, until they closed over him and he couldn't breathe. He heard the grind of his teeth and the rasp of his breath, and sweat from his forehead mingled with tears from his eyes and trickled down into his mouth so he wasn't sure if he was drowning in sea water or his own excreta. He tried to tell himself it wasn't happening, that it was all in the mind; but this didn't make his agony less real. 'Open your eyes,' a voice was screaming, 'and you'll be able to find a way out.' But another voice whispered, 'Hang on! Hang on! If you let this thing get the better of you it'll be with you always.' He tried to be calm. You know you aren't *really* pegged out in the sand, he told himself, and to prove it all you have to do is stand up . . . To his horror he couldn't do it; for the message sent out by his brain seemed to get lost on the way to his legs. He told himself not to panic: to do it bit by bit: first onto his knees. He managed that— though only after the sort of effort that made him feel he had run a marathon. But when he tried to stand, the *behouden huis* began to spin like a top, he felt as though hands were clutching at his throat, he swayed like a drunk and fell awkwardly, bringing down the tent and hitting his head on one of the supporting poles. It wasn't a heavy blow; but the shock, the pain and the fear that he was injured catapulted all other fears from his mind. He felt his head. Mercifully there was no blood; only tenderness and an embryo bruise. I'm OK, he thought. Thank God for that. He got to his feet, and, as his head cleared, it came to him that he was standing without swaying, and breathing without choking; the *behouden huis* was no longer spinning. Shock had succeeded where willpower had failed, and his claustrophobia had vanished, never to return. For an enemy once defeated loses its terror.

He collapsed on his carpet of seaweed, not caring that he was all tangled up with the tent, conscious of tiredness but at the same time elation. He told himself that he had won a battle, not a war, but this didn't diminish his euphoria. He fell asleep, knowing that only one thing mattered: he had won.

And in his dreams she came to him in the *behouden huis*, an amalgam of a girl he had known back home and the girl with the snow-white dogs. She was warm and comforting, and he held her close until the walls of the shelter dematerialised, and the two of them were walking hand in hand through the forest.

'Tell me,' she said, 'what makes you want to stay alive so badly?'

He woke shivering with cold, his head aching, and— he had to laugh—in his arms the pelt of one of the Weddell seals.

So much, he thought, for fantasies. So much for dreams.

Later that day, when he had put up the tent and cooked himself a meal, he made an inventory of his possessions. He didn't have to be an expert on logistics to work out that fuel and food were the Charybdis and Scylla on which his hopes of survival were likely to founder. He had enough fuel to keep his lamp burning for three or four hours a day and to cook himself a couple of meals, but none to spare for heating. He had enough tea and powdered milk to last virtually *ad infinitum*, and enough dehydrated vegetables and meat to last maybe eight weeks. But this wasn't anything like enough to see him through until the spring . . . It was now early May; it would be late September or early October before the first of the migrating birds and mammals (a potential source of food) returned to the Peninsula. How could he hope to survive for four months on nothing but tea and powdered milk? All he could do, he decided, was work out the minimum he needed each day to keep alive, eat that, and when there was nothing left hope for another miracle.

Unless, of course, he turned to cannibalism.

The *behouden huis* seemed to grow suddenly colder and darker.

It shocked him that the idea of cannibalism should have escaped from the secret places of his mind and was now flaunting itself openly as an option to be considered. He considered it. But even the thought of what would be involved made his mouth pucker with nausea. There were some things, he told himself, he could *never* do. And eating his commanding officer was one of them.

That is what he told himself.

Yet at the back of his mind was a seed of doubt. Your fine feelings are all very well, a voice whispered, now that your stomach is full and there's food in the larder; but how will you feel when hunger gnaws at you like a physical pain, you are dying, and the means of survival is lying there in front of you?

It was a long time that night before he slept.

A few days later there took place an event that he knew was inevitable but which he had nonetheless been dreading: the disappearance of the sun. On 19 May it failed to appear above the horizon . . . During the previous winter many of the special detachment had found it hard to come to terms with the loss of the sun; and *they* had had companionship, and the warmth and light of their hut to compensate them. Lockwood had no such compensation. He was faced with the prospect of sitting alone in the cold and the dark for something like 1,500 hours. When he weighed up the odds he had to admit that in all probability he'd never see the sun again. For several days after its disappearance he climbed to the top of his nunatak in the hope of getting another glimpse of it; but all he could see was a patch of anaemic pink in the sky. And it wasn't long before that too was gone.

With the disappearance of the sun he could feel winter, like the anaconda of some terrible nightmare, tightening its grip on him.

Next day he tried to work out a blue-print for survival. He must, he told himself, establish a routine he could keep to. For he knew that in the Antarctic winter, when a person's biological clock is deprived of warmth and light, it becomes disorientated. What both the mind and the body need is an artificial clock: the discipline of the same events taking place at the same time day after day: a rhythm to fall into.

In the weeks that followed he managed, by trial and error, to settle into such a rhythm.

He would stay in his sleeping-bag until 9 a.m. He didn't get up earlier partly because, like a hibernating animal, he wanted as much sleep as he could get; partly because his sleeping-bag was the warmest spot in the shelter, and partly because getting out of it wasn't much fun. For during the night condensation from his breathing as often as not turned to ice, and when he woke his head and shoulders were frozen solid to the bag and the bag frozen solid to the floor. (It was one of his less pleasant nightmares that one morning he would find himself entombed in ice, unable to move.) When at last he did get up he was sometimes so cold, stiff and cramped he could hardly move. To get his circulation going he did exercises, flailing his arms and kicking out his legs in an elephantine *pas seul*. Then, as soon as he was able to move freely, he lit his lamp and his paraffin stove. This was a moment to savour, as light, like a benediction, transformed the *behouden huis* from prison-cell to Aladdin's cave. It usually took about 40 minutes for the stove to bring water to the boil, and while he was waiting he checked that his possessions were in the right place and in working order— since the greater part of his life was spent in the dark, it was essential that he knew exactly where everything was and could lay hands on whatever he needed blindfold. Then came another moment to savour . . . Because there were so few events each day that he could look forward to, he elevated the making and drinking of his morning tea into a ritual: measuring out milk, sugar and six drops of lime juice as an antidote to scurvy with exaggerated care, making sure his mug was scrupulously clean, never failing to say grace:

'Thank you, God, for what I'm about to drink.'

And the sweet hot tea was therapeutic as communion.

When he had drank it, he turned his attention to the *behouden huis*. This, he frequently reminded himself, was his home: a place to be proud of, to keep shipshape and to improve. He was forever working on it, sealing up the crevices more tightly, levelling the floor, building an entrance-tunnel-cum-latrine. He would have liked to carry on with these 'home improvements' all day; but fuel was short, and a little before noon he would steel himself to put out his lamp. It was a moment he dreaded, for it heralded the long afternoon of inactivity.

Only those who have been held prisoner for long periods in grim conditions by hostile guards can have any idea what Lockwood went through that winter. By comparison those in 'solitary' are in clover; for prisoners in solitary enjoy adequate food, adequate warmth, light at the flick of a switch, and the knowledge that other human beings are near by. Lockwood, on the other hand, was perpetually hungry, perpetually cold, was condemned for 20 hours out of 24 to total darkness, and knew there was no other human being within 1,000 miles.

It was the loneliness that got to him most. There were times that winter when he felt as though he was the last member of the human race left on a dying planet.

Loneliness isn't easy to cope with . . . A couple of million years ago the species *Homo erectus* rose to prominence in the rift valleys of Africa largely because of its ability to communicate and act as a group, and today you will find the descendants of *Homo erectus* huddled together at one end of a beach while the other end remains empty. We are creatures of the herd, and have come to think of companionship as our birthright. This birthright Lockwood was now denied. Every afternoon he had six hours of utter darkness and aloneness to get through, from mid-day when he turned off his lamp until 6 p.m. when he turned it on again. During this time he couldn't sleep, because if he slept in the afternoon he found that he was unable to sleep at night; and he couldn't move about, partly because of the darkness and partly because he needed the warmth and protection of his sleeping-bag. So he had no option but to lie there, knowing he had to occupy his thoughts or go slowly mad ... He tried all manner of things ... He recited poetry. He had never been all that keen on poetry, but his mother had enjoyed reading him Macaulay's *Lays of Ancient Rome*, and he found he could remember great chunks of how Horatius defended some bridge or other over the Tiber; he could also remember (and had fun rephrasing) Alice's *Jabberwocky*. He played games: like the town game, when you chose the name of a town and then had to think of another one which began with the previous town's last letter—London, New York, Khartoum, Melbourne, and so on—you weren't allowed to use the same town twice and Halifax was banned. He relived incidents in his life that he had particularly enjoyed. He set himself problems and memory tests. And since he couldn't use his eyes he came increasingly to rely on his ears. He became adept at interpreting the nuances of the wind: the sigh of the thermals as they drifted in with the tide, the vibrating moan that heralded the blizzard and the screams that marked its climax and the buffeting gusts its wake. And when there was no wind he listened to the silence: the absolute silence of a world frozen to immobility: no movement, no light, no sound. It was as though the earth and everything in it lay in the womb of the Universe waiting to be reborn. Hang on, hang on, hang on, he told himself, and you'll be reborn too.

The hands of his watches, those afternoons, never moved as fast as he wanted them to.

He had two watches, his own and Ede's; and it is hard to see how he could have survived without them. They were the anchors that held him on an even keel, the stabilisers that brought order into a life which would otherwise have been chaotically timeless. He knew that his watch lost roughly ten seconds a day; Ede's as much again. And each evening at exactly 6 p.m. he made a ritual of winding and adjusting them before he relit his lamp and his stove.

This was another of the day's great moments, as the canvas of his tent was metamorphosed to gold and the walls of his survival shelter to ochre. And an even greater moment was to come. For just as, earlier, he had made a ritual out of making and drinking his tea, so he now made an even more meaningful ritual of preparing and eating his meal. Only those who have suffered hunger can understand how Lockwood felt during those evenings. Often as he measured out his dehydrated vegetables—so many tiny cubes of potato, so many of turnip, carrot or swede—his hands were trembling with excitement. Often as he prepared the seal-cuts which formed 90 per cent of his diet, he couldn't stop the saliva dribbling out of his mouth and turning to ice in his beard. And when at last he sat down to eat he forced himself to eat slowly, savouring each mouthful, feeling, like a person on a drip-feed, the life-force flowing back into his body.

After he had eaten—provided the weather was good enough—he took a turn outside: partly to get exercise and partly to get a change of scene.

In the Antarctic winter there is not a great deal of difference between the night-temperature and the day-temperature, and at night it is often easier to see because of the light from the moon and the stars. On evenings when the weather was settled, Lockwood often walked as far as the beach, his footsteps ringing out loud and clear but making no mark on ice as hard as adamant. The times he liked best were those rare occasions when the aurora wove its magic. One display in particular he never forgot.

It happened one evening towards the end of May, as he was about to crawl back into the *behouden huis*: a veil of silver streaking like a sidewinder from horizon to horizon. A pause, then another veil, this time of green; another pause, and then a veil of red. The light flickered and flared, faded and died; and Lockwood was wondering if the display was over, when a great Catherine-wheel of silver burst suddenly overhead: shafts of pulsating light that seemed to hang and sway like bead-curtains in the wind, now contracting now expanding, now fading now increasing in brilliance. Slowly the light ebbed away, until all that was left were a few wavering streamers, the dust flung out from the aurora's cloak. Again Lockwood thought the display was over; but again the sky exploded, this time into coruscations of red. It was as though, along the southern horizon, great tongues of flame thousands of feet high were leaping out of the ice. For several minutes shafts of red, crimson and vermilion were interwoven in a tapestry so bright he had to shade his eyes as he stared at it. Then once again the glory faded. But for more than an hour the southern skyline glowed a macabre rose-red, as though a little below the horizon a great city were being consumed by fire. And over everything hung a silence so absolute it was almost tangible, and a sense of peace beyond understanding.

But this sort of display only happened once in a blue moon. Most of the time the weather was too bad for Lockwood to risk going out, and the only exercise he got was walking round and round the inside of the *behouden huis*:

20 times clockwise, 20 times anticlockwise: round and round, again and again, like an animal in a cage. Until it was time to doss down.

He dossed down each evening at 9 p.m., by which time he was so cold it was a relief to crawl into his sleeping-bag. He was well aware of the importance of sleep, knowing it was a haven in which his body and mind could build up strength; and on good nights he sometimes managed to sleep for as much as twelve hours. But there were other nights—and they became increasingly frequent—when the cold kept waking him and shaking him as a terrier shakes a rat, and his mind kept wandering into channels that he wanted to get out of but couldn't. After such nights it was a relief to break the ice and clamber out of his sleeping-bag.

He was able for some time to keep to this routine. However, as the weeks passed and the weather became colder, he found himself growing weaker, both physically and mentally.

He grew weaker physically because he wasn't getting enough to eat.

Three cups of tea, a few ounces of seal meat and a few cubes of dehydrated vegetables a day were not enough to keep him in good health. He needed more food and more variety of food. In particular he needed the vitamin C that is found in fresh fruit and vegetables.

Initially he was able to live off the fat that was in his muscles. However, it wasn't long before his muscles started to waste away. He had then to live off his own protein. This was bad news: when someone is forced to do this, body-fat is converted to acid, which plays havoc with the lungs, the heart, and in particular the liver. As the weeks passed Lockwood found himself becoming increasingly dizzy and short of breath. His urine turned darker and his excrement more fluid. By mid-winter there were even worse signs. Ulcers began to form on the inside of his mouth, his teeth became loose in their sockets, and little yellow and purple bruises broke out in rashes across the joints of his arms and legs.

At first he refused to admit it. But there came a time when the symptoms were too obvious to be denied.

He had scurvy.

He wasn't an authority on scurvy, but he knew it had been the bane of seamen in the days of sail, and he could remember, as a schoolboy, reading an eyewitness account of it: *Our ship reeked of sickness and death . . . the cries of the afflicted would have moved stones to pity . . . Some looked like walking corpses, and death blew them out like so many candles . . . they passed nothing but blood, except for two or three days before they died when their excrement was like grey sulphur—and this was a sure sign that their hour had come.*

Not the end he would have chosen.

But it was no good, he told himself, feeling hard-done-by. The thing to do was to fight. Captain Cook, he seemed to remember, had 'conquered' scurvy by making his crew drink lime juice and eat fresh vegetables. How could *he* conquer it?

Well, he had a bottle of lime juice that had survived the attack, and for the last month he had been putting six drops each morning into his tea. Clearly this hadn't been enough. He doubled the dose. He realised that at this rate his lime juice would run out long before the end of winter; but it was no good, he told himself, doing things by halves.

Fresh fruit and vegetables were more of a problem. Indeed, his first thought was that in the middle of the Antarctic winter he had about as much hope of finding any as of meeting a dinosaur. Then he remembered that vegetables—of a sort—grew in the sea. Could it be that kelp and seaweed would do for him what limes and cabbages had done for Captain Cook? The trouble was that in winter the kelp and seaweed were encased in ice, a solid layer several feet thick. All sorts of plants and creatures continued to flourish on the sea-bed, but it was impossible to get at them. Yet the riches of the sea did, very occasionally, find their way ashore. Lockwood remembered that a couple of times last winter the special detachment had come across kelp and seaweed littering the beaches like jetsam from some fortuitously-lightened ship. None of them had had the scientific know-how to account for this; but marine biologists could have told them that when the weather is exceptionally cold, ice known as anchor-ice forms in mats along the top of the sea-bed. Under the tug of currents and tides these mats will sometimes break away, tearing off and carrying with them living organisms. The mats will then work their way to the surface and be drifted ashore.

Lockwood took to scouring the beaches around the tip of the Peninsula.

And eventually he struck lucky.

The night was still and clear, and he had ventured farther than usual from his *behouden huis* to a beach he hadn't been to before. At the water's edge he spotted something that stood out against the featureless expanse of white; it looked like a huge pile of lettuce speckled with black. On closer inspection the 'lettuce' turned out to be anchor-ice, and the specks of black a hotchpotch of algae, limpets, sponges and seaweed; there was even a starfish clinging against all probability to life.

Starfish with seaweed may not be among the great dishes of the world, but as Lockwood prised everything remotely edible out of the ice he was conscious of a feeling more deep-rooted than excitement and more enduring than relief. It was a difficult feeling to analyse. Perhaps the nearest he ever got to it was when he told a friend, years later, that there were times that winter when he'd felt as though he was physically part of Antarctica, as though he was caught up in the continent's perennial cycle of life, death and resurrection.

He had that feeling now. Very strongly. It was mid-winter: the only light was the light of the stars; it was minus 20°, and for hundreds of miles in every direction the world lay under a sheet of ice. Yet he had found life.

There was a lesson here, he told himself. The starfish had survived by blending into and becoming part of its surroundings. Surely anything a starfish could do, he could do too.

When he got back to the *behouden huis*, he started chewing the seaweed. It was so tough that with his loose teeth it took him ten minutes to masticate each mouthful. He realised he could make things easier for himself by boiling the seaweed; but he was afraid that this might reduce its vitamin content. So he kept on chewing, hour after hour, steeling himself not to gag as the tang of iodine seared his throat; telling himself anything that tasted so foul must be doing him good.

His scurvy wasn't cured. But its progression was halted, and its more distressing symptoms were, for the time being, alleviated.

Physically his decline was arrested.

Mentally it was another story. For as the cold, the dark and the loneliness weighed down on him, he was driven that winter to the very edge of insanity by two spectres: the image of his dream girl, and the prospect of cannibalism.

His dream girl came to him initially not as a lover but a friend who helped him clear the *behouden huis* of snow.

His survival shelter was screened from the prevailing wind, but during cyclonic storms it sometimes suffered the full impact of the northerlies: bludgeoning 120-knot gusts which ripped snow, ice, shingle and kelp off the beach and drove them near-horizontal against the dry-stone walls. The walls survived. But time and again, when the blizzards were at their height, the kelp and seaweed between the stones would be scoured away, and snow would come pouring in. At such times Lockwood had to work flat-out to plug the gaps and shovel away the snow. It was cold, back-breaking work. Often, when his hands and feet were numb, his clothes sodden and he was punch-drunk with exhaustion, he would be tempted to give up. What's the use of plugging the holes, he'd ask himself, when the kelp and shingle will only be blown out again? What's the use of shovelling away this lot of snow, when the next blizzard will bring in more? It was then that she came to him. When his hands were so numb he could no longer hold his bucket of seaweed, she would carry it for him; when his arms were so weak he could no longer lift his shovel, she would help swing it back and forth; and when the blizzard was over they would lie together in the tent. They didn't make love, because at such moments it wasn't physical love that Lockwood craved for. It was companionship.

'I'll never leave you,' she would whisper. 'I'll be beside you, always.'

Some men, when they woke and found themselves alone, might have felt cheated. But Lockwood felt more determined than ever to survive: to find one day a girl who really would be beside him, always.

Not all their meetings were so innocent.

Sometimes in the afternoons, when Lockwood had recited his poetry and played his games and tested his memory *ad nauseam*, he would be hard put to it to occupy his thoughts. Sometimes he would think about God, but God proved too shadowy and insubstantial for him to hang onto. It wasn't that he didn't believe in Him; it was just that he needed something more concrete to focus on. Sometimes he would think about his home and his family; this worked for a while but wasn't exciting enough to hold his attention for long. It wasn't that he didn't love his home and his family; it was just that Norwood and

Antarctica seemed to have about as much in common as Mercury and Pluto, and his experiences in the former didn't seem to have much bearing on what was happening to him in the latter. Sometimes he would think about girls. This was more exciting. However, he didn't have a great fund of experience to draw on, and he soon discovered that the images he could conjure up of the girls he had known at home were not half as exciting at the image of his fantasy girl.

At first he was content only to stare at her as she stood silhouetted against the green of the forest, her hair cascading over her parka. But one day she smiled at him, and turned and walked away through the trees; and in his imagination he followed her into the forest of his dreams.

It was at this stage that dreams and reality began to get mixed up.

So long as he was awake he was able to keep his fantasies under control; but when he was asleep it was a different story. Soon she was coming to him almost every night. Or rather he was going to her; because for a reason he couldn't understand she would never come into the *behouden huis*.

'But it's warmer inside,' he would protest.

'And more fun,' she whispered, 'in the forest.'

So they took to meeting where the snowline ended and the trees began. And, with every rendezvous, her legs seemed to get longer and slimmer, her eyes brighter, her body more desirable.

'Don't your knees get cold?' he asked her.

She laughed: 'You don't have to worry about *my* legs!'

Playfully, she shook one of the fir trees so that the snow cascaded down on him.

He woke wet and shivering. And despised himself.

He told himself he had to stop thinking about her.

This, however, proved easier said than done. He tried walking round and round his tent until he was dizzy and

132

exhausted. He tried going without sleep. But still she plagued him, her image materialising when he least expected it. He'd be watching the aurora, and suddenly she would be smiling down at him from the stardust. He'd be cooking his evening meal, and suddenly the gold of the flames would become the gold of her hair. He told himself, with some truth, that she was driving him mad.

As the days passed and he became more and more disorientated, a gradual change took place in their relationship. He began to think of her not as a loved one to be hurried to, but as a temptress to be avoided. Eventually she became equated in his mind with a mistress: an object of excitement tainted with guilt. He found himself hankering after her and yet not wanting to see her. One afternoon, he had what seemed like an inspiration. Their love-making had always been in the forest; so if he didn't want it to continue, all he need do was make sure he stayed inside the *behouden huis*. He walled himself in. 'I won't go out,' he muttered, as he hauled more and more stones across the mouth of the tunnel. 'And you can't come in.'

But it didn't work. That night he could have sworn he heard her footsteps. He told himself he must be hallucinating. But his ears wouldn't have it. For there was no doubt about what he could hear . . . Pad, slither, pad, pause. Pad, slither, pad, pause . . . It was as though she was working her way round and round the *behouden huis* on ill-fitting snowshoes.

I know, he thought, it's a polar bear! But even as the thought formed, he knew he was clutching at straws. There are no polar bears in Antarctica: nor, in winter, any other living creature.

From the far end of the tunnel came a thud, and a scraping and scratching.

The hairs pricked on the nape of his neck. He grabbed

his revolver. 'Go away!' he shouted. 'Go away! Or I'll kill you.'

There was a long silence. That's frightened her, he thought. The minutes ticked by, and there was no movement among the stones piled up across the entrance, and no more scraping and scratching; only little moans of wind, harbingers of yet another blizzard to come. He moved the seaweed from between a couple of stones in the wall, and peered out. The stars were hidden by cloud, and he could see nothing. Yet he had the feeling, very strongly, that something or somebody was watching him.

He crawled back into his sleeping-bag; but not to sleep.

Next morning he made a most unwelcome discovery. Part of his seal meat had turned putrid.

He had noticed while dismembering the seals that one was diseased. It was as well he hadn't eaten its meat, and had stored it separately from the rest; for although the cuts had been kept bone-dry and refrigerated, they had turned gradually darker and softer; and he now found to his horror that the meat had become the breeding colony of a myriad microscopic worms. This was a body blow. It was not yet midwinter, and in a few weeks he would be out of food. But it was no good thinking about that. He decided to carry the putrid seal meat down to the beach and throw it away.

As he crawled out of the *behouden huis* he swung his torch this way and that; but its beam illuminated nothing. There was no need, he told himself, to be afraid.

But he had gone no more than a dozen yards when he saw her: her eyes, like oriflammes in the night, staring at him.

He didn't believe it. He took a deep breath, turned away and counted to ten. But when he turned round again the eyes—the only part of her that was visible—were still there. And they were moving towards him.

One voice cried, 'Go to her.' Another cried, 'Stay where you are.' And a third cried, 'Run for your life.'

The instinct to survive is the most basic instinct of all. As the eyes came swaying towards him, Lockwood fled. He scrambled through the entrance-tunnel, clawed the loose stones into place behind him, and backed up against the farthest wall, jibbering with terror. He expected whatever it was would try to follow him in. But it didn't. And as the minutes passed and from the far end of the tunnel there was neither movement nor sound, his jibbering gave way to the occasional mutter, and his terror to bewilderment. What the hell was going on? He lit his lamp, sat down and tried to work it out.

One possibility was that he was going mad. But he told himself that people who were mad didn't sit down and try calmly to analyse what was going on. Another possibility was that 'she' was an animal. But the special detachment had lived in Antarctica for more than a year, and they knew from personal experience that all creatures left the mainland in winter: the only exception being Emperor penguins, which sometimes arrived in huge numbers in the coldest part of the year, to lay and incubate their eggs. So could 'she' be a lone Emperor, who had got separated from her companions? He doubted it. Her eyes weren't those of a bird, and there was something menacing about her that didn't equate with the friendly persona of a penguin. So what other possibilities were there? She could hardly be human, could she? A survivor from the destruction of their hut, a German left behind after the attack, Ramsden risen from the crevasse or Ede from beneath the overhang of the nunatak? Such ideas were too preposterous to deserve a second thought. But then so was every other idea he came up with. He told himself he *had* to be hallucinating. But when he pulled aside a patch of kelp from between the stones and peered out, the eyes were still there: twin orbs of gold now swaying rhythmically from side to side, now bobbing up and down as though she were curtseying.

Something snapped. It was like an explosion inside his head, and in a moment of clarity he saw it all. It was so simple. Why on earth hadn't he been able to work it out before? Eskimos lived on the ice, didn't they? They lived there all the year round: in igloos. So she must be an Eskimo girl. And her eyes must be swaying about and bobbing up and down because she was dancing: dancing a naughty dance to try and tempt him to come out of the *behouden huis* to make love to her.

But he wasn't going to be tempted. He stuffed the kelp back into his peephole, and told himself he'd pretend she wasn't there.

It never occurred to him, over the next few days, that he was going mad. He thought his behaviour was perfectly normal—as indeed for most of the time it was. He kept assiduously to his routine: doing his exercises, brewing his two cups of tea in the morning, cooking his one meal in the evening. The only way his behaviour deviated from the norm was that he didn't go outside, and spent more and more time peering out through his peep-hole to watch the little Eskimo girl.

The only part of her he ever saw was her eyes. Sometimes they would be motionless, and he could imagine her stretched out on the ice, staring at him, smiling. Sometimes they would be swaying to and fro, and he could imagine her dancing: dancing in a way that became more erotic each time he watched her. It was frustrating not to be able to see her. And as the days passed his frustration developed into an obsession. He couldn't keep away from the peep-hole. He would be patching up one of the walls when he'd feel an uncontrollable compulsion to go to the other wall and peer out to see if he could catch a glimpse of her. He would be brewing his tea when he'd feel an uncontrollable compulsion to see if she was still there, and the water would boil over as he stood staring into the darkness. At night her eyes were forever stalking him down the corridors of his dreams. 'She's calling you,' voices began to whisper. 'Go to her.' At first the voices were soft and hesitant; but as the days passed they became louder and more insistent, until their message seemed to reverberate from every corner of the *behouden huis*: 'Go to her. Go to her. Go to her.' He rocked to and fro, his hands clamped to his ears, his every instinct crying out that the voices were siren songs: that if he gave way to them something terrible would happen.

But in the end he *did* give way. Again, something inside his head seemed to snap, and he was stumbling down the entrance tunnel, his mind blank as a lemming's as it nears the edge of the cliff.

He was levering aside the stones when he trod on his torch.

He always kept his torch and his revolver (like all his possessions) in the same place, in this case close to the entrance of the *behouden huis*. And he always took them with him whenever he went outside: his torch for the obvious reason that it enabled him to see in the dark, his revolver in case (by some million-to-one chance) he came across another surviving seal that he could shoot. So he now picked up the torch and the revolver by habit, without thinking what he was doing. Then he was crawling into the night.

The first thing he saw was her eyes, unexpectedly close. He stumbled towards her.

'Who are you?' he shouted.

She didn't answer; but her eyes swayed higher, as thought she was getting to her feet.

He was almost on top of her before he realised something was wrong: terribly wrong.

Her eyes were not so much gold as red: red as discs of

blood. She stank to high heaven, a fetid, fishlike stench. She gave a rasping, excited cough.

He flicked on his torch and saw, spotlit in its beam, the sinuous ten-foot sea leopard, her mouth white with saliva, her teeth long and sharp as a tiger's.

She reared up. Her teeth slashed at his throat.

'Ahhhhh!'

As in some terrible nightmare that he was watching but had no part in, he heard his cry of terror echo and re-echo over the fields of ice. Then she was on him. As he tried to jump back his feet slid from under him and he felt himself, as in slow motion, falling. So this, he thought, is the end.

He had no recollection of firing. But he heard the shots ring out again and again and again until there was a metallic click and his revolver was empty.

The bullets splayed all over the place; but from a range of three or four feet not all of them could miss. One lodged in her heart.

One second she was poised for the kill. Next second the blood was thickening in her throat. She gave a bubbling cough-cum-sigh, and fell deadweight on top of him.

He lay rigid with terror, waiting. But the sea leopard lay even more rigid; and the first thing Lockwood felt was not the tear of her teeth but the dampness of her lifeblood seeping through his parka and onto his back.

He struggled out from under her body.

Icefields and nunatak were undulating as though in an earth tremor, and every time he tried to stand his legs gave way. So he sat beside the dead sea leopard, willing himself to stop trembling and sort out his thoughts.

His first thought was a bemused gratitude. He was alive. And, by a miracle, uninjured.

His second thought was, 'That'll teach you to lust after women!' For the shock made him realise that for the last few weeks he had been in cloud-cuckoo-land. It would be wrong to say that for the rest of his time in Antarctica he never thought about women again. But he never thought about them in quite the same way.

His third thought was 'food!' He could see that the sea leopard was piteously thin—for she too had been starving—but he reckoned there would be enough meat on her at least to make good the loss of his putrid seal cuts.

His fourth thought was one that he didn't care for. It drove all other thoughts from his mind. He put off doing anything about it for as long as he could; but in the end he went to look for the body of John Ede.

What he found couldn't be called unexpected—it was pretty obvious, wasn't it, that there could have been only one reason for all those thuds and grunts from beneath the overhang? All the same, as he stared at what was left of his commanding officer he was hard put to it not to be sick . . . He tried to comfort himself with the thought that this wasn't the *real* John Ede he was staring at. The *real* John Ede, he told himself, was in another world; what was left scattered about on the ice were his accoutrements, the trappings, not the man. Nonetheless he was conscious of an almost overwhelming sense of guilt. He dropped to his knees. He touched what was left of an arm.

'I'm sorry,' he whispered. 'I should have buried you.'

He wasn't so far gone that he really thought the Old Man answered. But he did have the feeling that in some curious way Ede was close to him: that he understood, and that if forgiveness was called for, he forgave him.

He dragged the sea leopard into the *behouden huis*.

He was bruised, exhausted and shocked, and what he really wanted was to crawl into his sleeping-bag, close his eyes and forget. But as he looked at the sea leopard he knew his life depended on how much meat he could get from her. And when he started dismembering the carcass everything else became unimportant.

He wasn't surprised to find she was injured—why else

139

would she have stayed behind when all other creatures had left? One of her flippers and her tail had been crushed by ice, making it impossible for her to swim. Unable to swim, she had been unable to hunt. Unable to hunt, she had been condemned to death by slow starvation on the mainland. By midwinter the wonder was not that she was pitiably emaciated, but that she still clung to life. He could imagine her picking up his scent, dragging herself to a position from which she could watch him, sensing that he too was starving, and waiting for him to die. When he showed no sign of dying, he could picture her nosing round the *behouden huis*, picking up a new scent, finding the body ... Sea leopards, a species of seal, are one of the few carnivorous mammals of the Antarctic—fish and penguins are their staple diet—and their cusped teeth are formidable. She would have had no difficulty tearing a human being limb from limb. Existing on such exotic and unfamiliar fare was another matter: the sea leopard was no more than the proverbial bag of skin and bone, and it didn't take Lockwood long to realise that his food-problem had been alleviated, not solved. She would provide him with sufficient meat for maybe a month. Then, once again, the spectre of starvation would be with him.

Nevertheless he slept well that night.

There were no eyes, flaunting and taunting.

He was alone.

And that was the way he wanted it.

Over the next few days the weather underwent one of those dramatic changes that are commonplace in the Antarctic. The canopy of mist-cum-cloud lifted, the temperature plummeted, and for night after night the stars pulsated with such brilliance they seemed to be burning holes in the sky. There was no aurora; but the scene was spectacular enough without it. Wordsworth once wrote that,

Waters on a starry night
Are beautiful and fair;

and icefields on a starry night are even fairer. There were times during those last few days of June when, as Lockwood crawled out of his *behouden huis*, the beauty of the night almost literally took his breath away. Another thing that took his breath away was the cold. As the night air hit him, he felt as though a metal door had been slammed into his face.

Early in July two things happened that turned out to be more significant than seemed likely at the time.

First, he discovered the leaf.

He was working on the walls of the *behouden huis* when he noticed a number of curious marks on one of the stones; they looked like hieroglyphics. Intrigued, he prised the stone from the wall and examined it under the light of his lamp. The marks turned out to be plant fossils, among them a perfectly preserved leaf, its every detail etched into the stone as clearly as though it were only yesterday it had become embedded there.

Lockwood was no expert on fossils; but one can't live for a year in the company of geologists without some of their knowledge rubbing off. The leaf, he told himself, was almost certainly a beech leaf (*Fagus antarctica*), a relic of the vast forests which had once covered Gondwanaland; and he recognised the stone as tertiary limestone. In other words, he was looking at something that had survived for fifty million years.

Lockwood's discovery was not that remarkable—many other people, before and since, have found fossilised plants in the Antarctic. But the more he looked at the leaf the more he saw it as a symbol of survival. He ran his fingers over the tracery of its veins, almost as clearly defined as on the day it had unfolded in the warmth of the Cenozoic sun. What would have been the last living creature, he wondered, to set eyes on it? Would it have been one of the last of the dinosaurs, or one of the first of the sabre-toothed tigers? Perhaps the great creature had touched the leaf as it lumbered past; and now, 18,000,000,000 sunsets later, twentieth-century man was touching it.

He carried the stone almost reverently into his tent and put it where the light from his lamp spotlit the fossilised leaf. It would, he told himself, be a reminder of how long it was possible to survive.

The other significant happening was that he stubbed his toe on the pile of uranium-bearing rocks—and cursed them.

He had stacked the rocks in an out-of-the-way corner, where one of the dry-stone walls abutted the nunatak. And one of them had rolled off the top of the pile and come to rest, half-hidden by seaweed, beside his tent. In the dark, he walked straight into it.

'Bugger!'

He hopped up and down, flexing his toes.

It wasn't the pain that worried him, it was the knowledge that in his weakened condition even a minor injury could lead to gangrene. However, when he took off his boot and had a look, it was obvious no great damage had been done; he was more shocked than hurt. All the same, he looked at the rocks reproachfully. 'Bloody lumps of lava!' he muttered.

It was the first time he gave vent to a feeling that had been building up inside him for quite a while: a feeling that the rocks had a lot to answer for. It was because of them, wasn't it, that the special detachment had come to Antarctica? It was because of them that his friends had been killed; it was because of them that he was now incarcerated in the *behouden huis*; and it was because of them that he couldn't quietly lie down and die but felt obligated to thresh about like a hooked fish on the off-chance of surviving and getting the rocks back to England . . . And all for the sake of making a bloody bomb!

It was a change of attitude that crept over him gradually and almost unnoticed; but it was nonetheless a radical change. He didn't hate the rocks—yet. But the seeds of hatred were there.

Not that it seemed to matter a great deal *what* he thought about the rocks. Because by mid-July he had again run out of food.

And he was dying.

A person who is well-nourished and fit can live without food for several weeks. Lockwood was neither. For months he had been on a diet only marginally above starvation level. He was now so weak that when he tried to do his exercises he kept falling over. His weight had dropped from eleven stone to seven. He had frostbite, enteritis and scurvy. When he ran out of food, his life-expectancy had to be measured not in weeks but days.

So when he had eaten the last of his meat and the last of his dehydrated vegetables, and all he had left was powdered milk and tea-bags, he told himself there was only one thing left for him to do: die.

He wondered if he ought to write a letter home—wasn't that what people in his situation usually did?—but there didn't seem anything he could say that wouldn't add to his parents' grief; and in any case the letter would probably never be found. So he settled into his sleeping-bag, and wondered how long it would take.

He had barely got comfortable when a voice whispered, 'You don't *have* to die, you know. The sea leopard didn't finish what she began . . .'

'No,' he said firmly. 'I won't.'

And he willed himself to sleep.

When he woke, he told himself there wasn't much point in struggling out of his sleeping-bag to make tea. However, almost at once a trite little adage began to hammer away inside his head—'while there's life there's hope'—so in the end he made the effort. Everything took longer than usual, and he was so weak he spilt some of his powdered milk; but the tea tasted good, and when he had drunk it he crawled back to his sleeping-bag. Wouldn't it be wonderful, he thought, if I could close my eyes and never wake up ... But he had an idea it wasn't going to be as easy as that ... He thought about all sorts of things that afternoon. He told himself that in wartime a lot of people died violently, and without a chance to make their peace with God; he had that chance, so he was luckier than most. And in another way he'd been lucky: he'd seen the beauty of Antarctica—not many people had done that. Rather to his surprise he felt more sad than afraid: sad that he'd never again feel the warmth of the sun, nor the freshness of the wind; never see that special brightness come into a girl's eyes, never linger over a kiss, never make love. He told himself it was wicked to be thinking of such physical things; he ought to be thinking of his immortal soul. The trouble was that when he tried to think about his immortal soul he got all out of his depth and confused, like a ship's captain who ventures into shallow waters without a chart. He leaned out of his sleeping-bag, picked up a strand of seaweed, crushed it between his fingers and felt better. I can't help it, he told himself, I'm a creature of the earth.

'And if you want to stay a creature of the earth,' a voice whispered, 'you know what you have to do.'

'No!' he whispered. 'I won't.'

He thumped his head into his sleeping-bag, and wondered if he ought to be thumping it against the wall of the *behouden huis*. That way it would be over quickly; that way he wouldn't be tempted. He tried to concentrate on tangible things. He listened. At first he could hear only the silence. But after a while he reckoned he could make out, very faintly, the sigh of the wind. The tide's coming in, he thought; and the wind's coming with it, in from the sea. It saddened him to think he'd never feel the wind again. And suddenly, quite out of the blue, he remembered glancing through one of his grandparents' books, the nineteenth-century *Lavengro*. Most of it he had found boring—unbelievably long-winded. But one passage had obviously lodged in his mind, for it came back to him now, almost word-perfect . . .

'Life is sweet, brother.'
'You think so?'
'Think so!—There's night and day, brother, both sweet things. Sun, moon and stars, brother, all sweet things. Then there's the wind on the heath. Life is very sweet. Who would wish to die?'
'I would. Have you thought of blindness, Jasper?'
'There's still the wind on the heath, brother. If I could only feel that, I'd gladly live for ever' . . .

He listened; and the sigh of the wind from the sea— or was it the wind from the heath?—was like a trumpet-call to life. 'You know you'll do it in the end'—the voice had a terrible inevitability about it. 'You might as well do it now.'

'I won't,' he whispered. 'I won't.'

On the second day after he ran out of food he never left his sleeping-bag; he told himself he could get out if he wanted to, but it didn't seem worth the effort. Much of the time he was in limbo, a sort of no-man's-land where fact mingled with fantasy. For his mind was giving way. This wasn't because he was consumed with fear or anxiety or guilt or anything as dramatic as that; it was just that his brain wasn't getting enough oxygen. It took him a long time to work things out, and some things he couldn't work out at all. In particular he couldn't work out what to make of the Old Man's last words . . . They kept coming

145

back to him ... 'I'll help you,' he had said. 'Remember that. I'll help you.'

What had he meant?

It would be crazy, he told himself, to pretend the words meant nothing; because Ede, that afternoon, had been perfectly lucid. So why beat about the bush? There was only one thing, wasn't there, his commanding officer could have meant, only one way his body could be of help to anyone once he was dead ... ? He was pulled two ways. On the one hand he felt that Ede, knowing exactly what he was doing, had suggested and indeed invited cannibalism. On the other hand the thought—let alone the act—of doing what would have to be done was so terrible he felt he could never bring himself to do it.

His fists beat a tattoo into his sleeping-bag. 'I won't,' he muttered. 'I won't. I won't. I won't.'

On the third day after he ran out of food—as though the Antarctic was underlining that it was about to claim him—there was a white-out: a blizzard in which falling snow and driven snow coalesced into a featureless curtain of white.

By now the pain of his hunger was like a rat gnawing at his stomach, and his mind was so far gone that it too was in a state of white-out, so he didn't know night from day, fact from fantasy, or right from wrong.

And it was then that he did what he had to do to stay alive.

There was never any doubt about *what* he did—how else could he have survived?—yet he had almost no recollection of doing it. For the human mind has a safety valve, amnesia, which blocks out events too terrible to bear the thought of.

For the rest of his life there were certain sounds that made Lockwood flinch, certain sights that made him turn away, and certain smells that made him gag; but for most of the time his secret remained a secret even from himself. That was how he stayed sane.

For the greater part of July he existed from day to day in a sort of vacuum. He didn't think of the future: neither the immediate future—of what he would do when there was no part of his commanding officer left; nor the long-term future—of what would happen if he survived and was rescued. It was enough that he was alive, and that the terrible things he had to do each day became gradually not so much an ordeal to be gone through with eyes tight shut as an accepted part of his routine.

As mid-winter passed and the days of total darkness could be counted on one hand, Lockwood's hunger might have been partially assuaged; but there was no such escape from his loneliness.

People who think they need to tune up their mental well-being sometimes go to a retreat (just as people who think they need to tune up their physical well-being go to a health farm). These people invariably find it difficult at first to adjust to their self-imposed segregation—and this is although they have only to walk through a door to return to the 'normal' world. Prisoners in solitary often find their punishment makes them feel rejected, denied the milk of human kindness—and this is although they know their captors are close at hand and keeping an eye on them. Hostages held by unsympathetic guards may suffer more; yet even they have *some* contact with their fellow-humans: a hand pushing in food, the grate of a key in its lock, footsteps in the dark. Lockwood, that winter, was denied even such peripheral contact with his species. He had no voice on the radio to listen to, no tape to remind him of other days, no living creature to touch, to see or to hear. Robert the Bruce in his cave had had his spider, the explorer in the desert has his sandfly, and the diver in the depths of the ocean his blind worm; but Lockwood had nothing. The only contact he had with another life-form was his leaf—and that was 50 million years old! No wonder he suffered the recurring nightmare that he was the last survivor on a dying planet, eating the last survivor but one. And no wonder that as Ede's body gradually disappeared, the ache of his loneliness became like the pain of a terminal cancer. He began once again to hallucinate. There were times when he thought he saw shadowy figures—his parents, school friends, Naval friends, girl friends—emerging from the walls of his *behouden huis*, and he would reach out his hands to touch them only to find they had vanished. And there were times when he could have sworn he heard voices—the chatter of a wardroom party, a girl's whisper in the dark—and he would answer and hear only the echo of his own voice. If only, he thought, I had something to keep me company: a one-cell protozoa in the seaweed, a wingless fly among the stones. But there was no trace that winter in the *behouden huis* of even such primitive forms of life.

But at least, he told himself, it looks as though I'll survive for long enough to see the sun. That should be back soon, and maybe its warmth will trigger off another miracle.

He asked himself what sort of miracle he'd like? Well, obviously a companion. But not a human companion, because it wouldn't be fair, would it, to ask anyone to go through what he was having to go through. Perhaps a dog? But then a dog would suffer too, and that wouldn't be fair either. Unless, of course, the dog was a husky . . . That's it, he thought, I'd like a husky: say the lead-dog from the team the girl used to drive through the forest? The lead-dog, he knew, was always a bitch. And he'd share everything with her: the good times and the bad, the blizzard and the aurora, the nourishment of his food and the warmth of his sleeping-bag; and they'd rough-and-tumble together, and he'd fondle her ears and she'd lick his face, and together they'd win through where neither of them could have won through alone, and never for the rest of his life would he want any other dog.

He knew it was only a dream. But what else did he have to live for?

Towards the end of July he took to crawling out of his *behouden huis* a little before mid-day in the hope of seeing the sun. Day after day he stared at the northern horizon, trying to convince himself there was a hint of light, but having always to admit it was a case of wishful thinking. He told himself to be patient, and dreamed of standing outside the *behouden huis* with his dog, and watching the great gold orb of the sun as it came welling up through the ice.

Sometimes his dreams were so vivid he could have sworn he heard her barking.

It was the barking that woke him. Only there was something not quite right about it. It was more like braying than barking: a cacophony of guttural '*kra-a-as*', faint at first but becoming louder, as though a herd of donkeys was coming towards him. He told himself it wasn't *really* happening; but when he shut his eyes and tried to go back to sleep the '*kra-a, kra-a, kra-a-as*' built up to a crescendo. He struggled out of his sleeping-bag, grabbed his torch and revolver, and crawled into the open.

What he saw remained imprinted in his memory, detail-perfect, until the day he died.

It was a night of exotic beauty. A full moon, hardly a breath of wind, and pockets of mist-cum-cloud hovering like ethereal castles over the ice. At first he couldn't think where the noise was coming from. Then he saw them: the little dumpy 'men' in their dress-suits of midnight-blue, cut away at the front to reveal the white of their shirts and the gold of their cravats: now standing hesitant, now throwing themselves flat on their faces and tobogganing forward over the ice: an advance guard of twos and threes followed by an army of thousands.

Only one creature, the Emperor penguin, ventures in winter onto the mainland of Antarctica. They come to lay and incubate their eggs. And out of all the thousands of beaches on the continent, the Emperor penguins had chosen Lockwood's to breed on.

His knees buckled, and suddenly to his embarrassment he was crying.

He hadn't cried when he stared at the charred bodies of his friends, nor when he left Ramsden in the crevasse, nor when he gave Ede his lethal injection, nor even when he ate him. But he cried now. And his tears were tears of joy. Because for the first time since the burning down of the detachment's hut it seemed possible that he was going to survive.

Resurrection

When the penguins were about 100 yards from the beach they came to a halt and huddled together. Lockwood was terrified they might about-turn and disappear as suddenly as they had materialised. However, after a few moments of indecision, first one group then another began to scramble up from the sea ice. They seemed to be moving awkwardly, and as they came closer he saw why. Many were carrying eggs, chalk-white ovals rather larger than a swan's egg, which they were balancing between their toes.

He made his way to the beach.

He longed to mingle with them, to touch them, play with them, feel the warmth of their bodies; but he was afraid they might turn on him, and, in his weakened condition, peck and bludgeon him to death. So he sat on a rock and stared at them. He stared at them hour after hour, afraid that if he looked away he might wake and find they had gone. Apart from the sea leopard, they were the only living creatures he had set eyes on for more than two thousand hours.

He recalled some of the stories that the detachment's amateur zoologist had told them about Emperor penguins: how they were unique in coming to breed on the mainland in mid-winter, rearing their young in conditions no other creatures on earth could survive in. This, the zoologist had explained, was because Emperor chicks mature slowly and need to be six months old before they can put to sea; the only time they can put to sea is when the ice melts in mid-summer; they must therefore be born in mid-winter. Another thing Lockwood could remember being told was that once the Emperors' eggs had been laid, it was the males who incubated them, while the females returned to the open sea to feed and recuperate. And indeed, as he now stared at his newly arrived companions, he realised that all those with eggs were males. But the more he thought about this, the more convinced he became that there was something odd about 'his' particular lot of penguins. Why were they arriving, complete with their eggs, so late in the year and at a new rookery, when normally one would have expected them to have mated, incubated their eggs and reared their chicks in the same place? Later, when he had time to work things out at leisure, he came to the conclusion that their original rookery must have met with some disaster. And in this he was right . . .

The Emperors had in fact come ashore at their usual time in May, and at their usual breeding-ground, an ice-shelf surrounded by high cliffs not far from the tip of the Peninsula. Here they mated—Emperors, like swans and wandering albatross, mate for life—and everything seemed to be going according to plan. A geologist, however, might have seen the writing on the wall. For the cliffs surrounding the ice-shelf were unstable. Over thousands of years snow had been piling up behind them in gargantuan 'dunes', and now, suddenly, the weight of this snow became more than the rock-strata could bear. Many of the female Emperors had laid their eggs, left them in the care of their partners and set off for the open sea where they would spend the next six weeks feeding, when several hundred thousand tons of snow, rock and ice came crashing down on the rookery. About half the penguins were killed or seriously injured. The survivors had one over-riding concern: their eggs. Few creatures are as devoted to their young as Emperor penguins. The parents share the job of incubating their single egg, feeding their chick and nurturing it to adolescence in what are arguably the most difficult conditions on earth. So the males were now in a quandary. Their rookery had become a place of death, with the cliffs unstable and liable any moment to avalanche again, and the ice-shelf fractured and liable any moment to break up. Yet if they left it, how could their females (who were feeding several hundred miles away in open water) find them when they returned? Some birds, including most of the injured ones, stayed put. The remainder, balancing their eggs on their clawlike toes, set out across the sea-ice to find a place where they could rear their young in safety.

A couple of days later they were hauling themselves onto the beach below Lockwood's *behouden huis*...

He welcomed them both as companions with whom he could face the rigours of the Antarctic winter, and as a source of food. He didn't particularly like the idea of killing them; but he hadn't battered three seals to death and eaten his commanding officer, only to let himself starve when food lay all around him for the taking. And in the small hours of the morning, when the mist had lifted and the icefields lay lacquered in the last of the moonlight, he went back to the *behouden huis* for his revolver.

Provided he made no attempt to touch them, the penguins ignored him; but whenever he tried to move an egg from between the toes of an apparently dozing Emperor, the bird came to life and struck at him. He was wondering which one he should kill, when the matter was more or less settled for him. Only a few yards from where he was standing, two of the adult males started to fight.

Emperor penguins are not usually belligerent. These birds, however, had had a lot to put up with. Many had lost their eggs and were on the *qui vive* to steal their neighbour's. So when one of the males shifted his position and his egg fell out from between his feet, another bird promptly pounced on it and hid it in the folds of loose skin beneath his stomach. The rightful parent, however, saw what happened. With an outraged '*Kra-a-a-ak!*' he set about the thief with flippers and beak. In normal circumstances the egg would have been given back; but deprivation had made the thief desperate. His own embryo chick had been crushed in the cliff-fall; he had joined the trek to a new rookery in the hope of finding another egg, and his paternal instinct was now too strong to be denied; he hung onto his prize with the despair of a creature who has only one thing to live for. The birds surrounding the combatants shifted uneasily. Because penguin eggs are fragile, fighting within a rookery is *verboten*, and on the rare occasions when there *is* a fight it is in the interests of the community to see it is brief. And final. As soon as the surrounding penguins saw that the thief was getting the worse of it, they turned on him, pecking and bludgeoning him until he lay motionless in a pool of blood.

Lockwood was probably right in thinking it was an act of kindness to kill him.

That morning he ate well. For the first time in 138 days he ate as much as he wanted to. For the first time in over 3,000 hours, when he had finished eating he felt neither hunger nor the fear of hunger. Perhaps only a child of the Third World can understand how he felt. He felt he had been brought to the heaven he had often dreamed of but had never expected to see.

Next day the cloud thickened, the wind strengthened, and by midnight a blizzard was trying to rip the *behouden huis* off the bottom of the world. Lockwood didn't care. He slept on, dreaming of steaks roasted, grilled, baked, marinaded, boiled, well-done and rare, and telling himself he was lucky: that not for many people do their dreams really come true.

The blizzard blew itself out in twenty-four hours; and by mid-morning on the penultimate day of July the sky was cloudless.

During the bad weather the Emperor penguins had stayed huddled together in a close-packed group; now they dispersed and took up positions round the beach like so many sentinels, watching and waiting. What they were watching and waiting for was the return of their females. It was, however, something a great deal more spectacular than a penguin which materialised that morning out of the ice.

It was 11.50 a.m., and for the past ten minutes Lockwood had been staring at the northern skyline. And this time, he told himself, he *wasn't* imagining things; this time the darkness *was* less absolute. A band of mother-of-pearl was welling up along the horizon. The mother-of-pearl became flecked with pink. The pink deepened. And suddenly great shafts of vermilion and gold—sunlight refracted by ice—began to cartwheel along the horizon like the spokes of a turning wheel. Then came the miracle that most of us take for granted, but Lockwood hadn't witnessed for 64 days.

Sunrise.

Only the upper rim of the sun appeared that morning. It cast no shadow and gave off no heat, and within five minutes it had vanished. But to Lockwood its return was an intimation of life.

He stood outside the *behouden huis* long after the last glimmer of light had faded, staring at the spot on the horizon from which the sun had risen. He was like a child of the desert who for the first time sees a river ... One of the most arid deserts in the world is the Karakum. Very occasionally (perhaps two or three times in a lifetime) the nomadic people of the Karakum will visit the only river that flows through their desert, the Amu Darya, the 'lifeline thrown down by Allah to a people dying of thirst'; and a child who has never had enough water in its life and has had to fight for and conserve the few drops it has, will set eyes for the first time on one of the great rivers of the world; and the child will stand and stare at the Amu Darya not just for a few minutes and not just for a few hours, but for day after day. For the child knows that what it is staring at is the be-all and end-all of its life, a phenomenon without which it wouldn't exist. And that is how Lockwood, now, thought of the sun. When it hadn't been there, the world had been dead and he had been dying. Now it had returned, the world—and he with it— was going to be reborn: as by a miracle, resurrected.

If, that morning, he had been with the detachment they would have capered about like a tribe of sun-worshippers; they would have snowballed one another, spliced the mainbrace and indulged in the twentieth-century equivalent of a fertility rite. But he was alone. He had no option but to keep his joy bottled up.

The cold that evening was sharp as ever; but as he paced up and down Lockwood hardly noticed it; he was co-cooned in the warmth of his thoughts. A week ago, he told himself, I'd given up hope. But the tide has turned. Now I've got food and soon I'll have warmth. Each day the sun will climb a little higher, and shine a little brighter; soon it will be strong enough to bring shadows; its warmth will melt the ice, and with the melt will come algae and lichen, and with the algae and lichen will come plankton and krill, and with the plankton and krill will come fish, and with the fish will come birds and mammals; and life will come back to a world that's been dead; and if I'm patient and careful and lucky I'll survive, and one day, God willing, I'll be rescued.

As though to remind him how far away any such rescue was, the weather that evening took a turn for the worse.

Before he dossed down he went to have a look at the penguins. Everything was unnaturally still, as though the night was holding its breath, and the moon was ringed by a succession of haloes. He knew the signs. They were in for a storm.

The penguins evidently knew it too. For the rookery had fallen silent, and even as Lockwood watched, the birds began to form into a phalanx—or perhaps 'testudo' would be more accurate: not so much a line of battle as a protective shield, with their shoulders interlocked and their backs to the rising wind. Soon every bird in the rookery was within the testudo, the stronger and more far-sighted in the centre, the weaker and those tardy in forming up around the perimeter.

The wind strengthened. Little flurries of snow came swirling in from the sea. The penguins locked their flippers together, hunched up their backs and waited. This was a battle they and their ancestors had been fighting for 100,000 years: a battle not one of them could have won alone, but all of them could win together. Soon the blizzard engulfed them: the sort of cold that freezes mercury solid, makes tin disintegrate into loose granules and shatters bars of steel: the sort of wind that never drops below 70 knots and gusts to 120; and the sort of snow that swirls like a maelstrom through a world devoid of light.

So they waited for the blizzard to end: the penguins in their testudo, Lockwood in his *behouden huis*.

The blizzard, however, showed not the slightest sign of ending. It screamed and clawed at them, day after day.

The *behouden huis* became like an outpost under attack. The wind battered it first from one side then from the other. Snow pitted into it like shrapnel. Its defences were breached, and for 36 hours Lockwood had no sleep as he worked non-stop to plug the gaps blasted out of the walls. If he hadn't kept at it he would have been buried by the in-pouring snow. Two things helped. He no longer felt alone; for weren't his friends the penguins alongside him, doing battle with the same adversary? And he had no worries about fuel or food; whenever conditions were good enough he lit his stove and cooked himself the sort of meal that for months he had dreamed of. And after five days of violence the blizzard ended as suddenly as it had begun.

A few minutes to midnight the wind was 50 knots, the cloud unbroken and the snow continuous. A few minutes after midnight the breeze was gentle, the last remnants of cloud were disappearing over the horizon, and it might have been a different world the moon was shining down on.

This was the worst spell of weather Lockwood had to endure that winter. In such terrible conditions he didn't see how any living creature could have survived in the open, and as he made his way to the beach he was filled with apprehension. He had visions of a mound of frozen corpses.

But the penguins were alive, and their close-knit formation was just beginning to break up.

During the blizzard the birds had been silent; but now, as though to celebrate their survival, they started a cacophony of '*kra-a-as*' and '*aa-acks*' which echoed round the rookery like a discordant thanksgiving. Some—especially those from round the perimeter—were so encased in snow and ice they looked as though they were literally frozen solid. But this was a problem they knew how to solve. They rolled over and over to break up the ice that clung to them; then they extended and flexed their flippers, shook loose their feathers and started to preen themselves. As soon as they were satisfied everything was in working order, the majority waddled off to take up their sentinel-like positions round the beach. A handful, however, remained close together, pecking at the ice as though searching for food. They seemed loath to move. And as Lockwood approached them he saw why.

During the blizzard the first eggs had hatched. A couple of dozen of the Emperors were now holding between their toes not motionless ovals of white, but moving bundles of grey: all soft down and beseeching beaks.

It seemed to Lockwood that the newborn chicks were going to have a problem. For there was nothing for them to eat ... Under normal circumstances, by the time the chicks were born their mothers would be returning from the open sea, sleek and fat and ready to feed them with regurgitated fish. The females from this particular rookery, however, had no means of knowing where their offspring were; and it seemed to Lockwood that the newborn chicks had little chance of surviving for long without food. As the days passed, and more and more chicks were born, and there was still no sign of the mothers, he became increasingly worried. It saddened him to think that the Emperor penguins had survived the blizzard (and everything else Antarctica had thrown at them) only to see their progeny die of starvation almost as soon as they were born. But there was nothing, he told himself, he could do about it.

Then he remembered there was one thing he *wasn't* short of: powdered milk.

Most people would probably have taken the view—very reasonably—that Lockwood was out of his mind: that the idea of saving a whole lot of penguin chicks by feeding them powdered milk was farcical. However, by this time he felt he was not only caught up in but was himself taking part in Antarctica's recurring miracle of resurrection; and he told himself he couldn't simply sit and watch his companions die. He had to do *something*. So he mixed a sachet of milk-powder with melted snow, heated it to what he hoped was blood temperature, put it in a thermos, and set off on his Mission of Mercy.

His efforts were not appreciated by the penguins. The parents were fiercely protective. As soon as Lockwood came near them they hid their chicks, drew in their heads and set up a belligerent hissing. He tried first to cajole them with gentle '*kra-a-as*'; then he tried to get hold of a chick by subterfuge; but at the end of an hour all he had to show for his pains were bruises and peck-marks, and his thermos had been knocked out of his hands and its contents spilt.

He mixed another lot of powdered milk, and tried again. He found a penguin who, he liked to think, was eyeing him with more curiosity than belligerence, and sat beside it. At first the penguin eyed him with suspicion; but after about ten minutes, as though deciding Lockwood was a harmless eccentric, he lost interest in him and began to fondle his chick.

The chick was a six-inch pyramid of soft grey down, with white circles round its eyes that gave it a 'wise-beyond-its-years' look, like a baby owl. Every time it opened its beak—and that was often—it let out a series of plaintive '*cheeps*', which reinforced Lockwood's conviction that it was starving. He poured out a mugful of milk, and put it down as close as he could to its parent. Maybe, he thought, his sense of smell will tell him it's food. But the penguin's reaction was disappointing. He peered at the mug as though it were an embryo killer whale. Eventually he gave it a tap with his beak. The metallic 'ping' seemed to confirm his view that here was a phenomenon not to be trusted. Balancing his chick between his toes, he backed away to seek safety within a circle of his companions.

A lot of people would have thought, 'If the stupid birds won't help themselves, why should I bother?' But it wasn't in Lockwood's nature to give up. There must be *some* way, he thought, of getting through to them. He left his mug in the centre of a group of penguins, sat on a rock and waited. He waited a long time. But all that happened was that he got colder and colder.

The breakthrough came by accident.

The parents, encumbered by their chicks, were clumsy movers, and eventually one of them blundered into the mug and knocked it over. The milk trickled out and coalesced into a pool of frozen crystals in a hollow in the ice. The penguins, Lockwood had noticed, often pecked at the ice, and one of them by chance happened to start pecking at the spot where the milk had coalesced. His reactions were almost comic in their predictability. After the first peck he stepped back, cocked his head on one side and peered at the ice in astonishment. Another tentative peck was followed by a succession of more enthusiastic ones. He let out an excited '*kra-kra-kra-a-aak*'. Another penguin joined him, and the sequence was repeated. Soon a circle of Emperors were pecking away at the ice long after the last of the milk had disappeared. Then came the moment that, for Lockwood, made it all worthwhile. The first penguin, who had managed to gobble up about half the milk-crystals before the others cottoned on to what was happening, regurgitated the unexpected nourishment for his chick. It may not have been the prettiest of sights, but at least, Lockwood told himself, one of the baby birds had, for the moment, been saved. He went back to his *behouden huis* and opened another sachet of milk.

What he didn't realise at the time was that the male birds were, in fact, able to keep their offspring alive (albeit for a short time only) by feeding them with a glandular secretion that was rich in protein. His efforts were therefore basically *de trop*. However, his concern did help him to establish some sort of a rapport with the penguins . . . The creatures of Antarctica have lived so long in isolation, they have no inborn fear of man. It was therefore easier for Lockwood to win the Emperors' friendship than if he had been stranded, say, in Africa with a herd of wildebeest, or America with a flock of flamingos. All the same, he had to suffer pecks and buffets, rebuffs and disappointments, before he became an accepted member of the rookery. But at last, after many misadventures and misunderstandings, there came a time when he found he could recognise individual birds, when the penguins came trooping over the ice to greet him on his 'milk-run', when after a blizzard they came (or so he liked to think) to look for him, when a couple were persuaded into his *behouden huis*, and one particularly trusting parent let him fondle its chick.

Only the deprived and the lonely can know how much this meant to him.

And as the penguins, that spring, provided him with two of the prerequisites of survival—companionship and food—so the sun was soon providing him with a third, warmth.

As in mid-winter he had made a ritual out of savouring his cup of tea and his single meal, so he now made a ritual out of welcoming the sun. Each morning, weather permitting, he would stand by his *behouden huis* waiting for the gradual lightening of the sky, the brightness along the eastern horizon, the shafts of red and gold, and finally the great pulsating disc of the 'mighty monarch of the world' as it heaved itself out of the ice. To start with, the sun sank back under the ice almost as soon as it had appeared. But gradually it rose ever a little higher, stayed in the sky ever a little longer, shone ever a little more brightly and gave off ever a little more heat. Soon Lockwood could make out shadows—the silhouette of a group of penguins, the wall of his *behouden huis*—and one day, almost too wonderful to be believed, for the first time in three months, he felt on his face a touch of warmth. It was the kiss of life: a caress he had longed for often but had many times despaired of ever feeling again.

He raised his face to the sun. Never for as long as I live, he thought, will I take you for granted.

By the end of August there were more signs that spring was in the offing. One afternoon, on his way to the beach, he heard the trickle of water. On the most northerly of the nunataks the ice was beginning to melt . . . Once or twice before, that winter, there had been a temporary thaw. But this was something more fundamental. This was the coming together of the components—water, minerals and warmth—from whose union there would soon stem an increasingly sophisticated chain of life—algae, lichen, plankton, krill, crustaceans, fish, birds, penguins, seals, whales . . . But all this, he knew, was way in the future. And for the time being the melt brought almost as many problems as blessings. For in the ever-increasing warmth of the sun, the ice-shingle-and-seaweed filling in the walls of his *behouden huis* began to disintegrate. Soon, each afternoon, little trickles of water were seeping out from between the stones and coalescing into puddles round the base of his tent.

He was trying one evening to channel the puddles away, when he heard the penguins singing. There was no other word for it: a *Te Deum* echoing and re-echoing round the icefields. For a moment he couldn't think what was happening. Then he saw them, silhouetted in the afterglow of the sunset: the females coming back from the sea.

Of all the images of Antarctica that lodged in his memory this was the most poignant.

The sun had set, but its splendour lingered on, transforming the pressure-ridges from grey to pink. Little patches of mist floated over the icefields, their lower strands in shadow, their upper strands transformed by the last rays of sunlight to cobwebs of gold. It would be difficult to imagine a more peaceful scene. But the penguins were anything but peaceful. Each and every one was staring seaward, quivering with excitement, and braying like a demented donkey.

For standing out against the skyline were two groups of little black dots: rather less than a dozen in one, rather more than a dozen in the other. As the dots came closer Lockwood's eyes confirmed what his instinct told him. They were penguins. Sleek and well-fed female penguins: now waddling forward in single file, now throwing themselves face down and 'tobogganing' towards the rookery on their stomachs. They made no sound until they came to the ledge where the sea-ice gave way to the land-ice. Then, as they leapt ashore, they too started to sing.

For this, Lockwood suddenly realised, was how the birds who had mated recognised one another: not by sight but by sound.

One might have thought that with several thousand penguins all braying their heads off, individual voices would never have been distinguished. This wasn't so. And soon the beach was the scene of ecstatic reunions. The moment a pair who had mated recognised one another's cries they rushed towards each other. They stood about three feet apart, their bodies bent backward, singing their love-song; then they touched beaks, touched breasts and began very gently to caress one another. Finally the male showed his mate their egg, or in the case of an early hatching, their chick. This triggered off another display of affection, the female crooning to the chick, fondling it, and encouraging it to settle between her feet. Then came the moment that not only cemented their relationship but ensured the survival of the species. The mother gave her chick its first meal of regurgitated fish.

Within an hour of their return all the females whose mates were still alive had found them, and one might have expected the reunited families to spend at least a few days together. It didn't happen. The males' paternal instinct may have been strong, but stronger still was the instinct to survive. They were starving. For the last couple of months, while incubating their eggs, they hadn't had a scrap to eat. The nearest food was away in the open sea, some 100 miles to the north; so the moment they were satisfied their progeny was safe and being looked after, they headed seaward. It would be six weeks before they were back and the family once again united.

From that moment, the mother birds returned in ever-increasing numbers. Soon there were more females than males in the colony, and a glut of food for the chicks.

In the months to come Lockwood saw a lot of the Emperor penguins. He and they were the only living creatures in a continent the size of Europe, and they shared everything: the cold and the blizzards, the silence and the solitude, moonlight and the aurora. He was subsequently to make friends with birds and mammals more graceful and some might say more endearing than the Emperors. But one's first love is something special; and for the rest of his life it was the tough little Emperor penguins who walked with him most often in his dreams.

By mid-September the melt had become a flood. Patches of rock were emerging like skeletal bones out of the ice; water was cascading down the north face of the nunataks, and Lockwood's *behouden huis* was more like a survival ark than a survival shelter.

Winter had given way to spring.

Soon, Lockwood told himself, more and more creatures would come flocking to the mainland: first a trickle, then a flood and finally those teeming millions of fish, birds and mammals which each year transform a once-dead shoreline into the most prolific breeding ground in the world. And last of all would come men.

Would the crew of the *Scoresby*, he wondered, still be keeping a look-out for survivors? Or would they have written off the detachment as dead?

Now that rescue had become a possibility—albeit still a distant one—he told himself there were things he needed to work out. How to ensure he was sighted, and that a ship approaching the Peninsula didn't pass by without realising he was there. And what to tell his rescuers when they asked the inevitable question, 'what happened to the others?'

The first problem, he decided, wasn't an immediate one. It would be the better part of three months before a ship could get anywhere near the Peninsula. It was too early to be thinking of building cairns, bonfires or beacons, or setting up a flagpole.

But the more he thought about the second problem, the more it worried him. For he didn't want his rescuers to find out about his cannibalism.

Common sense might suggest that *anyone* in Lockwood's situation would have reverted to cannibalism: that he had done nothing to be ashamed of, and had nothing to hide. And indeed if he had had someone to talk things over with, this is almost certainly the way he would have seen it. But he *hadn't* anyone to talk to. For something like 5,000 hours he was alone, most of the time entombed in the dark, his only companions his thoughts. No wonder introspection and a sense of guilt became his bedfellows.

So what *was* he going to tell his rescuers?

His first idea was that he'd tell them he was the sole survivor from the burning down of their hut. But the more he thought about this the more he realised it could lead to problems. Suppose, for example, after the war an expedition visited the site of their hut and uncovered the bodies, meaning to give them a decent burial; what would they think when they found that Ede and Ramsden were not among them? Or suppose Ede's body was found on the tip of the Peninsula; why, people would ask him, had he pretended his commanding officer had died in the hut, and why was nothing left of him but his skeleton? His rescuers would be kind and sympathetic, but they would want to know the truth. They would ask him questions he didn't want to answer, and he could picture himself trying to fob them off with half-truths and getting mixed up and resorting to lies and getting found out, until in the end he was forced to admit 'I ate him'. And in a nightmare scenario he could picture the way they would look at him. In their eyes would be pity, but the sort of pity they might have felt for one of the world's untouchables.

I'll have to work out *very* carefully, he thought, what to tell them.

In the end he decided to stick as close as possible to the truth. To say that he, Ramsden and Ede had survived the holocaust, and had set out for the tip of the Peninsula. Ramsden was no problem; all he had to say was that the petty officer had fallen into a crevasse and been killed, and that would be that. As for Ede, he'd say he had been terribly injured and had died during their journey—no one would expect him to remember exactly where. And so long as he stuck to this story, he didn't see why it should be doubted—provided, that is, he got rid of the Old Man's body.

I must find a safe place, he told himself, to bury him.

His first idea was to lower him, weighted down, into the sea. Then he remembered that storms can wrench even quite large objects off the sea-bed, and currents can swirl them for hundreds or even thousands of miles. He didn't care for the thought of a half-eaten corpse being washed up on the coast of South America. There was also the drawback that the sea-ice was still almost three feet thick; getting Ede's body to the bed of the sea and anchoring it there would be difficult if not impossible. Better, he told himself, to bury him among the rocks of the Peninsula.

It was a couple of weeks before he found a suitable place; a deep ravine bisecting a plateau that was too far from the *behouden huis* to be visited by his rescuers, and too bleak and cheerless to invite a visit from anyone else. It took him a very long time to hack out a grave at the bottom of the ravine, loosening the rocks with an improvised crowbar and making sure he left no trace of his excavations. It saddened him that he was giving a man he had liked and admired so furtive a resting-place. No panoramic vista of the land he had loved, no cross, no inscription, no flowers; he couldn't even manage a tear.

What sort of person have I become? he thought, as he lowered all that was left of the Old Man into the pit. And he was filled with a sudden desire to go from one extreme to the other: to build a great cairn on top of the grave, to surmount it with a cross for all to see and an epitaph for all to read. Then there would be nothing to hide: no need for evasion and deceit . . . But this, he knew, wasn't the road he was going to walk down. Some secrets are best kept hidden.

By the time he had buried Ede the sun was setting. It was a lovely evening, with the mountains bathed in the last of the sunlight, their icefalls and glaciers burnished with gold, their peaks thrust up like cones of fire into a sky of applemint green. This, he told himself, was how the earth had been once, ought to be always, but was in danger of never being again. And not for the first time the contrast made him think: Antarctica before the coming of man, all peace and beauty and tranquillity; and Antarctica after the coming of man, a hacked-up and half-eaten corpse shovelled guiltily into a secret grave.

Sleep didn't come easily that night. And when he did at last drop off, he dreamed—a dream which, had he related it to Hugh Dempster, would have given the psychiatrist food for thought. He dreamed that the uranium-bearing rocks piled up in a corner of the *behouden huis* burst suddenly into flame. Only the flames were no ordinary ones. They burned with a terrifying out-of-this-world intensity, and when they subsided what was left was a pile not of ash but of skulls.

Next morning he moved the rocks out of his *behouden huis* and stacked them at the side of the nunatak. They were a problem, he told himself, he could do without. And indeed he soon had more pressing things to think of. For as winter gave way to spring he had to face both a new adversary and the return of an old one.

His new adversary was damp.

Week after week a *mélange* of sleet-cum-rain-cum-banks-of-fog came swirling in from the sea. It was like being trapped in a vast refrigerated sauna. Each afternoon the melt turned the walls of his *behouden huis* into waterfalls. It was impossible to keep anything dry. Everything—his tent, his sleeping-bag, his clothes—was either veneered with ice or sodden with moisture. In terms of physical discomfort he had as hard a time that spring as he had had in winter, and it wasn't long before his health again began to deteriorate. He developed a cough and renewed symptoms of his old adversary, scurvy.

Scurvy isn't the easiest of afflictions to live with. One of its side-effects is depression; and more than once as the sun disappeared for days on end behind the rain clouds Lockwood was tempted to give up, to close his eyes and hope that never again would he have to open them. At such times, when he was confined for long spells to the *behouden huis*, he yearned above all for a companion. And one afternoon he found one.

He was plugging up the gaps scoured out of the walls by the melt, when he saw something move. When he shone his torch on it he saw it was a tiny fly, no more than a few millimetres long. It had a semi-transparent body, no wings, fragile legs and a head about the size of a pin, and it was crawling very slowly over a slab of granite. A biologist would have told him that wingless flies exist in a micro-climate which bears little relation to what we call 'the weather'. Lockwood, however, saw the little creature as a harbinger of summer. Anxious not to let it out of his sight, he carried the slab of granite into his tent, and spent the rest of the afternoon watching the fly as it crawled end-lessly round and round the rock.

'What are you looking for?' he asked it.

The sound of his voice was an alarm bell. What in God's name am I doing, he thought, talking to a fly? And why have I brought it into the tent? Probably all it wants is to get back to the seaweed it crawled out of. He replaced the rock in the wall of his *behouden huis*.

But he didn't forget the fly. Several times that evening he went to see how it was getting on, and before he dossed down he went to say goodnight to it. It was still on the same rock, but now, as though exhausted, it didn't move. He hoped it was all right. That night he dreamed about it: that it became his friend; that each morning it came out of the stonework to greet him; that he taught it to crawl onto his hand. And in his dream he forgot the fly was wingless, and watched enchanted as it flitted from rock to rock, looped the loop, and settled upside down on the roof of the *behouden huis*. But when he came to look for it in the morning it was gone.

He went scrambling about on hands and knees, shining his torch into crevices in the rock.

'Where are you?' he kept muttering. 'Are you all right?'

Eventually he found it. On its back. Dead.

Why it had died he didn't know, but he felt responsible. 'Poor little bugger,' he muttered. 'You'd still be crawling about, wouldn't you, if I'd left you alone.'

Three weeks passed before he saw another sign of insect life.

Almost as soon as the melt got under way a chain of freshwater pools had formed round the base of his nunatak; and gradually, as the sun gained strength, the rocks round the edge of these pools became coated with algae. This was good news for Lockwood. In the hope of alleviating his scurvy he took to collecting the algae, boiling it and drinking it. One afternoon he had dislodged a rock from the edge of the pool and was scraping off the algae, when he saw clinging to its undersurface a mass of microscopic creatures. He thought at first they were tiny black beetles, but as he looked at them more closely he realised they were eight-legged mites, primitive cousins of the spider. Very carefully he put the rock back. He didn't disturb the mites, but spent the rest of the day studying them, trying without success to work out the purpose of their scurrying hither and thither.

A week later he made a more interesting discovery.

One of the pools at the foot of his nunatak was a place of rare tranquillity. It was sheltered from the wind and warmed by the sun, and the melting ice flowed into it in a gentle trickle. It had been the first pool to spawn algae and lichen, and now as Lockwood walked past it one evening on his way to the rookery he saw that its water was not, as usual, crystal-clear, but mottled pink. On looking at the pinkness more closely, he realised it was made up of a myriad living creatures, that he was staring at a shoal of minuscule shrimps. They were using their comblike legs to tear algae off the rocks and stuff it into their mouths. He sat watching them until it was dark, wondering if they could be the first of the many creatures who would soon be coming to Antarctica to breed.

At the time he never got round to working out *why* so many birds and mammals should flock each summer, in such enormous numbers, to breed on one of the bleakest shorelines on earth. It was happening. That was miracle enough. It was only years later, when he was back in England, that he became interested in the whys and wherefores of the stupendous proliferation of life in which he had been caught up.

The prerequisites of life on earth are water, warmth and minerals. The tropical ocean basins, which one might have expected to be the cradles of life, are often devoid of minerals; they are the deserts of the sea. The sub-Arctic and sub-Antarctic basins, on the other hand, are rich in minerals; and in several parts of these oceans, wind, swell and currents combine to churn up the minerals from the sea-bed and bring them to the surface. Nowhere on earth are there fiercer storms, steeper swell or more violent currents than off the coast of the Antarctic Peninsula. So the surface waters around the Peninsula are unusually rich in mineral-nutrients. In winter these are kept locked up, as in a tomb, by the sea-ice. But each spring, as the sea-ice melts, the waters of Antarctica come alive. They change colour; and they change consistency, as in the warmth of the sun the minerals are transformed by photosynthesis into the most prolific crop on earth: plankton. First to form is the vegetable phytoplankton—billion upon billion of microscopic one-cell diatoms. Individually these are too small to be seen by the naked eye, but collectively they form into vast mats of green-brown 'scum', which drift hither and thither on the surface of the sea. (The name plankton means 'something that drifts about aimlessly'.) These mats often cover hundreds of square miles, and show up on satellite pictures as clearly as the glittering ice-caps.

From this vegetable phytoplankton stems the animal zooplankton: billion upon billion of herbivores which feed off the mats of 'scum'. The majority are smaller than a grain of rice, but they are multitudinous as the sands of the desert. If you collected together every species that exists on earth—all the insects from the rain forests, all the mosquitoes from the swamps, all the locusts from the deserts, all the fish from the sea, and all the grazing herds from the plains—their combined number would be less than the number of copepods (the smallest of the herbivores) which feed each year off plankton. In a second of sunlight a million are born. In a second of storm a million die. In the second a whale opens its mouth ten thousand are swallowed. They are forever eating and being eaten by one another. And, more importantly, they provide sustenance for creatures that come from the four corners of the earth to feed on them. For the great thing about plankton is that it is a crop which never fails, which doesn't depend on wind or rain or some complex system of propagation, but which proliferates each year simply through the warmth of the sun. It is partly because this food chain is so reliable that it is used by such a vast multitude of invertebrates, crustaceans, fish, birds and mammals—almost 40 per cent of all living creatures depend on it for their survival.

Lockwood, from his vantage point on the tip of the Peninsula, was to have a grandstand view of this amazing resurgence. Soon, within walking distance of his *behouden huis*, one beach was to become the breeding-ground of 100,000 crabeater seals, and another that of 250,000 Adélie penguins; one cliff-face was to become the breeding ground of 10,000 Dominican gulls, and another that of 100,000 Antarctic petrels. Their sheer numbers never ceased to amaze him. What would have amazed him even more, had he thought about it, was that for every creature he saw on the land there was a multitude of others in the sea that he never saw. For the birds that nested and bred in the cliffs, and the seals and penguins that hauled up and bred on the beaches needed enormous quantities of fish to sustain them; to sustain the fish there had to be even more enormous quantities of krill; and to sustain the krill there had to be astronomic quantities of herbivorous and carnivorous zooplankton. It has been said that there are probably more living creatures each summer in the waters round Antarctica than there are grains of sand in the Sahara. No other place on earth enjoys such a dramatic burgeoning of life.

First to arrive to feed off this cornucopia were the birds.

One afternoon towards the end of September Lockwood was trying to dry out his sleeping-bag during a rare spell of fine weather, when something—it could have been a passing shadow or the rustle of wings—made him look up. And there they were, the most beautiful of all the birds of Antarctica: a pair of snow petrels, flying low over the sea-ice towards him. He had a good view of them as they passed almost directly over the *behouden huis*: black eyes, black beak, black feet, and the rest of them pure white. One moment they were there, next moment they were gone. He ran round the nunatak to try to spot where they had landed, but they had vanished as though they had never been. He told himself it didn't matter; somewhere on the Peninsula they were about to nest, harbingers of the battalions to come.

That night he dreamed he was one of them: that now by sunlight, now by moonlight, he flew low over the sea, dived into waters teeming with fish, and swooped in and out of the ice-caves at the foot of the bergs. And ever at his side was the mate he longed for.

A few days later the battalions began to materialise. He was on his way to the rookery when he was aware of movement high up in the cliffs. The birds were well camouflaged and it was some time before he spotted them: about a dozen Antarctic petrels, handsome birds with chocolate-brown wings and tan underbellies. They were working in pairs, shovelling away the winter snow with their bills and feet, preparing the ledges for their nests. That night he dreamed he was one of *them*: that he and his mate were building a nest for their chick.

Not many birds arrived during the next 48 hours, and Lockwood was soon to know why. The weather deteriorated. Soon a full-scale blizzard was lashing the Peninsula: driving rain, hundred-knot winds, and huge waves flinging shingle half-way up the beach and spray almost to the top of the cliffs. He hoped the petrels had found safe ledges on which to build their nests. The blizzard lasted two days, then ended as suddenly as it had begun, and the night of 2nd October was still and quiet.

For a reason he couldn't account for he found it difficult to sleep. He had a faint but persistent headache, and a feeling that something was about to happen. The thought came to him suddenly and quite out of the blue:

I hope there's not going to be an earthquake—the Peninsula, he knew, was on a fault line, and several of the offshore islands were active volcanoes. It was 2 a.m. before he fell asleep.

It seemed to happen the moment he dozed off. First the noise, like a train approaching fast through a tunnel. Then the vibration, as though the earth was quivering like ill-set jelly. My God, he thought, it *is* an earthquake! As in a nightmare too horrible to be believed, he saw the nunatak collapsing on top of the *behouden huis*, and the *behouden huis* on top of him. He had never leaped faster from his sleeping-bag, and out through the entrance-tunnel. Half-way down the tunnel he realised it wasn't the earth that was vibrating, it was the sky. What in God's name, he thought, is happening?

As he staggered into the open the noise was so deafening that though he clapped his hands to his head he felt his eardrums were about to burst. Only a strip of sky was visible where, along the horizon, the moon hung low over the sea-ice. The rest of the sky was blotted out by a heaving, moving, living canopy. Birds. About 50,000 of them.

For weeks the petrels had been massing on the islands of Tierra del Fuego, waiting for good weather. As soon as the depression which had kept Lockwood in his tent moved away into the Weddell Sea, they set out on the final stage of their migration. Over the Drake Passage they had flown low, to avoid the worst of the wind. Then as they neared the coast of Antarctica they spiralled up in a great cauldron, like an inverted waterspout, to search for the familiar outline of their rookery. For several minutes they wheeled and circled. Then, as they sighted the cliffs behind Lockwood's *behouden huis*, the 'waterspout' collapsed, and the birds *en masse* came plummeting earthward. The noise of their descent was like the roar of a waterfall. The noise of their alighting was louder still: a deafening clap-clap-clap of wings as 50,000 petrels pulled out of their dive, hovered, jostled for position, alighted, took off and alighted again in their search for an unoccupied cranny on the cliffs which for generations had been their breeding ground.

It was bedlam. But gradually, as more and more birds found a resting-place, the noise subsided and the sky cleared. Soon it was just another dawn—except that Lockwood now had a surfeit of neighbours.

More petrels arrived during the next few days. For a while they had the Peninsula to themselves. They took possession of the sunniest and most sheltered crevices on half-a-dozen rockfaces and settled down—or so they thought—for the breeding season. However, it wasn't long before other species turned up.

Lockwood was no ornithologist; but in his efforts that spring to get to know his companions two things were in his favour. Although there was soon an enormous number of birds nesting on the Peninsula, the number of different species was small. In the average British county or North American state there are probably at any one time some 200 different species of bird. In the whole of the Antarctic Peninsula there were, that spring, no more than thirty species. The birdlife of Antarctica is multitudinous but not diverse. Another thing to help him was that the different species arrived at different times and nested in different places—the penguins on the beaches, the petrels and fulmars and terns in the cliffs, and the gulls and cormorants in the rock-scree. The proliferation of life that was about to take place was by no means as chaotic and haphazard as it appeared to be.

After the Antarctic petrels came the Wilson's petrels, although their first visit was a brief one. One morning Lockwood noticed about a dozen birds hovering over the sea-ice with their legs dangling down beneath them. These, he told himself, must be the birds that seamen in the days of sail had called 'Jesus birds', because they

176

looked as though they were walking on water. (Some people reckon that the name petrel is a derivation of Peter—that is, Saint Peter—who also tried his hand at walking on water.) However, the sea-ice had not yet melted, and there was no water for this lot of petrels to walk on; by mid-day they had given up and were heading for the offshore islands.

A few days later there was another mass influx: about 25,000 fulmars: big, elegant, grey-and-white birds twice the size of the petrels, who set about 'persuading' their smaller cousins to vacate the best of the rock ledges. Lockwood was intrigued by the way they did this. His first impression was that the birds fought and the weaker was driven off; but as he watched more closely he saw this wasn't the case. A fulmar would hover over the ledge that it wanted; it would shriek and posture and threaten, but it would never attack. If the nesting bird was intimidated and fled, the ledge would change hands; if it held its ground the fulmar would try elsewhere. There was no bloodshed. No killing.

It made him think. The beaches of the Peninsula were soon to be so crowded with seals and penguins that he could hardly set foot between them, and the rock-ledges so jam-packed with nests that the birds were literally touching. Territory was at a premium. But it was not something the creatures of the Antarctic fought to the death over. They jostled, quarrelled, threatened and defended. But they never killed unless it was for food: a code violated only, he told himself, by the misnamed *Homo sapiens.*

One morning towards the end of October, when the wind was from the east, he heard an almost lyrical crooning. It sounds, he thought, as though another lot of penguins has arrived.

It was not till he came to the beach where, in mid-winter, he had found the starfish that he spotted them: about 100 squat little figures with black backs and creamy-white 'shirt-fronts': Adélie penguins. They were strutting about on the rocks at the edge of the sea-ice, their flippers spread sideways and their beaks pointing skyward, not so much braying as singing. They took not the slightest notice of Lockwood as he walked to within a few yards of them and sat on an outcrop of granite. At first he was intrigued; but as for hour after hour the penguins did nothing but walk round in circles, posturing and crooning, he got both cold and bored. He was about to return to his *behouden huis* when the volume of crooning increased, and the penguins lined up at the edge of the ice staring seaward. How they knew that more birds were approaching Lockwood was never able to work out; but after about a quarter-of-an-hour a cluster of dots appeared on the horizon: dots which as they grew larger he identified as more Adélie penguins, advancing in line abreast on the beach. The moment they heard the crooning of their mates, they too burst into song. They rushed forward faster and faster till they came to the little five-foot cliff which divided the sea-ice from the land-ice. Lockwood thought they might have a job scrambling over it; but the Adélies took off like so many jump-jet Harriers, came soaring over the cliff with the *élan* of salmon leaping a waterfall, landed with a thud that made him wince, and at once picked themselves up and started rushing hither and thither in search of last year's mate. The moment a pair recognised one another they began the same ritual as their cousins the Emperors: singing their hearts out, bowing, nodding, posturing and eventually gently touching. By the time it was dark and Lockwood was heading back for his *behouden huis,* the birds who had found their mates were already scraping together stones and building a nest, while the others remained lined up along the top of the ice-cliff staring hopefully seaward.

Over the next few days Lockwood revisited the rookery several times. Within twenty-four hours the number of birds had risen to 3,000. Within forty-eight hours it had risen to 30,000. Within a week there were 300,000 Adélie penguins in the rookery, nesting in pairs, spaced out at almost exactly four feet apart—close enough for the penguins to threaten but not to peck one another. In the centre, where it was safest, were the wise old birds who had arrived early. Round the perimeter where it was more dangerous were the younger birds, some still seeking a mate, who had arrived late. The bedlam of their mating and nesting could be heard five miles away. There was a lot of jostling and a lot of threatening and quarrelling. But again, no killing.

In the months to come Lockwood spent a fair amount of time watching the Adélie penguins. He saw the male and the female sharing every pleasure and every chore: saw the two of them collecting pebbles for their nest, taking turns to incubate their egg, feeding their chick, protecting it from skuas and leopard seals, teaching the *crèches* of baby penguins to walk and to swim, and finally leading them out of the rookery and into the open sea. He saw accidents, deaths and a lot of things that made him sad. But he never saw one penguin kill another.

This confirmed his belief that the creatures of the Antarctic had more sense than men. They would be better off, he told himself, without us. And this in turn strengthened his feeling that the uranium-bearing rocks stacked up outside his *behouden huis* would be bad news for Antarctica's multitudinous wildlife. For if uranium was all that important, its discovery would surely bring men flocking to the bottom of the world.

He told himself he was silly even to be thinking of these things. What he ought to be concentrating on was his rescue.

For with the melting of the sea-ice, rescue was beginning to look not only possible but probable.

He knew that somewhere beyond the horizon the sea-ice was melting, because each day he saw the birds in their millions heading north in search of food which they could only be getting from the open sea. How far offshore this open water was he didn't know—it could have been 50 miles, it could have been 500—for there are huge annual fluctuations in the extent of the pack-ice that girdles Antarctica. He could only hope that the thaw, this season, would be widespread and would come sooner rather than later. And if it came sooner, it might be little more than a month before a ship was able to push through to the tip of the Peninsula.

How could he be sure that if a ship did come, it would spot him?

His first step was one he agonised over for days. He didn't want to do it, but in the end he decided to quit the *behouden huis* which had served him so well in winter. One reason was that the melt had transformed his 'cave' into a channel through which water was continually flowing, so that his tent was forever awash, and his clothes, food and cooking gear were never dry. Another reason was that the *behouden huis* couldn't be seen from the sea; it blended too well into the nunatak. The new site that he chose for his tent was more exposed and a great deal less comfortable, but he reckoned it would be sighted by a man with binoculars from half-a-mile offshore.

Once he had moved house, he started thinking about a bonfire, a flagpole, heliographs and an SOS.

The difficulty was that he had virtually nothing to burn, and whatever he put outside quickly became sodden. In the end he decided to make a cache of things like spare clothes, penguin fat and a small tin of kerosene, and keep them in his tent, ready to be taken out and set alight the moment a ship was sighted. He also had problems with his flagpole. He managed to make one, using the slats and runners from his sledge; but every time he put the wretched thing up the wind blew it down; so that too had to be left ready to be hoisted at the last moment. His heliographs he made out of tin cans. He had saved about a dozen, with the idea originally of making them into fish-hooks. Now he scrubbed them and polished them and edged them into crevices in the north-facing slope of his nunatak. When the sun was shining they were effective. The trouble was that the sun, that spring, didn't shine all that often.

So he pinned his hopes on his SOS.

His first idea was to find a patch of snow that was visible from the sea, and form the letters SOS on it out of bits of rock. But on every north-facing slope the snow was now melting so fast that the areas of snow were getting smaller and the areas of rock larger; this meant that the SOS he formed one week might be invisible the next. He therefore decided to find a slope where the rock was one colour— say grey granite—and form an SOS on it out of rocks of another colour—say yellow sandstone. He knew this would take time; but time was one of the few things he wasn't short of.

His first step was to find a slope which could be easily seen from the sea. This involved trekking over the ice, about half a mile offshore, and eyeing the tip of the Peninsula as it might one day be eyed by the crew of the *Scoresby.*

His venture onto the sea-ice brought him new friends: Weddell seals, creatures who lived not close-packed on the beaches like penguins, but spaced out in small family groups on the ice. On his first reconnaissance Lockwood spotted two females and their pups, the latter so small he reckoned they were only a few days old. They were sunning themselves at the edge of a breathing-hole.

As he approached he expected them to slither into the water and disappear beneath the ice. But they didn't. They stared at him without fear. So he settled down to watch.

For a long time nothing happened: the seals were happy in the warmth of the sun and that was enough; but eventually his patience was rewarded. One of the females nuzzled her pup into the water and started to teach it to swim. Newborn seals, like newborn humans, have an affinity with water. They float naturally. They don't, however, swim naturally. This is a skill which has to be taught. And as Lockwood watched, he could only marvel at the mother seal's gentleness and patience. At first her pup was a reluctant pupil. Like a child who has first swallowed salt water and then got knocked over by a wave, it tried to scramble back to *terra firma*. But its mother, with nuzzles and trills, persuaded it to persevere until eventually the two of them were circling, somersaulting, playing and diving—leaping half out of the water, expelling the air from their lungs, then staying submerged for several seconds. The lesson went on for something like half-an-hour, and not once did the mother show a hint of roughness or impatience.

After a while Lockwood became aware of a sensation that puzzled him: he felt he was being watched. He stared at the ice and the sky, half expecting to see some predator approaching, but there seemed to be no sign of danger. He told himself he must be imagining things. Yet the feeling persisted, and eventually his ears gave him the clue he needed. As well as the trills of the mother seal and the high-pitched yaps of her pup, he became aware of another sound, a succession of grunts, so faint as to be almost inaudible. Slowly he moved to the edge of the breathing-hole. And it was then that he saw him: a shadowlike shape motionless beneath the ice. For a moment he was afraid it might be a sea leopard or even a killer whale. Then he realised it was the father: keeping guard, encouraging.

He would have liked to go on watching the family for hours; but he told himself he would be well advised to get his priorities right. He hadn't yet found a site for his SOS.

He saw it in the last of the evening sunlight: a gently-sloping apron of granite on the central headland. It was some way from his tent, but in every other respect it looked ideal. He'd start building his SOS, he told himself, in the morning.

However, when he got back to his tent, it wasn't his SOS that occupied his thoughts. It was the seals.

He felt drawn to them, as though in some curious way he was bonded to them and their lives and his were intertwined. What was it, he asked himself, that he found so attractive about them? He decided it was their innocence. He could walk up to them and they didn't run away. He could stand among them and they showed no fear. They had the insouciance of young children before they learn the ways of the world. Maybe, he thought, all creatures were like this when the world was young, before the coming of man. And maybe that's the way things were meant to be, and Antarctica is the only place left on earth that's still got it right . . . For the first time in six months, as he boiled the water for his evening tea, he wasn't concentrating on what he was doing. He was still trying to work out exactly what it was that bound him to the seals when he reached for his saucepan. And his hand closed not on the handle but the rim. He leaped back, cursing. The saucepan went flying. And boiling water cascaded all over his foot.

'Bugger!'

He hopped up and down, wringing his hand, flexing his toes. He was hurt, frightened, shocked and above all angry with himself for being so careless. He knew that in his condition *any* injury was likely to be serious. So how could he minimise the damage? The great thing, he seemed to remember, was to keep the burnt area cool and clean; so he'd better get his boot off. He stuck his injured hand in the snow and with his other hand started fumbling with the laces. He had a job undoing them—it was amazing how clumsy he was with only one hand—but at last he managed to loosen his boot and lever it away.

183

He peeled off his sock and saw that his instep was swollen, red and beginning to blister. And painful. He stuck his foot as well as his hand in the snow, and felt exceedingly sorry for himself.

He expected, as he got over the shock, to start feeling better. But it didn't happen. He started feeling worse.

When a person who is fit suffers from shock they have a reserve of strength to fall back on to help them regain their equilibrium. Lockwood had no such reserve. And the trauma of his burns now began to trigger off just about every other ailment that his body had been heir to. His knees and wrists began to ache with a dull, pulsating throb—and that was the aftermath of his scurvy. His eyes began to smart—and that was the aftermath of his snow-blindness. And he became suddenly aware of his physical deterioration. It was as much as he could do to lift his foot from the snow; and when he looked at it, he was appalled to see not only how burned it was but how skel-etal. There was practically no muscle: just bare bone and tatters of red skin, darkening.

And suddenly it was all too much for him. He had had enough. He didn't want to fight any more. He wanted to close his eyes and sleep; and if he drifted from sleep to unconsciousness and from unconsciousness to oblivion, well that, he told himself, was the best thing that could happen. He slumped face-down in the snow.

'Remember your promise to the Old Man,' a voice whis-pered; but he told himself that Ede was in some place where he had no need of promises.

'What about the rocks?' the voice went on. Sod the rocks, he thought, we're better off without them.

He shut his eyes. And tiredness, coldness and the ache of his hand and foot engulfed him like a succession of waves which swirled him away, rolling him over and over, until they cast him up on an unknown shore where he lay splayed out, unmoving and uncaring. He might never have moved again if it hadn't been for the birds.

He had been lying in the snow for only a couple of minutes when he heard the clap-clap-clap of wings, growing louder, coming closer. He opened his eyes, and saw them as they emerged out of the storm clouds and passed low over his tent: the epitome of all the wild and graceful creatures of the Antarctic, a pair of wandering albatross. Probably, he thought, they are looking for a site for their nest—lucky things. There'd be no nest, he told himself, for *him* to build. No young to rear. For a reason he didn't understand, he felt a sudden urge to have a last look at the world he was about to say good-bye to.

The storm clouds were gathering, and the pack-ice was lacquered gold by the setting sun. Along the northern horizon the sky was applemint green. And when he least expected it, he saw her again. His fantasy girl, staring at him from the edge of the pine forest. Only this time she was different: sort of shadowy and insubstantial, and dressed in very different clothes—what looked like a Wren's bell-bottoms. And she was pleading with him. He could hear what she said quite clearly: 'Please, James! Don't go somewhere where I can't reach you.'

If only, he thought, I could touch her: just for a moment. He staggered to his feet and reached for her, and blundered into the tent. Pain knifed through his hand and foot. And the shock of seeing his fantasy girl and the shock of his pain jerked him back to reality. Did he really, he asked himself, want to die?

He found himself weighing up the pros and cons dispassionately, as in some academic exercise. On the one hand there'd be no more loneliness, no more pain, no more hunger, cold and damp, no more having to cope with the frailties of his body; there'd be peace. On the other hand, had he struggled so far down the road to survival only to quit in the final straight? And what about all the things in life he'd never known and would be missing out on? The most basic instinct of all took over: the instinct to survive. He half-hopped, half-crawled into the tent, opened his first aid kit and set about dressing the burns.

He did everything by the book: small and frequent sips of water, and the burns kept dry and clean with the air circulating round them; and, in the days ahead, gentle exercise but nothing strenuous. He was terrified of gangrene. But he was lucky. For a couple of days the burns got no worse; then they began, very slowly, to get better. He had a good supply of fuel and food in the tent—seal blubber to burn, penguin cuts to eat—so he was able to keep movement to a minimum. And at the end of ten days he was walking with no more than a slight limp, and able to use his hand without too much discomfort.

His thoughts turned again to his SOS.

He would probably have shifted camp in any case to be close to his work, but since he now needed to cut down on walking because of his injuries, the move became imperative. The site he chose was far from perfect— windswept and none too level—but it was visible from the sea and close to the apron of granite on which he was planning to form the letters. The letters themselves he reckoned he'd be able to make out of lumps of sandstone quarried from the base of one of the nunataks. He set himself the target of a letter a week.

It was dull and difficult work. Each slab of sandstone had to be prised out, broken up into roughly the right size, dragged a couple of hundred yards and left in exactly the right place. The slabs couldn't be too big, or he would have a problem moving them; and they couldn't be too small or they wouldn't be seen. His only tools were a snow-shovel and a makeshift crowbar, and, to drag the stones into place, a sling made out of his sledging harness. On days when the weather was bad he wasn't able to move any stones at all. On days when the weather was good he'd move up to a dozen.

While working, he kept an eye on the ice. There was no indication yet that it was melting close inshore; but he could tell by the behaviour of the birds that it was melting not so far out to sea; for the terns, petrels and fulmars left for their feeding ground later and returned earlier— an indication that they had less distance to travel. And one evening in early November he noticed a faint blue haze—like bluebells seen through mist—along the northern horizon. He took to climbing one of the nunataks before he dossed down, and peering seaward. He *thought* the blue was getting more distinct. And closer. But he wasn't sure. Until at last, after a particularly warm day when the light was unusually clear, he saw something that he hadn't seen for seven months. Along the skyline a riband of pure blue.

The open sea.

He wasn't given to histrionics. He didn't fling his cap in the air and caper about, and he didn't fall to his knees in prayer. He simply sat and stared at the riband of blue, and told himself it stretched unbroken all the way to England.

He knew that rescue was still problematical. *Scoresby* might never come; or she might pass by and never see him. Yet he felt elation building up inside him like flood water behind a dam. He scooped up a handful of snow and let it run through his fingers. What was it that chap in the book had said about the sun, the moon and the stars and the wind on the heath and life being sweet? He knew the feeling.

All he had to do now, he told himself, was wait.

Over the next few weeks he fell into a routine which afforded him something deeper than happiness. Each morning he checked his flagpole, his embryo bonfire, his heliographs and the stones of his SOS. This didn't take long. And then, for almost the first time since the burning down of the detachment's hut, he had comparative warmth, plenty to eat, and time on his hands.

He settled down to enjoy the companionship of the birds and the seals.

By now there were something like ten million birds on the tip of the Peninsula: rather less than half of them penguins (mostly Emperors, Adélies and Chinstraps), rather more than half of them seabirds (mostly petrels, terns, skuas and gulls). The majority of the adults spent most of their time courting, mating, nesting, incubating their eggs and caring for their chicks. Some species flew and fed by day, some by night. Some nested on the cliffs, some in the coastal scree, some on the beaches, and some (a very few) in the mountains of the interior. They ate plankton, krill, crustacea, fish and insects; they ate corpses, faeces and food that was in the process of being regurgitated for others; they ate anything defenceless, injured or dying. They were not at all the sort of birds that might have featured in an old-fashioned Disney cartoon. But Lockwood loved them: loved them for their energy, their toughness, their exuberance, and for their sheer guts in making a go out of life on a shore which a couple of months ago had seemed sterile as the moon.

There were also getting on for a million seals on the tip of the Peninsula, most of them Crabeaters or Weddells. Whenever Lockwood went trudging over the sea-ice he came across them in small communities, with several families sharing a breathing-hole. He was intrigued by their eyes: huge, moist and infinitely appealing. Seals' eyes, in fact, only appear to be large and moist because they have spherical lenses and soft retina to help them see underwater; but Lockwood didn't know this, and it looked to him as though the seals were forever crying.

This bothered him.

'Don't cry,' he'd whisper. 'I'll never hurt you.'

And the seals would let him walk up to them, touch them and play with them, their beautiful eyes all the time overflowing with tears. It became an obsession with him to find out *why* they were crying. He'd sit for hours by their breathing holes, talking to them. Eventually he decided they must be crying because they were afraid: afraid that more men would be coming to the Antarctic and they would be killed.

'Don't worry,' he told them. 'I'll see nobody kills you. I promise.'

And the music of their calling came to him softly through the ice, like a muted symphony. Poor things, he thought. All they're asking is to be left alone.

It never occurred to him that solitude had made him unbalanced. It seemed the most natural thing in the world that he should talk to his friends and be anxious about their future. And his anxiety for the seals brought to the surface the doubts and fears which for some time had been at the back of his mind: what the hell was he going to do with the uranium-bearing rocks?

Slowly but irreversibly, over the last few months, his attitude towards them had changed. The more he came to terms with and grew to love Antarctica, the more he came to think of the rocks as evil. And not merely as an abstract evil, but as the specific evil which would bring about the desecration of the land he loved. For it seemed to him that if uranium was really all that rare and all that valuable, then as soon as men knew it existed in Antarctica they would come flocking to the continent in ever-increasing numbers. As in a vision of Armageddon, he saw the peaks of the Peninsula torn apart by opencast mining, and the wildlife of the Peninsula butchered, as men exploited and fought over the bottom of the world in the same way that they had exploited and fought over every other part of it.

It was a vision that was to trouble him for the rest of his life.

So as he sat outside his tent that summer in the surprisingly warm polar sun, he was torn two ways. One voice whispered it was his duty to hand the rocks over—especially as many of his friends had died in search of them. A second voice whispered that he had another and more compelling duty, to say nothing about them. Then a third voice muttered, 'Sod it. You've enough on your plate without bothering about the bloody rocks. Just concentrate on staying alive and getting rescued.'

And this was the voice he listened to. Each day he monitored the gradual disintegration and recession of the ice. And one afternoon, after an unusually long spell of sunshine, he noticed a flock of Wilson's petrels hovering no more than a couple of hundred yards offshore. As he watched them, one after another, plummet seawards, he suddenly realised they were fishing in a lead of open water.

He knew then that he wouldn't have long to wait.

Antarctica, however, had one last surprise for him.

About a week after sighting the Wilson's petrels, he woke one morning feeling slightly sick and with a headache. More often than he cared to remember he had woken cold, aching and so weak he could hardly move; but he had seldom woken with a headache. He expected it would soon disappear. But it didn't. It persisted into the afternoon, so slight as hardly to bother him, more inexplicable than uncomfortable. He decided to go for a walk.

He hadn't gone far before he realised that everything was unusually still and quiet. There was no wind and no movement in the sea. Even the birds had fallen silent; they were huddled motionless as dummies on their ledges of rock, with none of their usual and noisy taking off and landing. The seals were behaving oddly too; they had moved away from the beaches and were slithering about, restless, on the rock-scree about 100 yards inland. He wondered if there was going to be a storm. He had already checked the barometer, and it had read steady and high; but he knew that Antarctica's moods could change with catastrophic suddenness. He told himself he had better keep close to his tent.

It happened without warning. A continuous, ear-splitting crack-crack-crack, as though a giant in the sky was ripping up a bolt of calico. For a moment he couldn't think what was happening. Then he saw that half-a-million petrels were taking off almost simultaneously. For a moment the noise of their beating wings made his senses reel. Then as they gained height the noise subsided, and he was left staring at a cloud of little black dots disappearing not to their usual fishing grounds in the north, but to the lonely reaches of the ice-sheet in the south. Where on earth, he thought, do they think they are going? And what made them take off so suddenly, as though they sensed danger?

His headache seemed to be getting worse—probably, he told himself, because of the noise—and he decided to go and lie down. He was only a couple of hundred yards from his tent. However, half-way there he began to feel so sick and dizzy he wondered if he was going to make it. For Christ's sake, he thought, what's the matter with me? For the last few yards he was so disorientated he didn't feel safe standing up; he crawled into the tent on hands and knees. Once inside he felt a little better and somehow safer. He took refuge in his sleeping-bag, and about the time the sun was setting drifted into an uneasy sleep.

It seemed as though his head had barely touched the pillow when he was catapulted awake. The earth was vibrating, and there was that terrible roaring again, rushing towards him like a train through a tunnel. It's all right, he told himself; it's only the birds coming back.

191

Then he realised it *wasn't* all right. This time it *wasn't* the birds. This time it really *was* an earth tremor.

He was half-way out of his tent when the earth moved under his feet. It was a moment of absolute terror. He had always thought of the earth as stable and permanent—'solid as a rock'. Now he knew better. It was a ball of liquid fire encased in a paper-thin crust, and he was standing on that crust and it was quivering like jelly. He didn't know what to do: rush back to his tent, throw himself to the ground, run—but where could he run to? So he simply stood there, retching at the stench of sulphur, conscious of the fires below, terrified he was about to be tipped into some reeking crevasse, and flinching as a nearby cliff collapsed with a roar like an avalanche, until after something like half-a-minute he became aware that the rumbling had subsided and the earth was no longer quivering.

It was over.

And he was alive.

It was some time before he felt able to move—quite illogically he was afraid that if he moved he might trigger off another tremor. But at last he plucked up courage to take stock of what had happened.

There seemed to be surprisingly little damage. No chasms had opened up in the ice, and the cliffs surrounding his tent were still standing. He was making his way down to the shore when he suddenly noticed the seals; they were again acting strangely, backing away from the water. His first thought was 'please God, not another tremor'; his second was, 'if they're heading for higher ground, maybe I should, too'. It was then that he heard a sound he couldn't place: a sort of whispering sigh, like the wind through distant trees. He stared out to sea, where the sound seemed to be coming from, and saw what looked like a bar of moonlight advancing on the Peninsula. If he hadn't still been in shock he would have worked out at once what it was. In fact the tidal wave hit the shore almost before he realised the danger.

It was only a little tidal wave—the sort that might be expected after a 3.5 earth tremor—but it landed with an almighty crash, raced up the beach, and came swirling over the rocks where only a few hours earlier the newborn seal pups had been lying beside their parents.

How, Lockwood wondered, had they known? Even as he stared at them, and almost as soon as the undertow had subsided, they came slithering back to the rocks at the water's edge. If they reckon it's safe, he thought, that's good enough for me. He crawled back into his sleeping-bag, shut his eyes, and fell almost immediately into the deep dreamless sleep of those in shock. Only once did he stir and come close to waking, as, in the false dawn, half-a-million petrels came back to their nests in the cliffs that encircled his tent.

Next morning he expected the tip of the Peninsula to look different; he felt there ought to be something to show for the drama of the night. At first glance everything seemed very much as it was before; but on closer inspection he found that the world had indeed been reshaped. He was checking that the stones of his SOS hadn't been moved, when he noticed, at the bottom of the apron of granite, tiny wisps of smoke coiling out of the rock. He noticed too that the seals were giving that part of the apron a wide berth. He approached with caution. What he saw didn't look all that spectacular; it only became spectacular when he thought about the cataclysmic forces that had brought it about. For more than 200 yards along the shore the rocks had been levered up, in an almost straight line, a height of some five or six inches. What he was staring at was an embryo fault, the sort which in a million years could become a rift valley. It came to him that not far beneath his feet were rivers of fire, and the earth's crust where he was standing was unstable. He backed away. and hastily moved his tent off the apron of granite.

That afternoon he came across more evidence of the after-effects of the tremor.

He was on his way to collect lichen from the pool where, long ago, he had found freshwater shrimps, when he pulled up short. Everything looked different. The north face of his nunatak simply wasn't there. The slopes of snow-cum-ice had vanished, and in their place lay an excrescence of newly-fallen rock. His 'cave' had vanished too, and with it his *behouden huis*. He remembered the great roar as the earth tremor had built up to its climax. So this, he thought, is where the cliffs collapsed.

His first thought was: 'If I hadn't moved I'd have been buried alive.'

His second thought was: 'Well, that takes care of the uranium-bearing rocks.' For he could see that they were now well and truly buried beneath several hundred thousand tons of granite and schist.

The irony of it made him think. Men had searched for the rocks in about the most testing conditions on earth; they had suffered for them, killed for them, died for them, turned cannibal for them. And now Nature, in a moment of casual puissance, had put them out of everyone's reach.

He wasn't sure if his overriding emotion was regret or relief. It saddened him that he wouldn't now be able to keep his promise to Ede, and that his friends had died for nothing. On the other hand, now the rocks had vanished as though they had never been, no one need ever know they had been discovered. So if he said nothing about them, there would be no great uranium-rush to Antarctica. And his friends the seals, the penguins and the seabirds would be left in peace.

He made sure that the rocks had indeed been buried beyond all hope of recovery. And he made sure that the earth tremor hadn't disturbed Ede's body. Then, once again, he settled down to wait.

It was an almost pleasurable routine that he now settled into. In the mornings he would check the paraphernalia of his rescue. In the afternoons he would talk to the great multitude of his friends with whom he shared the bottom of the world. And in the evenings he would work out exactly what he was going to say when he was rescued.

He decided that his best hope of being spotted lay with his SOS and his bonfire. So he checked each day that the stones were in place and clearly visible, and that the wherewithal of a bonfire was dry and at hand.

The afternoons were the times he liked best. Then, if the weather was good, he would mingle with the penguins, seals and seabirds. By this time he was not only at ease with them (and they with him), he felt he was one of them, taking part, like them, in the miracle of the earth's annual resurrection. And this was perhaps the most abiding of all his impressions of Antarctica: that he was a creature of the earth; not so much an individual, as a living, breathing, working part of our planet's continuous affirmation of life.

Each evening he reminded himself that he could any moment be rescued, and that he needed to work out exactly what he was gong to tell his rescuers. He had two secrets to hide. To avoid any suspicion of cannibalism, he needed to dissemble about what had happened to Ede. And to safeguard his friends the birds and the seals, he needed to dissemble about the uranium—to pretend it had never been found. He went over what he was going to say again and again. It would be all too easy, he told himself, to make a slip. He would need to be very, very careful.

One morning, about three weeks after the earthquake, he was cooking breakfast outside his tent, when for no particular reason he looked up. And there was *Scoresby* standing in towards the tip of the Peninsula.

Nemesis

Rehabilitation

It was the moment he had hoped for, but now it had come he wasn't prepared for it. His brain refused to accept what his eyes were telling him; he thought the minesweeper must be a mirage; if he blinked she would be gone. He blinked. But *Scoresby* was still there. And it came to him in a moment of incredulity that she was no figment of the imagination. She was real.

But had she seen him?

He made a dash for his tent, dragged out his heap of spare clothes and blankets, dowsed them with fuel, and tossed a lighted match onto them. There was a muffled explosion and a sheet of flame, but not much in the way of smoke, and he realised that to give off the sort of column of smoke that would be spotted he needed to burn something more solid. He hesitated, but for a second only; then he was dragging his sleeping-bag out of the tent and flinging it onto the fire. If the minesweeper didn't spot him he was dead, with or without a sleeping-bag. If she *did* spot him he wouldn't need a bag; it was a cabin that night he'd be sleeping in. As in a vision of paradise he saw a bath filled with hot water, and a bed made up with sheets. He threw his last pieces of spare clothing and his last drops of kerosene onto the flames, and a column of smoke went spiralling into the sky. There was a moment of silence. Then three times the bellow of *Scoresby*'s fog-horn rang out above the cries of the seabirds.

They had seen him.

He was saved.

Against all the odds he had made it.

He watched as in a dream while the minesweeper hove-to and lowered a boat. Then a wave of about the last emotion he expected swept over him: fear.

For nine months he hadn't spoken to a human being; what should he say to the men who had come to rescue him? For nine months he had slept in his tent; would he be safe anywhere else? And his friends the birds and the seals: did he *really* want to leave them? And the tranquillity of the ice and the beauty of the aurora; would life ever be the same without them? He was seized by an almost overwhelming compulsion to run away, to hide: to cling to the world that he knew and had come to terms with.

He told himself it was crazy to be feeling this way. But he couldn't help it. As the longboat neared the shore, he had to make a conscious effort to walk down to the beach. Would the crew, he wondered, recognise him? Would he recognise them? And what should he say to them? What was it that explorer-fellow Stanley was supposed to have done: raised his hat and held out his hand and said 'Doctor Livingstone, I presume?' He let out a cackle of laughter that sounded uncomfortably like a maniac's. God help me, he thought, I've gone mad. What will they think of me?

The prospect of other men's eyes on him made him suddenly conscious of his body: his skeletal limbs, his scurvy-bloated stomach, his filth, his hair and his beard half-way to his waist. I bet, he thought, I stink like a polecat. And again the impulse to hide engulfed him: so strongly that to overcome it he had to sit down.

It was a funny thing, but the moment he sat down all the strength seemed to drain out of him . . . Up to now it had been willpower as much as anything that had kept him going: the knowledge that every second of every minute of every hour of every day his survival had depended on his own unaided efforts. Now other people had appeared on the scene, he told himself it was up to them to make decisions. Let them, he thought, do whatever has to be done. I don't want to fight any more.

The longboat grounded. Four men scrambled out. Two stayed by the boat. The other two came towards him. The crunch of their footsteps on the gravel sounded loud and somehow menacing. And again he felt fear: as though the men approaching him were gaolers, come to drag him to some place he didn't want to go to. One of them—he could tell by the thread of red between the gold braid on his arm that he was a doctor—was speaking. His voice sounded harsh and unfamiliar, though his words were comforting.

'Thank God we've found you.'

The other man was looking this way and that; he seemed puzzled. 'Where are the others?'

He didn't know what to say. He was afraid that if he said anything he'd blurt out, 'I ate them.' So he simply shook his head.

He saw the horror come into their eyes. First horror, then pity.

The doctor held out his arms. 'Come on,' he said. 'We've come to take you home.'

He tried to stand; but his knees buckled and he was conscious of a sudden pain in his chest. He would have pitched face-down onto the shingle if the doctor hadn't jumped forward and caught him.

They had had the foresight to bring stretchers with them, and they lowered Lockwood onto one of them, covered him with blankets and carried him to the boat. Then they were heading for the *Scoresby*. He had a vague recollection of spray flying over the gunwale and into his face, more pains in his chest, and the doctor sitting beside him and holding his hand and saying over and over again: 'You're OK. You're safe.' Then a rust-stained hull blotted out his view of sea and sky, and he was aware of men leaning over the deckrail and peering down at him.

'Just the one, sir,' he heard the doctor shout. 'And I need to get him to sickbay.'

As they hoisted him aboard, the pains in his chest seemed to be getting worse, and he was finding it difficult to breathe. What on earth, he thought, is the matter with me? He was conscious of steel decks and bulkheads, the throb of engines, a pervasive stench of diesel, men moving aside as he was carried past, a pristine bunk with sheets on it, hands loosening his clothing, an oxygen mask clamped to his mouth, and a welcome spin into oblivion.

It was the oxygen that prevented his embryo heart attack being anything more than a tremor: a tremor so slight that if there had been such a thing as a Richter scale of heart attacks his would have registered less than one. By mid-day he was propped up in his bunk, sucking an orange, and not quite able to believe that he was back in a world in which there were human beings.

While Lockwood was being cared for in the sickbay, a second and larger landing party went ashore. They scoured the three headlands, hoping against hope to find survivors, expecting to find bodies, but in fact finding nothing. Nothing, that is, apart from Lockwood's tent which together with its few contents they brought back to the ship. Before *Scoresby* continued her patrol her commander wanted to be sure there was no chance of other survivors still being alive in another part of the Peninsula.

'I need,' he said to the doctor, 'to talk to him.'

The doctor was not too happy about this. 'Go easy with him,' he said. 'God knows what the poor devil has been through.'

So they made their way to the sickbay, and the commander asked Lockwood, very gently, what had happened to the rest of the detachment. And Lockwood was very calm and perfectly coherent. He explained about the U-boat attack, their trek to the tip of the Peninsula, the death first of Ede and then of Ramsden, and the winter that he had spent alone in his *behouden huis*.

When he had finished, the others didn't say much, but he could see they were moved. And before the commander left he laid a hand on Lockwood's shoulder. 'They'll give you something more than a putty medal for this,' he said, 'Now relax. You've not a thing to worry about. We'll soon have you back in England.'

A few minutes later the tempo of *Scoresby*'s engines increased.

Lockwood shut his eyes. 'We're leaving, aren't we?' he said.

The doctor nodded.

'Can I go on deck? To say goodbye?'

The doctor was surprised. He thought his patient would have seen more than enough of the prison he had been incarcerated in. But he said, 'If that's what you want. Why not?' So they festooned Lockwood in blankets and rugs and wedged him into a sheltered place in the stern, and let him watch the receding coastline.

It was a peaceful scene. There was not much wind, and a line of nimbo-stratus was drifting slowly in from the west. For a while the coast of Antarctica was bathed in sunlight, its icebergs and snowfields bright white in a light that was unbelievably clear. Then rainclouds drifted across it and it was gone, and something told him he would never see it again.

He shut his eyes—as he was to shut them often in the years to come—and once again he was there, with the seals and the seabirds, the snowfields and the aurora. And he realised to his great embarrassment that his face was wet with tears.

'Don't worry.' He felt the doctor's hand on his shoulder. 'It's all over.'

'I know,' he said. 'That's why I'm crying.'

*   *   *

Lockwood's initial debriefing turned out to be less of an ordeal than he had feared.

Scoresby's captain was a young RNVR lieutenant-commander, not a great deal older than Lockwood. He knew nothing of the detachment's top secret mission, he had simply been told to keep an eye out for them, and for the sole survivor his ship had picked up he felt nothing but admiration. He saw no reason to press him to answer questions that he obviously found distressing—though he did wonder why Lockwood seemed so ill at ease and defensive when asked about some of his experiences. It's almost, he thought, as though he has something to hide. However, he told himself that if there *was* a mystery, it wasn't his job to unravel it. *This officer*, he wrote in his report, *has been through the most terrible ordeal. It is a miracle he survived. Not surprisingly he is still confused and reluctant to talk about some of his experiences. It is therefore suggested no further debriefing is carried out until he has had a chance to recover both physically and mentally.*

This very sensible advice was not followed.

Less than a week after his rescue, Lockwood was put ashore at Port Stanley, and there waiting for him was a commander from MI6 who had flown out from England to give him a full debriefing.

It would be unfair to condemn the Admiralty for insensitivity. The special detachment had been on a top secret mission which could have had considerable influence on the course of the war. No wonder the Admiralty wanted to know what had happened to it. In particular they wanted to know if the detachment had found uranium; and if they had, whether there was the slightest possibility that the Germans had somehow got hold of it.

The man they sent to the Falklands to question Lockwood about this—a Commander Middleton—started off by being understanding and patient. However, he was a highly intelligent man; and it didn't take him long to realise that the young sub-lieutenant was holding things back. He didn't know what, or why, but his orders had been to find out what had happened to the detachment, and he intended to do exactly that.

Lockwood now found himself in the situation he had foreseen and dreaded: faced with questions he didn't want to answer. Many times as Middleton was asking him about the detachment's geological field-work he was tempted to blurt out that yes, they *had* found uranium. But one thing always made him hold back. The commander would ask some question that he didn't want to answer, and he would shut his eyes, and a vision—always the same—would come to him. He would be looking down on a waterway lined on one side with flat-topped icebergs and on the other with snow-covered mountains, and the sea would be alive with dolphin and whales, and the beaches dark with seals and penguins so close-packed a man couldn't set foot between them, and the sky would be filled with seabirds wheeling, soaring and diving, and the air would be vibrating to a cacophony of brays and barks and croons and trills; and he knew this was no dream, this was the real thing. Then Middleton would repeat his question. And Lockwood's vision would change, and he would be standing at the top of a snowslope, retching, staring down at a circle of charred timbers and limbless corpses, and the only movement would be a little coil of smoke seeping out of the wreckage, and everything would be silent as the grave; and he knew that this too was no dream, this too was the real thing, this was Paradise after man had paid it one brief visit.

Now a lot of people might take the view that the comparison wasn't a fair one: that Lockwood's ordeal had left him unbalanced. That may be. But rightly or wrongly it was now, in Port Stanley, that he made up his mind that never, for as long as he lived, would he tell anyone about the uranium they had found in Antarctica. It might, he told himself, be inevitable that the continent he loved would one day be desecrated; but he wasn't going to be responsible for its desecration. The more testing Middleton's questions became, the more he fell back on a defence that couldn't be breached.

He said he couldn't remember.

It was the solution to every problem, the way out of every difficulty. Each time he was asked a question he didn't want to answer, he would look at Middleton very straight and say, 'Sorry. I can't remember.'

And the commander knew he was lying, but there wasn't a thing he could do about it. His report to the Admiralty was an admission of failure.

The basic facts, he wrote in his conclusion, *are beyond dispute. The detachment was attacked by a German landing-party, almost certainly from a U-boat, and its base destroyed. Three personnel survived the attack, but only one, Sub-lieutenant Lockwood, survived the ensuing winter. In normal circumstances one would have expected this officer to provide information from which the whole story could be pieced together. However, Sub-lieutenant Lockwood appears to have serious physical and mental problems consequent upon his privations. He is unco-operative and unwilling to talk about many of his experiences.*

Rehabilitation is therefore recommended under the aegis of a qualified Naval psychiatrist, who hopefully may be more successful than I was in overcoming this officer's inhibitions and apparent loss of memory.

A couple of weeks after this debriefing, Lockwood was on his way to England in a destroyer.

The destroyer was one of few warships guarding a large number of merchantmen. Her ship's company were overstretched. They were well disposed towards Lockwood, and perfectly willing to be friendly. However, he spent much of his time in the sickbay, and when he did appear in the wardroom it seemed obvious he didn't want to discuss his experiences. In actual fact, Lockwood would have been glad of a confidant; but there was a problem. He was neither secretive nor deceitful by nature, and it distressed him that he'd be having a friendly conversation with someone – say about seals or icebergs – when the person he was talking to would, in all innocence, start asking questions about one of the things that Lockwood didn't want even to think of; and he'd find himself having to be guarded and evasive to prevent the truth slipping out, and in the end he'd have to revert yet again to saying 'I can't remember'. Until the things he *said* he couldn't remember got all mixed up with the things he *really* couldn't remember, which made him think, 'Sod it. I'll say I can't remember a thing.'

And this was his state of mind when he walked into Hugh Dempster's consulting rooms in Haslar.

*   *   *

Hugh Dempster was right in thinking that Haslar wasn't the place for the young lieutenant (Lockwood's promotion had come through while he was on his way back to England) and that what his patient needed was not counselling, but peace and quiet and a chance to pick up the threads of his life in his own way and his own time. And it was largely due to the psychiatrist's recommendation that Lockwood was sent first to a Naval convalescent centre in Rustington, then on indefinite leave.

It was the period of grace he needed to get back to an even keel.

Rustington was therapeutic. By the spring of 1944 the threat of invasion had diminished; so had the threat of major *Luftwaffe* raids. Lockwood was able to go for long walks along the promenade, albeit behind festoons of barbed wire and the occasional unmanned pill-box.

His four weeks at home were even more healing. His parents quickly realised there were things their son didn't want to talk about, and this they accepted. 'Let it be,' his father said to his mother late one night after Lockwood had gone to bed. 'It's enough he's alive. And with us. He'll tell us what went on when he's ready.' And if Lockwood had been allowed to spend more time at home he might indeed have eventually told his parents everything.

However, almost exactly three months after his rescue, he was judged fit if not for active service at least for a desk job. On 20 May, 1944 he was appointed meteorological officer to the Royal Naval Air Station of Benbecula in the Outer Hebrides.

Jeanie with the light brown hair

Benbecula turned out to be a sort of stepping stone. It bridged the gap between Lockwood's physical involvement with Antarctica—when he was actually there—and his subsequent cerebral and emotional involvement with it, when for some 40 years he worked for the British Antarctic Survey. You could say it was a pivot round which the wheel of his life turned full circle.

He settled down there a great deal better than might have been expected.

The Naval Air Station was situated on the north-west tip of the island; there was nothing between it and America but 3,000 miles of sea, and it was the ideal place for a loner: all peat, mist, soft light and gentle colours and about a thousand seabirds to every person. Flying duties were shared between the Navy and the RAF. The former operated a squadron of Swordfish, the latter a flight of Wellingtons, both carrying out anti-submarine patrols over the Western Approaches. Lockwood's job was to forecast the sort of weather they would be flying in, and it was important he got it right. If he didn't, it was all too likely that one of the snail-like Swordfish, encountering winds stronger than forecast, would run out of fuel before it got back to base, or one of the antediluvian Wellingtons, encountering colder conditions than forecast, would ice-up and crash.

Lockwood soon proved himself a first-rate met officer, both skilled and dedicated.

His skill stemmed largely from the fact that his experiences in the Antarctic had made him adept at piecing together forecasts from data collected on the spot. On the Peninsula he had found he could often anticipate changes in the weather by noting things like the colour of the sky at sunset or the feeding behaviour of the sea-birds. And the skills he had learned in the Antarctic he now put to use in the Hebrides.

His work provided him with two things he particularly needed: a link with the past and a refuge from the emotional problems of the present. During much of his time on the Antarctic Peninsula, he had, as one of the detachment's meteorologists, kept a written record of temperature, wind, precipitation and pressure. Now on Benbecula he found himself doing the same. And the continuity was comforting. He found it comforting too to have something to take his mind off his disabilities. For he still weighed less than eight stone, his hair was snow-white (and was to remain snow-white for the rest of his life), his speech was slow and hesitant, and his eyes seemed often to be staring at things other people couldn't see. His fellow officers knew that he had had a hard time on some top secret mission, and went out of their way to make him feel at home. For this he was grateful; but in a way their kindness made things more difficult. Everyone wanted to be friendly, wanted to talk, wanted to help. Yet there were things he had no intention of talking about, and secrets he had no intention of sharing. At Haslar he had sought refuge in silence. Now on Benbecula he sought refuge in work.

The Swordfish and Wellingtons were expected between them to provide continuous air cover over a large section of the Western Approaches; this involved a lot of night flying, and a lot of flying in bad weather. Lockwood's predecessor had been competent, but he had made mistakes: aircraft had been lost; aircrew had been killed. Lockwood was determined that if lives were lost it wouldn't be through shortcomings of his. He put in a request to see the Station Commander, and made the point that if the Commander wanted to stop losing aircraft he ought to upgrade and pay more attention to his met section. Met officers in those days were not considered among the *élite*; they lacked the technical status of, say, doctors or engineers, and their work was notoriously fallible. However, the Station Commander was impressed by Lockwood's arguments, and agreed to let him have most of what he asked for—more sophisticated equipment, additional personnel, improved radio facilities, more time for briefing the aircrew, and an ancient utilicon to help him get round the airfield.

With these additional resources, Lockwood set about improving the standard of weather forecasting. He initiated a new regime, with his instruments being read not twice a day but three times—at 8 a.m., 4 p.m. and midnight. He had a radio-operator listening out round the clock to pick up transmissions by ships or aircraft on patrol in the Atlantic. He got permission to fly in both a Swordfish and a Wellington so that he could see for himself the sort of conditions their crews had to cope with. He unearthed and studied old records in the hope of finding seasonal weather patterns. If any of his personnel grumbled at having to work too hard, he took on their duties himself.

And as the amount of data on which forecasts were based increased, so the forecasts themselves became more reliable. The change was neither sudden nor dramatic; but as the months passed the aircrew began to realise that Lockwood's prognoses were more often right than wrong. He became a respected member of the airfield's *dramatis personae*, turning up at all hours in his battered old tilly to read his instruments, and standing for hours at the end of the runway sniffing the wind, or making notes on the behaviour of the seabirds. Sometimes in the small hours of the morning, when the only other lights in the airfield were from the control tower, the striplight would still be on in the met office as Lockwood pieced together a new chart, and when it was finished he'd make his way to the operations room. 'That Swordfish off the Rosemary Bank,' he'd say. 'Tell them the wind's veering north and strengthening. It'll soon be 30 knots.' And his message would be passed on, and the task of the Swordfish observer would be made that much easier and the danger of the plane being blown off course and lost that much less.

By mid-summer Lockwood's fellow-officers had him sussed out. He was a man with a past that he didn't want to talk about: a loner, who was too good at and too wrapped up in his work to be lonely.

Then came the incident which set the seal on his growing reputation.

The night of 2–3 July didn't seem in any way out of the ordinary. The temperature may have been a bit lower than usual for mid-summer, and the stars a bit brighter, and there were concentric, well-defined haloes round the moon; but no one on the airfield had the slightest premonition of what was in store. Before Lockwood dossed down he made his routine check of the midnight readings: pressure 30.2 steady, temperature 41°, wind north-westerly light—nothing to worry about there; and no radio signals to suggest that anything unusual was going on in the Atlantic. So why, he wondered as he walked back to his cabin, was he conscious of a vague unease? It must, he told himself, be the haloes round the moon. They reminded him of those harbingers of the blizzard, the bright concentric circles which only a few months ago had lit up the night sky over his *behouden huis*.

It was the silence that woke him. It was the early hours of the morning, and no birds were singing. He peered out of his cabin window, and the hills on the neighbouring island of North Uist looked so close that if he reached out his hand he could touch them. He checked his cabin barometer. It read 29.9 falling: not a big fall, but one that *could* be significant. He dressed, called for his utilicon and was driven to the end of the runway. He got out his binoculars and studied the sea and the sky. He would have liked to study the seabirds too, but there weren't any. This worried him. It was the hour before sunrise, and gulls and cormorants ought to have been congregating on the offshore rocks in their thousands. Yet there wasn't one in sight. He asked his Wren driver to take him to the control tower, and ran up the stairs to the operations room.

The duty officer was surprised to see him. 'You're an early bird, James!'

'What aircraft are up?'

'A Stringbag and a Welly.'

'Have they signalled any change in the weather?'

'They haven't signalled a thing. There's a convoy coming in. And we've radio silence.'

'Jesus wept! That's the last thing we need!'

'Why? What's up?'

'I think we're in for a hurricane.'

The duty officer looked at the cloudless sky and the windsock hanging limp from its moorings. 'You sure?'

'I can't be sure. But I'd take a bet on it. Can you recall the aircraft?'

There was a long silence, then: 'Sorry, James. With a convoy coming in, and U-boats about, I daren't break radio silence.'

Lockwood took a deep breath and picked up the duty officer's phone. 'Emergency,' he said. 'Give me the Station Commander.'

The conversation that followed was brief and to the point.

'Captain speaking.'

This is the met officer, sir. I think we're in for a hurricane.'

'A hurricane! . . . Hang on a minute.'

He could imagine the Station Commander getting out of bed, surveying the peaceful scene through his cabin window and thinking 'the silly bugger needs his head testing'.

'What makes you think we're in for a hurricane?'

'The barometer's plummeting, sir. 'And'—he hesitated—'what really worries me is the birds. They've disappeared.'

A long silence, then, 'Right. Leave this with me.' And the phone went dead.

He reckoned the Station Commander must have thought he was mad and gone back to bed; but after a couple of minutes the tannoy burst into life. 'This is the Captain speaking. Duty watch to the hangars. At the double. Repeat at the double. Secure all aircraft.'

Heaven help me, he thought, if I'm wrong.

But he wasn't wrong. A little after sunrise a fitful wind came swirling out of the north: a wind that even in midsummer was cold enough to make the men manhandling the aircraft stamp their feet and blow on their fingers. By 9 a.m. all the Swordfish and Wellingtons had been wheeled into their hangars and lashed down. And this was as well, because the wind began suddenly to slam this way and that in gusts of increasing violence, a prelude to the sort of elemental fury which Lockwood had experienced often enough in the Antarctic but never expected to face in the British Isles.

The hurricane that hit the west coast of Scotland in the summer of 1944 was one of the worst in living memory. Men and women were killed, crofts were demolished, great swathes of forest were devastated, fishing vessels were torn from their moorings and flung ashore, and aircraft left in the open were blown over and destroyed. Almost the only airfield that *didn't* suffer damage was Benbecula. For they and they alone had been forewarned.

After this Lockwood came to be regarded as something

of a guru, and met officers from other airfields and shore establishments began to consult him and make use of his expertise. He slowly built up the reputation—well deserved—of being a first-rate meteorologist.

By the winter of '44, although the war was far from over its end was in sight, and people were beginning to think about what sort of job they'd be able to get when they were demobbed. It occurred to Lockwood that he might be able to make a career out of meteorology—maybe in the peacetime Navy. However, there now occurred an incident which put paid to *that* idea.

He was summoned to London for 'a medical'. And the medical turned out to be the excuse for another debriefing, another attempt to get to the bottom of what had happened on the Peninsula. Once again, Lockwood found himself faced with questions he didn't know how to answer. Once again he found himself repeating parrotlike, 'I can't remember.'

He realised he had a problem. It wasn't that he wanted to forget Antarctica. Far from it. He thought about it almost every hour of every day. In the diurnal gathering of Benbecula's gulls, he was reminded of the greater and more primordial massing of Antarctica's terns. In the beauty of Benbecula's northern lights, he was reminded of the more spectacular beauty of Antarctica's aurora. In the peace of the Hebridean moors, he was reminded of the even deeper peace of the Peninsula's ice sheet. In the soft eyes of the highland cattle, he was reminded of the tear-wet eyes of his friends the seals, and once again he would be walking among them, talking to them and promising them that no one was ever going to hurt them. It wasn't Antarctica he wanted to forget, it was man's desecration of it. However, it seemed that the Navy wasn't prepared to let him forget this desecration. Or the part he had played in it.

When he got back to the airfield he did a great deal

of thinking. Two things troubled him. He could see the Admiralty's point of view. They still suspected he hadn't told them the truth, the whole truth and nothing but the truth about what had happened in the Antarctic. They had given him counselling, rehabilitation and a great deal of time to recover from his ordeal, and they now expected him to come clean. And this, he told himself, was likely to be an ongoing situation. As in a moment of clairvoyance, he saw the file on the special detachment lying in the Admiralty vaults marked not only 'Most Secret' but 'Do not close'. And he realised that if he wanted peace of mind, he would be well advised not to join the Navy but to distance himself from it . . . Yet if he didn't throw in his lot with the Navy how was he going to make a career for himself in meteorology?

The idea came to him one evening as he was trying to work out the airfield's mean average temperature for October. He had in his possession a mass of statistics about the weather on the west coast of Scotland. Somewhere— passed on by the special detachment to Port Stanley— there was a mass of statistics about the weather on the west coast of the Antarctic Peninsula. If he could get his hands on the latter, he would be in a unique position to compare the climates of these two very different places, and maybe come up with some new ideas on global weather patterns. And if he could get his findings published, that surely would help to make him an employable meteorologist.

Persuading the Admiralty to grant him access to the Port Stanley statistics wasn't easy; but in the end he managed it and set to work.

It was the start of a lifetime of research: research which he found all the more enjoyable because it enabled him to keep in touch with the continent he loved.

He decided to call his thesis *A Comparison of Katabatic Winds off the Coast of Antarctica and the Coast of Scotland,*

and he was getting on rather well with it when he suffered an unexpected setback.

He fell in love.

Wartime liaisons between officers and other ranks were officially frowned on but unofficially recognised as inevitable, and Lockwood was guilty of one of the more common solecisms when he fell for his Wren driver.

Her name was Jean Lumsden. She was a quiet, rather shy girl, with too wide a mouth, too snub a nose and too many freckles to be beautiful in the classical sense, though the consensus of opinion among the aircrew whom she sometimes drove between wardroom and control tower was that she was decidedly all right. Her father was a crane driver in Southampton Docks, and she had joined the Wrens in the hope of ending up in Portsmouth, close to her parents. She was therefore none too pleased to find herself posted to Benbecula—about as far in the British Isles from Portsmouth as it is possible to get! However, she settled down happily enough, being popular with the other girls because she was easy-going and ready to give a helping hand whenever and wherever it was needed. Indeed it was because she *was* so easy-going that she found herself driving Lockwood ... Some of the Wren drivers had specific duties, others worked in a pool. When Lockwood was given his own transport he was told he could also have his own driver. It was a job none of the girls fancied. It wasn't Lockwood they objected to, it was the antisocial hours, and in particular the midnight drive each night to the compound where Lockwood read his instruments; Jean Lumsden let herself be talked into volunteering for a job that nobody else wanted.

They got on well, in a quiet sort of way, from the start. Lockwood was pleased that his driver seemed such a pleasant, attractive and undemanding girl. Jean was pleased that her passenger seemed kind, considerate and unlikely to make a pass at her in the met compound. Both were shy with members of the opposite sex, and both were inhibited by their difference in rank—for some time they were excessively formal: he called her Miss Lumsden, she called him sir. It was the seabirds that brought them together.

Lockwood spent a fair amount of time studying the gulls, skuas and cormorants which nested in their tens of thousand around the airfield; but not being sure if the powers that be would regard this as work or recreation he never, when he was bird-watching, used his official transport. One afternoon he was walking round the perimeter track *en route* to the shore, when Jean drove past in their tilly. She pulled up.

'Do you want a lift, sir?'

He asked where she was going, and she said 'to the north hangars.' The north hangars lay close to the old coastguard's track by which he got down to the shore. So he thanked her and climbed in. For a while they drove in silence. Then, thinking that perhaps some explanation was called for as to why he hadn't asked her to drive him, he said, 'I'm going bird-watching.'

'I know, sir.'

'I don't think the Admiralty would call that "official duties", do you?'

She reckoned he was being over-conscientious, but didn't like to say so in case he thought her forward and pushy, so she just said, 'Perhaps not, sir.'

There was another silence. Then, as they drew up outside the hangars, he asked her, 'Are you interested in birds?'

'I've not thought about them a lot. But I think I *could* be. If I knew more about them.'

'Sometimes,' he said, 'I *do* need to watch the birds as part of my duties—if I think we're in for a storm, for example. Perhaps you could drive me then? The track's OK, so long as you take it slowly.'

'Yes of course, sir.' She hesitated, then smiled and added, 'I'd like that.'

He thought that when she smiled she looked very attractive. It would be nice, he told himself, if he could get her to smile more often.

So every now and then the two of them played truant—or that is how they always thought of it—and drove to the tip of the island, where years ago there had been a lighthouse but now there was nothing but a prospect of rocks and a riot of seabirds. It was a wild place. Even on calm days the swell from the Atlantic came creaming over the rocks like avalanches of milk; on days of storm spray was flung 200 feet into the air and 200 yards inland. Jean learned a lot about seabirds on their visits to the tip of the island, but not a lot about Lockwood. It was common gossip on the airfield that he had been through some terrible ordeal in the Antarctic, and she hoped he would tell her about it. However, it didn't take her long to discover that Lockwood's past was something he preferred to keep to himself. At first this didn't bother her; but as they saw more and more of one another and came increasingly to like one another, his reticence worried her. We'll not get beyond birdwatching, she thought, unless he feels he can trust me.

A few weeks later an unexpected incident brought matters to a head.

The sun was setting, and they were coming back, rather later than usual, from the rocks at the tip of the island. Everything was very still and very quiet, with no wind and little drifts of sea mist forming in hollows on the airfield. They were driving round the perimeter track when a pair of gulls, frightened by the noise of the tilly, took off from almost under their wheels. Before Jean had a chance to brake, they hit one. They both flinched, and, looking back, saw a crumpled heap of feathers, twitching.

'It wasn't your fault,' he said. 'Would you stop?'

She pulled up and switched off the engine, and he got out of the tilly and walked back to the gull. He took a careful look at it, then, with a wrench of his fingers, broke its neck. Its wings jerked once, then it stopped twitching. He was laying it on the grass at the edge of the perimeter track, when he realised the girl was standing beside him. 'I didn't want to leave it to suffer,' he said.

She nodded. 'I know. But I don't think I could have done that.' She took his hand. 'It was'—she hesitated—'very brave of you.'

As their fingers interlocked he didn't do anything dramatic like flinch or recoil. But he did withdraw. 'We'd better,' he said, 'be getting back.'

She looked at him very straight. 'Why?'

'Why what?'

'Why do you always draw back? When I try to get close to you?'

'I'm sorry, Jeanie.'

'Don't be sorry. Just tell me why.'

His eyes took on a glazed, unfocused stare that she knew only too well. He was retreating into a world in which she had no place.

'Please,' she said, 'don't go somewhere where I can't reach you.'

He was torn two ways. He longed to talk to her, to share with her the things that meant so much to him. But a voice whispered 'if you tell her some things you'll end up telling her others. Do you want her to know you're a cannibal? Do you want her to know about the uranium?'

'We're late,' he said. 'We'd better be getting back.'

They drove the rest of the way to the wardroom in silence.

Neither of them found it easy to sleep that night. They both sat up into the small hours, thinking.

Lockwood told himself he was a fool. Here was a girl he was coming to love and who seemed to love him, so why weren't they sharing *everything* as lovers ought to . . . ? The truth was—though he didn't like to admit it—he still hadn't recovered from the trauma of his experiences in the Antarctic. Not so long ago he had been on the edge of death for month after month; he had been so hungry he had hacked up and eaten his commanding officer, and so mentally deranged he had wept at the death of a fly and hallucinated over a naked Eskimo girl. Wounds that deep don't heal overnight, and his love affair had come too soon after his ordeal for him to cope with it. Given time, he would very likely have started by telling her some things and ended by telling her everything. But right now what he wanted above all was to be left in peace, to forget. Maybe, he thought, if I pretend the problem isn't there it'll go away, and we'll be able to carry on as before.

But Jean wasn't prepared to go along with this. She was a direct, uncomplicated girl who liked direct, uncomplicated things; and it seemed to her that Lockwood had too many hang-ups for them to have the sort of relationship she longed for. He was the first person she had ever met with whom she felt she could share the rest of her life. But he, it seemed, didn't want to share his life with anyone. That, she told herself, was not as it should be. She decided to have things out with him.

A couple of days later their tilly was parked on the edge of the perimeter-track; he was studying the gulls and the skuas through his binoculars, and she was waiting in the driver's seat. After a while she came and stood beside him. She was very unsure of herself.

'James . . .'

He looked at her uneasily. 'Yes?'

'Just for a moment. Please. Could you think about us? Not the birds?'

His unease escalated: 'What about us?'

'Why,' she said, 'can't you tell me what happened in the Antarctic? I know something terrible happened. And

I want to *help*. But'—it added to her embarrassment that she knew she was blushing and close to tears—'every time I try and get close to you, you sort of slam a door in my face . . .'

This was the last thing he wanted. This was another interrogation, all the harder to bear because his interrogator was someone he cared for. 'Please, Jeanie. I don't want to talk about it.'

The far-away look was back in his eyes, and she knew he had retreated to a world where she couldn't get through to him. Well, she didn't intend to grovel, and she didn't intend to cry; if this was the way he wanted things, so be it. She walked slowly back to the tilly, and sat in the driver's seat and stared at the headland where they had spent so many hours together watching the seabirds, and thought of all the things that might have been.

When he had made sure that the gulls and the skuas were feeding as usual, he too came back to the tilly and climbed in beside her.

She didn't look at him: 'To the wardroom, sir?'

'Yes, please.'

Several times on their way to the wardroom she thought he was going to say something. But he didn't. 'Least said,' he told himself, 'soonest mended.'

But that's not the way it turned out.

A couple of weeks later the Wren officer in charge of transport asked for volunteers to be transferred to Lee-on-Solent. This was one of the few Fleet Air Arm airfields earmarked for post-war expansion; it was also close to Southampton Docks. Jean volunteered that afternoon, and within 48 hours was on her way south. At least, she thought, I'll be close to Mum and Dad . . . She wrote Lockwood a letter which, nearly fifty years later, was found among his personal effects. In the letter she told him what she had been too shy to tell him to his face: how much she loved him. 'But if we can't walk everywhere together,' she wrote, 'I think we had better walk alone.'

It was something he was totally unprepared for. He took her letter to the tip of the island, and read it and re-read it and read it again. Then he sat for hours staring at but not seeing the seabirds, and telling himself what many wiser men have told themselves before him—that you never know what you want till it's gone.

*   *   *

Again he sought refuge in his work.

A Comparison of Katabatic Winds off the Coast of Antarctica and the Coast of Scotland was published in December 1945, and much to Lockwood's delight it appeared not only in a couple of meteorological journals but also in *The New Scientist* and *The Geographical Magazine.* What people liked was the combination of specialised research and personal experience: a combination that enabled Lockwood not only to explain natural phenomena—in this case the violence of the coastal winds—but to bring them to life.

His *Katabatic Winds* brought him to the attention of people outside the Services, and in the spring of '46 a young man from the Colonial Office telephoned and asked if he could come and see him. Their meeting turned out to be the bit of luck for which Lockwood was long overdue.

The young man said that his name was Vivian Fuchs, that he was about to start working for a department of the Colonial Office known as the Falkland Islands Dependencies Survey, and that he was helping to get together a team to carry out a programme of scientific research in the Antarctic. They were, he added, looking for a meteorologist.

The two men sat up late into the night, talking. It soon became apparent that they had fundamentally different ideas about Antarctica. Fuchs wanted to go there to do

223

field-work, with the idea of maintaining a British presence on the continent. Lockwood wanted to stay in England and co-ordinate a programme of research, and in particular meteorological research. But over-riding these differences was the fact that they both had a deep and abiding love of the continent. This was what bound them together. And this was what counted.

A fortnight after Fuchs's visit, Lockwood received a letter from the Colonial Office. There would be a job waiting for him, he was told, as soon as he was demobilised, with the Falkland Islands Dependencies Survey.

It was a dream come true.

* * *

Not many people spend virtually the whole of their working life serving one master. But Lockwood did. He joined the Survey in the summer of '46 and retired in the spring of '87.

One might take the view that he worked for an obscure government department for a not very generous salary, and became so obsessed with his work that he missed out on many of the better things in life: he never, for example, married or had children or the companionship of a woman with whom he couldn't stop holding hands; nor did he have anything grand in the way of a home. One might, on the other hand, regard him as a man ahead of his time: one of the first people to see Antarctica as a well from which the rest of the world could draw knowledge, and also one of the first protagonists in the fight against pollution. Whichever view one takes, the facts are these . . .

He started work at the Survey's headquarters in Cambridge on 2 July, 1946. And right from the start he was happy there. His job enabled him to keep in touch with the continent he loved and was to remain faithful to for the rest of his life. During the war he had been almost a physical part of this continent, grafted onto it as mistletoe to a tree. If he had had to sever this connection, he would have been bereft. As it was, his job ensured that his ordeal in the Antarctic, far from being a transitory wartime experience, turned out to be the fulcrum in which the remainder of his life—and indeed his death and the aftermath of his death—was forged.

To start with, the hierarchy at the Survey regarded him as a bit of a maverick: there were raised eyebrows in the Colonial Office, for example, when he asked for the results of his meteorological research-work to be sent to Moscow and Buenos Aires. However, Lockwood insisted that the weather knew no frontier and in the end he got his way—partly because of his status and partly because of his presence. In 1946 few people had ever set foot on the mainland of Antarctica, fewer had wintered there, no one had ever wintered there alone. Although he never thought of himself as such, Lockwood was something of a legend. As for his presence: he had always been good-looking, and his spare frame, white hair and haunted eyes now gave him a *cachet* of distinction. Women often thought him not only distinguished but attractive, the more so perhaps because he studiously distanced himself from them. In his eyes, no woman ever measured up to his 'Jeanie with the light brown hair' as he came nostalgically to think of her, and besides, he reckoned that if he wasn't prepared to share his secrets with anyone then he shouldn't get close to them. Plenty of people who never married, he told himself, led happy and useful lives. He would be one of them. He would devote his life to Antarctica.

And that is the way it was.

The '50s and '60s were years of quiet content for Lockwood, and he came to love both Cambridge and the unobtrusively beautiful country round it. He rented rooms in a farm on the road to Ely, driving to work each day in the sort of car that wouldn't have a hope nowadays of passing its MOT. He didn't make friends easily, but the friendships he did make tended to last for life: his secretary, who was forever leaving him to have children and then forever coming back; one or two of his colleagues at the Survey; one or two lecturers in the University colleges, and a couple of local farmworkers. Most of his pleasures were low-key: the occasional drink with friends in the pub, bird-watching in the fens, sailing his battered old dinghy on the Broads, long walks over the big flat fields with his dog.

He acquired his dog by accident. One day a miserable-looking puppy, thin and collarless, turned up on the farm. Lockwood first fed it out of pity, then became attached to it. It grew into a large and rather ungainly animal of doubtful ancestry, with a penchant for knocking things over, especially when in pursuit of bitches or cats. He and Lockwood developed a very satisfactory relationship. They were both loners, and they each did their own thing, by themselves when they felt like it, together when it suited them. Sometimes for day after day Clueless (as Lockwood called him) would disappear; and sometimes for day after day he would leap with an almighty crash into Lockwood's car and come with him to the Survey's laboratories, where he would inspect all the sites where he knew he would be tolerated, choose the most comfortable and sleep until his master was ready to take him home. It was perhaps inevitable that as the years passed Clueless came to spend less and less time on his wanderings and more and more with Lockwood, until by the time he was old he was attached to his master like a shadow. When he died, Lockwood felt the resurgence of an emotion that he thought he was immune to: loneliness. But, as ever, his work was an antidote.

And it wasn't long before his work became not only increasingly important but increasingly seen to be important. The reason for this was the International Geophysical Year of 1957–58.

Scientists had known for some time that Antarctica was the ideal place for research: that it was, in the words of the nineteenth-century Swedish explorer Otto Nordenskjold, 'a vast refrigerated storehouse of knowledge'. For locked up beneath its ice-sheet the secrets of the earth still lie uncontaminated, as they were before the coming of man. In 1957 the scientists of the world got together, and teams from twelve nations set up more than 50 research-stations on and around Antarctica; then, in an unprecedented example of international co-operation, they pooled the results of their work. In this scientific extravaganza the Survey (now re-named the British Antarctic Survey) played a leading role, and Lockwood found himself in charge of the meteorological research work carried out at the Survey's research base at Halley, on the periphery of the Weddell Sea.

Those who took part in the IGY were determined it should be more than a nine days' wonder, and that research and co-operation shouldn't be limited to one year only, but should continue and eventually become accepted as the norm. From this determination sprang the Antarctic Treaty.

This deceptively simple piece of legislation—it has only 14 articles and can be read in ten minutes—is based on the assumption *that it is in the interest of all mankind that Antarctica shall continue for ever to be used exclusively for peaceful purposes . . . and* (the) *facilitation of scientific research*. Its signatory nations—and there are now more than 40 of them—undertook to adhere to certain basic principles, such as restricting military activity on the continent, and banning nuclear testing and the dumping of radioactive waste; they also agreed to conserve the continent's resources and protect its environment. The treaty came into force in June 1961, and was to be binding for thirty years.

It would be difficult to overstate the importance of the Antarctic Treaty to scientists in general and to Lockwood in particular. For him, it was the guarantee not only that his work would continue, but that its findings would be disseminated. And the more research-work he and his colleagues carried out at Halley, the more it seemed to them important that people all over the world were made aware of what they were discovering. Lockwood published a number of papers on his Halley researches; and if these are listed in chronological order they tell a story: *Keeping Track on our Depressions: the Low Pressure Systems of the Southern Ocean* (1950), *Frozen in Time: the Climatic Record of the Polar Ice Sheets* (1955), *Heavenly Bodies: a Study of Aurora and Geocorona* (1960), *The Ionosphere: a View from the South Pole* (1964), *Atmospheric Research in Antarctica* (1970), *The Morphology of Ozone* (1977), *An Equation for Disaster: 1 Atom of Chlorine = Minus 100,000 Atoms of Ozone* (1981), *The Hole Truth* (1986). Initially his researches were concerned with the surface weather, latterly they were concerned with the atmosphere.

It isn't easy nowadays to say who ought to be credited with a particular scientific discovery, for research is very much a team effort; the scientist who has the bright idea in the field, the technician who tests the idea in the laboratory, and the PR man who writes up the report are nearly always different people. Certainly Lockwood never claimed to have 'discovered' the hole in the ozone layer. Nevertheless it was his team at Halley, working under his directives, who first gave warning of the dramatic decrease in oxygen atoms in the atmosphere over Antarctica.

Discovering and monitoring this decrease was only a small part of Lockwood's work. It probably wasn't even the most important part. It was, however, the part that grabbed the attention of the public. For the idea of a hole in the sky through which the injurious rays of the sun could beat down on the earth in unfiltered savagery was a vision of the apocalypse that the man in the street could understand and be afraid of.

Shortly before he retired Lockwood published *The Hole Truth*, in which he set out, for laymen, the results of his Halley research.

We may be able, he wrote, *to abuse the earth and get away with it. But we abuse the atmosphere at our peril.*

I can't see life on earth coming to an end because we cut down our rain forests or exhaust our stocks of fish; for the earth is tough and man adaptable; if we cut down one lot of trees we can plant another, if we kill one lot of creatures we can breed others. I can, however, see life as we know it coming to an end if we tamper with our atmosphere; for the atmosphere, in more ways than one, is beyond our control, and if things go wrong up there we may never be able to put them right.

One function of the atmosphere is to regulate the strength of the sunlight that gets through to the earth. About 15 miles above the surface of our planet is a comparatively thin layer of oxygen atoms (O_3); this is the ozone layer; and it is these 'dense' oxygen atoms—as distinct from the more common oxygen molecules (O_2)—which absorb and block off the potentially lethal ultra-violet radiation in the rays of the sun. If this ozone layer were to disappear, so that the sun's rays got directly through to the earth, that would very likely be the end of all of us.

Scientists working in the Antarctic have recently discovered that at certain times and in certain places, the ozone layer is rapidly diminishing. Indeed, above Antarctica it has diminished to such an extent that there is now a hole in it.

Scientists also know the cause of this. A substance which shouldn't be in the atmosphere at all has recently been detected there: chlorine. And this chlorine is combining with the oxygen-atoms to form chlorine monoxide, an alien compound which interacts with and destroys the ozone layer. Scientists know too where the chlorine comes from. It comes from a family of chloro-

fluorocarbons—man-made industrial gases—currently used in refrigeration units, aerosols and plastic foams. These chlorofluorocarbons (CFCs) are now being pumped into the atmosphere at the alarming rate of 60,000 tonnes a year.

One disturbing result of this diminution of the ozone layer has been particularly noticeable in the southern hemisphere. Yesterday, our parents lay on the beaches of Australia without sunblock cream, and suffered few ill-effects. Today, our children smother themselves with sunblock; yet in spite of this, there has been a marked increase in recent years in Australasia of skin cancer and cataracts, both directly attributable to increased radiation from the sun.

All this doesn't mean that the sky is about to cave in, and the end of the world is nigh! However, it does mean, I believe, that we have been given a warning. A specific warning to stop polluting our atmosphere with CFCs. And a more general warning, that if we are going to alter our environment (and it seems obvious this is what we are going to do), then we need to monitor the alterations that we bring about carefully and scientifically.

By far the best place in the world for scientific research is Antarctica. The conditions there are pristine, the infrastructure is in place—more than 40 permanently-manned research stations—and the process of disseminating whatever knowledge is gained is well established. One thing that has particularly helped Antarctica to become 'a continent for science' is the Antarctic Treaty. It is therefore of some importance that when this Treaty comes up for renewal in the early 1990s it is ratified. For the Treaty is a guarantee of research. And without research there may be no survival.

This was his apologia. And his swan song. A year after it was published, he retired.

*   *   *

He retired partly because he was over 65, and partly because in the last few months he had been experiencing a tightness in his chest and a tingling in his arms, and his

230

doctor had prescribed an aspirin a day and told him to take things easy. He would, he decided, make a clean break with the Survey, but would continue working as long as he could for SCAR, the Scientific Committee for Antarctic Research, of which he was a long-serving member.

His friends assumed he would stay in Cambridge. Lockwood, however, had other ideas. Common sense told him that at the age of 66 his heart condition was likely to get worse rather than better, and the last thing he wanted was to be a burden to those he was fond of. He decided to retire to a part of the world he had loved as a child, but hadn't been back to for 50 years: Cornwall. In the autumn of 1986 he took a month's holiday, and went there to look for a house.

He found it almost by accident. The wind was cold and the sea flecked with white horses as one morning in early November Lockwood and his dog set out to walk the cliff path that ran from the mouth of the Helford River to The Manacles. At the top of an incline, a vista opened up ahead which wasn't beautiful in the conventional sense but which gave him a feeling of quiet satisfaction. Nestling beneath the cliffs was a village of grey-stone walls and grey slate roofs—referring to his map he saw it was Porthallow—its only links with the outside world two single-lane roads zigzagging through a mosaic of gorse-encircled fields. It looked a good haven to drop anchor in; but he told himself not to get excited because there probably wasn't a house for sale within miles. However, he was lucky. Almost the first thing he saw as he left the cliff path and came into the village was a big red 'For Sale' notice on one of the fishermen's cottages that lined the harbour. He made a note of the Estate Agents. And a couple of months later the cottage was his.

He would have been happy to slip away from the Survey without fuss, but his colleagues weren't having that: he was far too well-respected and far too well-liked. There were parties and presentations, and more cards to wish him God Speed than he had room for in his office. On his last evening, he joined the Director for a farewell drink. The two men had always got on well, and the Director wanted to make one last effort to prevent their parting having the sort of finality that Lockwood seemed set on. They stood, savouring their whisky, looking out across the fields that surrounded the Survey's headquarters.

It was, Lockwood told himself, all very different from when he'd first joined the Survey. In those days they had existed in Nissen huts and borrowed laboratories, and had been trying to raise money to set up their first Antarctic base. Now they had an imposing purpose-built headquarters, equipped with the latest computer technology; they operated their own ships and their own aircraft; they had the use of satellites; they controlled four permanently manned research stations.

'James, you're daydreaming!' the Director's voice brought him back to the present.

'I was back in the Nissen huts. Trying to keep warm.'

'We've come a long way since then. Thanks to people like you . . . But I've been thinking. What are you going to do with yourself in this Porthallow place?'

'I'll have my dog. And my seabirds. And my work for SCAR.'

It sounded to the Director like 'ye-olde-cottage-with-honeysuckle-round-the-door': a myth seen through rose-tinted spectacles. 'Will that be enough to keep you out of mischief?'

'I hear what you're saying. But it's what I want.'

The Director could recognise a brick wall when he hit one. 'Well, all I can say is what was said in the speeches. *Please* don't forget us. *Please* keep in touch. What else are friends for?'

He was touched—as he'd been touched by the warmth

that his departure seemed to have engendered among the Survey's rank and file. 'We can keep tabs on one another,' he said, 'through SCAR.'

For a while they talked of the work that Lockwood would be doing for SCAR. There would be no problem, the two men agreed, with the scientists. There never had been. Even during the Cold War and the Falklands War, research-workers from the USA and the Soviet Union and from Britain and Argentina had worked together, shared accommodation, pooled knowledge, and helped one another in emergency; the scientists had been far better ambassadors for peace than the politicians. But they both felt there might be problems with the Conservationists and with one or two governments. The Conservationists wanted the Antarctic Treaty given *more* teeth, and the continent turned into a World Heritage Area. One or two governments wanted it given *fewer* teeth, so that its natural resources could be exploited commercially. Pleasing everyone was not only going to be difficult; it was going to be impossible.

They stayed talking into the small hours. And after a fair number of whiskies, they shrugged aside the cares of the world and the problems of SCAR as a snake sloughs off the skin it has grown too big for, and what they were left with was what lay under the skin: half a lifetime of friendship.

Lockwood didn't drive home that night. He dossed down in the Survey's guest-suite. And about the last thing he was conscious of was the Director's hand on his shoulder, and a voice that seemed to come from a very long way away saying, '*Any*thing you want. *Any* time. We'll be here.'

*   *   *

It isn't true that if you retire to some corner of rural England you'll be ostracised by the locals. You'll only be

233

ostracised if you are forever comparing your new home with your old, or if you try to push in rather than fit in. Lockwood made neither of these mistakes. And the people of Porthallow soon accepted him for what he was: an idiosyncratic loner, who was fond of children, birds and dogs. It made things easier for him that he knew more than a little about the two subjects round which life in Porthallow revolved: the sea and the weather. Mutual wariness soon gave way to mutual tolerance, and, in time, tolerance gave way to affection. At the end of the year Lockwood wrote to the Director: *I've made a number of very good friends here, and now feel quite at home. So much so that, instead of looking forward to the SCAR meetings I'm thinking of giving them up, because they take me away from my dog, my seabirds and the village I seem to be falling more and more in love with.*

However, there came a time when the SCAR meetings took on an unexpected urgency. For the Antarctic Treaty was coming up for ratification, and several governments—including the British—were dragging their heels when it came to signing the protocol. Lockwood was in frequent touch with the Director about this, and a fragment of one of their conversations was soon to bring him sleepless nights.

'Things are looking better, James.' The Director was more optimistic than usual when he telephoned one evening towards the end of May. 'I reckon we'll sign. So long as nothing happens to rock the boat.'

'And what *might* rock the boat?'

'Why, you know. If we suddenly find the world's biggest oilfield. Or a volcanic vent full of diamonds. In our sector. The sort of thing that'll make the government say: "Hold on! That's ours. And we're going to exploit it."'

Such a discovery was, they both felt, highly improbable. Nonetheless Lockwood was conscious of a vague unease. It was as though he had a premonition that the ghosts from his past had been scotched, not laid, and were about to be resurrected.

*　　*　　*

He had just come in from watering his tomatoes when the telephone rang. 'Saint Keverne 130613.'

'Is that Mr James Lockwood?'

The voice was one he didn't recognise. 'It is.'

'Commander Burnett speaking. You don't know me. But I'm with MI6.'

He assumed that the call had something to do with his work for SCAR. Now how the devil, he wondered, have MI6 got involved? 'Yes, commander? What can I do for you?'

'Have you seen the morning papers?'

'No. We're out in the sticks here. The papers haven't come yet. Why do you ask?'

There was a longish pause, then: 'I apologise for jumping the gun. But when you *have* seen the papers, I think we ought to talk.'

He had a sudden sense of foreboding. 'Would you mind telling me what this is about?'

There was an even longer and slightly awkward silence, then the dozen words that turned his world upside down. 'I gather the Chileans have found a body. On the Antarctic Peninsula.'

It was as though he had been flung into an ice-cold bath. Flung into it, and held there. He closed his eyes. But no matter how tight he shut them he could still see the dismembered corpse being dug out from the ravine. And once again he could hear the crunch of his knife on bone, and taste the sweet-sourness of human flesh. And it came to him that time hadn't healed his wounds. It had merely covered them up.

Burnett suggested he came to see him next morning—

235

'say about 10 o'clock'—and Lockwood was too deep in shock to think of a way out.

As he put down the phone, he was conscious of a familiar tightness in his chest. He half-ran, half-hobbled to the local post-office-cum-newsagent and bought one copy of every paper they had.

The discovery of the body could hardly be said to have hit the headlines. Indeed, it was only when he got back to his cottage and spread the papers all over his sitting-room floor that he found mention of it. Then, on page 16 of *The Times*, under the heading 'News in Brief', he read:

ENTOMBED IN THE ICE

Chilean scientists, working from a research station on the Antarctic Peninsula, have discovered the body of an unknown seaman. It is thought the man may have been a member of the top secret Naval unit which operated in Antarctica during the Second World War.

He hoped some of the other reports might say more. But they didn't. There were no details of precisely where the body had been found, and no mention of it being dismembers—though that, he told himself, was hardly likely to have passed unnoticed. He paced up and down, telling himself to keep calm. But after a while he realised he was walking not up and down, but round and round: twenty times clockwise, twenty times anti-clockwise: like an animal in a cage. Don't panic, he told himself, you're not *really* back in the *behouden huis*. He made himself a pot of tea; but that didn't seem to do him much good, so he poured himself a whisky, but that didn't do much for him either. His mind seemed to have gone numb. After a great deal of agonising, he decided that all he could do was wait for

Commander Burnett, hear what he had to say, and play it by ear.

Sleep was a long time coming that night. And when he did at last drop off, he dreamed of things he hadn't dreamed of since he lay in his cabin in Benbecula.

Next morning the staff-car pulled up outside his cottage on the dot of 10 a.m. As Burnett got out, Lockwood thought for a moment he recognised him. Then he realised it was the species that was familiar, not the individual. For Burnett looked the same, spoke the same, and probably, he told himself, thought the same as so many of those other officers of the Royal Navy who, long ago, had suspected that more had gone on in Antarctica than met the eye. He thanked Lockwood very politely for seeing him at such short notice, and came straight to the point.

'What did you make of the newspaper reports?'

'They don't give much detail, do they?'

They sat by the window in Lockwood's sitting-room, looking out across the bay. It was a peaceful scene. Porthallow is sheltered from the prevailing wind, and there was hardly a ripple that morning on the sea; only a faint dappling beneath the cliffs leading up to The Manacles. But things are not always as innocent as they seem. The dappling was caused by a current which swirls seaward to lose itself among the jagged Manacle reefs, where wind, wave and current meet in a maelstrom the more deadly for the quiet water that leads up to it. So it was with their conversation: polite and innocuous on the surface, until suddenly and before he realised how it had happened Lockwood was swept into the vortex.

He reckoned he was parrying Burnett's questions without giving too much away, when the commander seemed suddenly to lose patience. 'I don't think you quite realise the position you're in.'

He wasn't sure what to say to that, so he said nothing.

The commander stubbed out his cigarette. 'Stalling and

saying 'I can't remember' isn't a card you can play any more. Not now we've found the body. Because what a story that body tells . . . ! But I've good news for you. We're not interested in what happened to your commanding officer. We don't want to know about that. What we're interested in is the uranium. So now—after all these years—will you please tell us where you found it?

Again his mind went blank. The worst of his nightmares was turning into reality. The secrets he had kept for 50 years were being brought into the open and flung into his face. He realised the commander was speaking to him.

'Can I have your attention, Mr Lockwood?'

'I can't remember,' he said.

'Let me tell you the story as we see it . . . In the 1930s the Colonial Office sent a team of geologists to survey the Antarctic Peninsula. Now I hope you've taken that in. We're talking about a British survey, by British geologists, in British territory, sponsored by the British government. They found traces of uranium. That didn't mean a lot at the time. But during the war uranium became important. So on Churchill's orders a Naval detachment was sent to look for it. Now I hope you've taken that in, too. We're talking about an official wartime mission, authorised at the very highest level. Now *you* know what happened to that mission. *We* can only guess. If there'd been no survivors, the Admiralty would probably have written the whole thing off, and that would have been that. But when they heard there *was* a survivor they said, "Good. We'll get him to tell us what happened." But you wouldn't tell them what happened, would you? You were asked again and again and again. And you said you'd lost your memory. Now why, I wonder, was that?'

'I can't remember,' he muttered.

Burnett looked at him critically. He could find no excuse for what Lockwood appeared to have done in the war; but he couldn't help, now, feeling sorry for him. 'It's no good any longer,' he said, 'saying you can't remember. Not now the body has turned up.'

He stared out of the window. The tide must have turned, he thought; the boats are swinging round on their anchors. 'I can't remember,' he said.

'Perhaps it will refresh your memory,' the commander went on, 'if I tell you there was a message on the body.'

He stared at him blankly.

Burnett spelt it out, as to a child one thinks is being deliberately obtuse. 'The petty officer was holding his diary in front of him. As though he wanted everyone to read it.'

It was several seconds before Lockwood realised what he was being told.

For fifty years it had been his ultimate nightmare that the half-eaten body of his commanding officer would be disinterred. When he heard a body had been found, he had taken it for granted it was Ede's. But it seemed this wasn't the case. It was Ramsden's. Things were happening too fast for him. He covered his face with his hands, and rocked to and fro like a child, and heard a voice that he didn't recognise as his own repeating over and over again 'I can't remember'.

They went on talking for more than an hour that morning. Lockwood, however, never had any clear recollection of what was said. For he was unable to think coherently, let alone answer questions coherently. In the end Burnett realised that he'd need more than one bite at the cherry to get what he wanted out of him. So choosing his words carefully, he suggested an adjournment.

And that is what they agreed: Lockwood should have 48 hours to think things over, then they should meet again for what the commander euphemistically called 'another chat'.

How Lockwood longed, during these 48 hours, for a friend to turn to, a shoulder to lean on. But there was a problem here: the same problem as he'd had to face in *Scoresby*'s sickbay, Hugh Dempster's consulting rooms, and the headland white with seabirds on Benbecula. If he divulged some secrets, he'd have to divulge others, and he'd very likely end up having to admit to cannibalism. That, he realised, was the nub. Rightly or wrongly, fifty years ago he had been determined not to admit to cannibalism; and he was determined not to admit to it now. He told himself that if he wasn't prepared to be honest with his friends and tell them *everything*, then he shouldn't involve them at all. So, not for the first time in his life, he sat down to work things out for himself.

He started making notes. By the end of the evening he'd exhausted two writing pads, his wastepaper-basket was overflowing, and all he'd come up with were two questions and two decisions. The questions were:

1 Exactly what had Ramsden written in his diary?
2 What did the Admiralty want from him, and why?

The decisions were:

1 He would never admit to cannibalism.
2 He would never disclose the whereabouts of the uranium.

When, 48 hours later, Burnett was once again ensconced in his sitting-room, and making polite comments about the view over Porthallow harbour, Lockwood put the first of his questions to him.

The commander, it seemed, had anticipated this. He opened his briefcase, and took out half-a-dozen A4 pages, neatly typed. 'These are the extracts from the diary that'll particularly interest you,' he said. 'They indicate that when Ramsden fell into the crevasse, your commanding officer was still very much alive—whereas you pretended he was dead. And they prove that you found uranium and were bringing back samples—whereas you pretended you knew nothing about it.'

He looked at the flawless, double-spaced typing. 'How do I know this is a true record?'

It was a mistake; and he regretted the words even as he heard himself saying them.

'Mr Lockwood!' There was both outrage and contempt in the commander's voice. 'It is *you* who play games and tell lies, not the Admiralty. If you insist, we can surely show you the diary. It has been flown back to England. And it's being held as evidence, in case there's a Court of Inquiry.'

A Court of Inquiry was the most terrible of his nightmares. As though to block out even the thought of it, he focused his attention on the extracts from Ramsden's diary. And as he read, the years rolled back, and once again the three of them were jam-packed together in their tent, and he was asking the petty officer not to disclose where they'd found the uranium—'in case the diary gets into the wrong hands'. It was ironic, he thought, that the diary had fallen into very different hands from those he had been afraid of at the time. But he was thankful nonetheless to find that Ramsden had—as ever—obeyed orders. There were many references to the uranium-bearing rocks that they were carrying with them, but no hint of where they had come from.

He handed the pages back. 'Thank you. Now what do you want from me?'

'We want to know where you found the uranium.'

'But why? After all these years?'

Burnett was exasperated. When he'd been given the job of extracting the truth from Lockwood about what had happened to the special detachment, he had immersed himself for days in the files in Admiralty archives. He was familiar with everything said at the debriefings; familiar too with the doubts that had been felt by many of the Sea Lords over parts of Lockwood's story. And when he combined the evidence of the files with the evidence that had now come to light in Ramsden's diary, he reckoned, not to put too fine a point to it, that Lockwood was a traitor. How else would one describe a serving officer who, in wartime, for reasons known only to himself, lies about the death of his commanding officer and withholds vital information about his mission from his superiors? He said quietly, 'You're in no position to ask questions. I've been ordered to get to the bottom of the Ede affair, and I intend to carry out my orders. I hope we can do this on a person-to-person basis. But if we can't, I shall convene a Court of Inquiry.'

He shut his eyes.

Burnett felt a stir of pity; but not enough to deter him from doing his job. 'I've been told,' he said, 'to offer you a deal. You tell us where the uranium is. We'll drop inquiries about what happened to Ede.'

His first thought was, 'It's a lifeline! Grab it!' Then he asked himself why the lifeline should have been thrown. And a suspicion he didn't care for took root in his mind, and, having taken root, burgeoned. 'Why,' he said, 'are you so interested in the uranium?'

'Because it's valuable.'

'But not *that* valuable. Nowadays.'

'Well, I suppose there *is* another reason. The Ede file has been festering in our archives for years—like a running sore. Now we've got Ramsden's diary, we've a chance to get to the bottom of things. Tidy up the loose ends. Close the file.'

He wasn't convinced. 'Surely it would be simpler to let sleeping dogs lie?'

Burnett's patience snapped. He had to admit that on the face of it Lockwood seemed a well-balanced, mildly-distinguished and rather pleasant old man. But this didn't alter the fact that 50 years ago he appeared to have been a cross between a war criminal and a traitor; and in the commander's eyes he deserved to be held to account. 'I must ask you,' he said, 'to give me a straight answer to a straight question. Where did you find the uranium?'

He screwed shut his eyes. 'I can't remember,' he whispered. 'I can't remember, I can't remember, I can't remember.'

Burnett put the typewritten pages back in his briefcase. He stood up. 'You give me no option,' he said. 'I shall ask for a Court of Inquiry.'

Lockwood knew he wasn't bluffing. 'Hang on! I need time to think.'

'How much time?'

'Say a week.'

'Too long.'

'But I've things to do. People to talk to.'

Burnett hesitated. 'Right,' he said slowly. 'I'll contact you a week today. And please'—almost as though he was ashamed of what he was doing, he put his hand on Lockwood's shoulder—'don't make things hard for yourself.'

*   *   *

When he had gone, Lockwood stood staring out of the window and seeing things that weren't there. I know why they want the uranium, he thought. If they find uranium, it *will* be like finding the world's biggest oilfield. Or a volcanic vent full of diamonds. It'll give them the chance to say 'Hold on! That's ours. And we're going to exploit it.' And that will give them an excuse not to sign the Treaty. And that will be the end of Antarctica as a continent of peace.

It came to him that he was back where he had been fifty years ago: the keeper of secrets which were likely to have a very considerable bearing on the future of the continent that he loved. He had safeguarded her secrets then. How, he asked himself, could he do otherwise now?

The next week was—mentally if not physically—the most difficult in Lockwood's life. He didn't spend sleepless nights agonising over his decision. He had made that. That was settled. What he did agonise over was the inevitable consequence of his decision: the Court of Inquiry.

In recent years there had been a number of war crime trials, and his feelings about them had always been equivocal. He had felt sorry for the often frail old men in the dock, but had told himself there was no time-barrier to justice, and the accused probably deserved to be brought to account. He had noticed how much interest—and indeed how much hatred, bitterness and passion—some of these trials evoked. And he told himself it would very likely be the same with his. He could visualise the headlines: 'War Hero Accused of Cannibalism'. For he reckoned the prosecution would do all they could to discredit him, in their efforts to make him disclose the information they seemed to want so badly. I'll have to get a good lawyer, he thought. But then he thought again. For how could he expect a lawyer (or anyone else) to help him if he wasn't prepared to tell them the truth, the whole truth and nothing but the truth—including the truth about his cannibalism? Perhaps, he thought, I can defend myself.

How he longed, that week, for a friend he could talk things over with. It wasn't that he was short of friends. For no sooner had reports of the body in the ice appeared in the press, then people not only from the Survey but from all over the world started ringing him up: 'Do you know who the man was?' they would ask him. 'Was he one of your chaps?' Uncertain how to ward off his friends without appearing churlish, he fell back on a stock reply: 'It all happened a very long time ago,' he heard himself saying, 'and it's something I want to forget.' He knew he wouldn't be allowed to forget for long; but at least for the moment the ambivalence of his reply spared him the sort of questions he didn't want to answer.

Sometimes, after a particularly difficult phone call, he

would be tempted to throw in the sponge and give Burnett the information he wanted. He would tell himself that uranium wasn't all that important nowadays, and the fact that it lay close to the surface of Antarctica, apparently crying out to be extracted, probably wouldn't be enough to dissuade the British government from ratifying the Treaty. But at the back of his mind was always a seed of doubt: a lingering suspicion that the uranium *might* be the last straw which would tip the scales against ratification. For he knew that the idea of opening up the Antarctic for commercial exploitation had powerful advocates.

What strengthened his resolve in these moments of doubt were the images (or to use an old-fashioned word, visions) which had meant so much to him 50 years ago, and which now kept coming back with a vividness that time had sharpened rather than diminished. And one moment he would be looking out on a narrow seaway, lined by flat-topped bergs and snow-covered mountains; and penguins in their hundreds of thousands would be nesting along the shore, and seals would be somersaulting in the water, and birds would be wheeling in the clear blue sky; and the bedlam of their courting, mating, feeding and rearing their young was like a *Te Deum*, an affirmation of life. And next moment the scene would change, and he would be staring down, retching, at the remains of the detachment's hut and the snow incarnadined and headless corpses, and the only movement was a coil of woodsmoke spiralling up from the charred timbers, and over everything hung the silence of death.

What's the point of waiting a week? he thought. I've made up my mind. I'm not going to change it. He telephoned Burnett, and said that he was sorry, he still couldn't remember where they had found the uranium.

*   *   *

A few days later he got a phone call from the Director. 'James! What's this about a Court of Inquiry?'

He had hoped that the convening of the Court would be done discreetly; but this, it seemed, wasn't to be. I'm told it'll be happening,' he said, 'in about a month.'

'Is this something to do with that body in the ice?'

'It is.'

A long pause, then, 'I'm coming to see you.'

He was saying, 'Really that isn't necessary,' when he realised the Director had hung up.

It wasn't what he wanted. He reckoned a *tête-à-tête* was bound to be difficult, because there were so many things he was not prepared to talk about, even with his best friend; he could foresee yet more questions that he didn't want to answer. However, their get-together turned out to be a good deal less stressful than he had feared. The Director made it clear he had come to help not to pry— 'tell me as much or as little as you like,' he had said—and on this basis Lockwood was glad of his companionship. It was some time before they got down to the nitty-gritty. In fact it was not until they were returning that evening from the Five Pilchards that Lockwood said matter-of-factly: 'You needn't worry about what I'll tell the Court.'

'If you're not worried, then neither am I.'

'I've taken advice. And I've got the answer.'

'Which is?'

'I shall defend myself. And I'll say nothing. I'll exercise my right to silence.'

The Director was somewhat taken aback. 'Is that a good idea?'

'You obviously don't think so!'

'I just don't know, James. Lawyers can be the very devil. A clever one will make even the squeaky-clean seem dirty. And'—he hesitated—'if you don't answer questions, won't that give a bad impression?'

'Maybe. But that's not what matters.'

246

The Director decided to keep his doubts to himself. He took his friend by the elbow, guiding him round a puddle in the street. 'All I can say is, whatever you do, it's not only me who's behind you. It's every man and every woman in the Survey. Any time you need us, we'll be rooting for you.'

He was more touched than he cared to admit. He was touched too by the concern shown by his friends in Porthallow.

Not that he spent a great deal of time in Porthallow in the weeks immediately before the Court's first sitting. For he decided to go to London. He moved into a friend's flat in Lambeth, so that he could have easy access to the files in Admiralty archives. For although he had decided to remain silent throughout the proceedings, he wanted to know what evidence was likely to be produced.

He was amazed at how bulky the Ede files were. They took up almost the whole of one shelf in Room 102, where documents categorised 'Confidential' were kept under nominal security. As he began to thumb through the mass of letters, signals, orders and requisitions, the years rolled back, and once again he was the only living human being within 500 miles: alone with the ice, the aurora and the clamour of seabirds. And as he stared at the faintly-yellowing pages, it came to him that the past was more important to him than the present.

He became, for a short period, a regular habitué of Room 102; and the time that he spent there wading through the documents enabled him to tie up a number of loose ends . . . He had often wondered why—since the uranium was apparently of such vital importance—the Navy hadn't questioned him more rigorously on his return to England. It now became clear from the files that this was because he had had a protector. *In my opinion*, Hugh Dempster had written, *it would be wrong to interrogate this officer further since it would be injurious to his mental stability.*

You might also like to consider the point that if the facts of a further interrogation were made public, this would do no good to the Navy's image, since we could be accused of flouting those principles of mercy, decency and respect for the individual for which we are supposed to be fighting. It made him realise just how indebted he was to the psychiatrist. I'm glad, he thought, I answered that Christmas card he sent me!

One other problem was solved. It had always surprised Lockwood that there had apparently been no further attempt, after the war, to find the uranium. He now discovered there *had* been an attempt, but that few people knew about it, because it had failed. It was known that the original '30s survey had found uranium close to the surface. The post-war survey had therefore made soundings to a depth of no more than 50 feet. And 50 feet was no longer deep enough. Because in the glacial valley where, during the war, Ede's geiger counters had gone berserk, the ice-fall had collapsed—brought down by the same earth tremor that had demolished Lockwood's *behouden huis*. The uranium was therefore no longer near the surface; it was buried under 200 feet of glacial ice.

He was pleased to have these points cleared up. What wasn't so pleasing was that the records showed there were people at the Admiralty who, right from the start, had suspected Lockwood was guilty not only of cannibalism but also of murder. He could see the rationale of their thinking . . . Three members of the Ede detachment had survived the burning down of their hut; but only one— and he desperately short of food—had survived the following winter. The one survivor was unable (or was it unwilling?) to say what had happened to the others, or where their bodies were. So perhaps he had eaten them. Or even killed them and eaten them. That would explain his efforts to pretend he had lost his memory. It would explain, too, why he was so reluctant to talk about certain aspects of what had gone on in the Antarctic . . . The finding of

Ramsden's body and Ramsden's diary might have cleared him of one crime, but it must have seemed to implicate him more deeply in the other. It might now be obvious that he hadn't eaten his petty officer; but it seemed increasingly obvious that he must have eaten his commanding officer. Why else should he have pretended he was dead when he was still very much alive?

Lockwood could see that the Court would feel he had a great deal of explaining to do. And if he remained silent there was only one conclusion they were likely to come to.

You can escape all this, a voice whispered. All you have to do is tell them where you found the uranium.

*   *   *

A week before the Court was scheduled for its first sitting, Lockwood returned to Porthallow. He felt he needed a haven before the storm.

It was not an easy week. The Director was on the phone a couple of times about the Antarctic Treaty. 'Bloody politicians,' he muttered in an uncharacteristic moment of frustration. 'They *still* haven't ratified. It's as though they're waiting for something. God knows what.' Lockwood could hazard a pretty good guess as to what it was they were waiting for; and next morning, as though to confirm his suspicions, Burnett was on the phone to him. 'Mr Lockwood! Would you please spare me a moment of your time?'

'Of course.'

'I want to make one last effort to persuade you to change your mind.'

'Sorry,' he said. 'My mind is made up.'

The commander was on the phone for the better part of half-an-hour, using the well-tried combination of carrot and stick. He said that if Lockwood co-operated and told them where the uranium was, then the Court would bring no charges of cannibalism or murder. But if he didn't co-operate, the Court would crucify him.

Eventually Lockwood's patience snapped. 'I can't remember,' he shouted. 'I can't remember, I can't remember, I can't remember.' He was still shouting 'I can't remember', when he realised he had slammed down the telephone.

For the rest of the day he felt very much alone. For there was no one with whom he felt he could share *all* his secrets, no one he could talk to, completely openly, about both his cannibalism and the uranium. Never, he told himself, had there been anyone close enough to him to share *those* secrets with.

The idea came to him that evening as he was listening to a programme on the radio about the songs of Stephen Foster. He told himself it was a ridiculous idea—bizarre would hardly be too strong a word for it. Yet it kept nagging away at him. And that night he dreamed of things he hadn't dreamed of since he had lain in his cabin on Benbecula.

By morning his idea had become an *idée fixe*. He rang Directory Enquiries; and when at last he had got the number he wanted and the person he wanted, he said: 'I wonder if you can help me? I want to try and trace someone I served with in the war . . .'

He knew the odds were against him; and he could hardly believe his luck when, 48 hours later, he was given an address which had been checked and checked again. He was so surprised to get the address, he wasn't sure what to do with it! In the end he decided the best thing would be a letter.

It was by far the most difficult thing he ever had to write. To start with he found himself watering things down so as not to distress her. Yet he knew very well that watering things down negated the whole purpose of the exercise. So in the end he told her everything.

When the letter was finished, he was conscious of a feeling that surprised him: a feeling of peace. It was as though, like Atlas freed of the world, he had sloughed off an almost physical burden.

He had been vaguely aware, while he was writing, of the moan of wind and the lash of rain. But now, looking out of his sitting-room window, he saw that the rain had stopped, the clouds had lifted, and the sky was bright with starlight and moonlight. All that was left of the storm was a bludgeoning wind.

He was tired; but he felt too elated and in a curious way too happy to sleep. What he felt like was a walk.

His dog could hardly believe her luck when at 1 a.m. he started putting on his boots. She rolled onto her back and started chewing at his laces. But when he opened the front door a strange thing happened. She wouldn't come with him. She crept back, as though afraid, and lay down on her blanket at the side of the Aga.

Now that, he thought as he headed up the cliff-path, is a funny thing. She's never acted like that before.

*　　*　　*

It was a splendid night for walking, and he decided to follow the cliff-path to a headland that looked out on The Manacles; the reefs were always a spectacular sight in the aftermath of a storm. It took him an hour to get to the spot from where he could look down on them, and they were indeed a sight worth looking at: great waves one moment streaming over the rocks like cataracts of milk, next moment sluicing back to leave them glistening with phosphorescence: a mill-race in which nothing could live. Half-a-dozen steps, he thought, and there would be no more problems, no more pain. He sat down near the edge of the cliff.

The scene reminded him of Antarctica: all brightness and light and sort of untarnished. He shut his eyes, and once again he was in the familiar channel with the seals somersaulting, and penguins braying and seabirds wheeling. He waited for the scene to change, as it had always changed before. But this time there was no vision of the apocalypse; this time his friends the creatures of the wild stayed with him. He couldn't think why. And he didn't want to try to work it out. It was enough that they were there, and he was with them and at peace.

He would have sat there till sunrise if he hadn't felt suddenly cold. As he got to his feet, he realised his mouth was dry and he was short of breath. I've been overdoing it, he told himself; I'd better get to bed. He was about half-way home when he remember his dog. It was funny, he thought, how she had seemed suddenly afraid and reluctant to come with him; he hoped she wasn't sickening for something. Thinking of his dog, he didn't pay much attention to where he was going.

The gulls were sleeping at the side of the path, and he nearly trod on them. They took off, with a clatter of wings, from almost under his feet.

As he leaped back, startled, pain seared through his chest, and gulls and cliffs and sea and sky coalesced into a great white net into which he was falling, falling, falling, and the net, by some process he couldn't understand, became metamorphosed to snows of Antarctica, and he reached out his arms to welcome them, and fell into them and through them and into some place beyond.

He was unconscious before he crumpled face-down across the path, and dead before the frightened gulls had flown full circle and returned to their nest.

'Home is the Sailor . . .'

The Antarctic Treaty was indefinitely extended by a protocol signed on 2 October, 1991, in Madrid. One of the last nations to sign was the British. A new clause was the introduction of a 50-year moratorium on mining.

* * *

Soon after the Treaty was ratified, the Survey's research vessel RRS *Bransfield* left for Antarctica. She carried her usual quota of scientists, equipment and stores, plus a special addition to her manifest which was there by order of the Director . . .

About a week after Lockwood's death the Director's secretary got a phone call she wasn't sure how to deal with. 'A Mrs Jean Martin wants to talk to you,' she told him. 'She says it's personal.'

The name didn't ring a bell, but he asked his secretary to put her through.

The Director and Jean Martin talked for quite some time, and as a result of their conversation Jean arrived next afternoon at the Survey's headquarters in Cambridge. She hadn't lost her freckles, or her shyness, or her directness; and the years had been kind to her. 'It's very good of you,' she said, 'to see me.'

'I'm glad to meet you. A friend of James is a friend of mine.' He gestured to a chair. 'Have you brought the letter?'

She took a large brown envelope out of her handbag. 'I did warn you! There's fifteen pages!'

'No problem. But are you sure you *want* me to read it?'

'Please. It's not'—she hesitated—'personal. At least not in the usual way. I don't think you'll find it embarrassing.'

He smiled. 'That's not quite what I meant, Mrs Martin. What I meant was James has obviously told *you* things that he didn't tell *me*. Are you sure you want me to know these things?'

She nodded.

So he read the letter.

When he had finished it, he walked to the window and stood looking out at the slim grey spires and the big flat fields, and thought of the times he and James Lockwood had looked at the same scene together. He was more moved than he cared to admit. 'He was a good man,' he said at last. 'So . . . what do you want me to do with the letter?'

'I hoped,' she said, 'you'd keep it. As a record. I mean, you've archives and that?'

'You don't want it published?'

She shook her head. 'If he'd wanted it published, he wouldn't have sent it to me.'

'And you don't want to keep it?'

'No.' She sensed his surprise, and said quietly: 'I've a husband and children and grandchildren. They're my life now. And I'm happy. I don't *want* a ghost from the past. But I *do* want to be sure his letter's in good hands. And never ever lost.'

'Never is a long time! But I give you my word. We'll feel privileged to have it in our archives.'

She thanked him as though she meant it, and he thought that was probably it. But after a moment's hesitation she said unexpectedly: 'I hope you don't mind me asking. But where is he going to be buried?'

It was a question he had given some thought to. 'Well, he didn't have any close relatives, you know. I'm his executor. So I suppose it's up to me . . . I thought of Porthallow. He loved it there.'

254

'He loved Antarctica more.'

He was considerably taken aback. 'You're not suggesting we bury him in Antarctica!'

'Well, I was.'

'I'm afraid,' he said, 'that's out of the question.'

He expected her to drop the idea, but she didn't. 'I know,' she said, 'it would be expensive. But if it *is* possible, my husband thinks we could afford it.'

'Well, it certainly *would* be expensive. But that's not the real problem.' He explained to her in some detail how everything that went on in Antarctica was meticulously scrutinised and controlled, and how scientists were going to extraordinary lengths to make sure the continent remained unpolluted. 'So you see, *nothing* can be buried there. Even the scientists' excrement and urine have to be collected and flown out!'

He hoped that now she realised it was impossible she would forget it. Instead, she looked at him very straight and said, 'I was afraid there might be difficulties. But it's something that *ought* to happen.'

'Mrs Martin! Can you give me one good reason why he ought to be buried in the Antarctic?'

'Because,' she said, 'that's what he would have wanted.'

For a second time he got up and walked to the window. She's right, he thought. She's right. And what else is there to say? 'I'm very much afraid,' he said, 'you may be asking the impossible. But I'll do what I can.'

She didn't press him for promises. She got up and held out her hand. 'Thank you, sir. For everything.' She hesitated, then added shyly. 'He wasn't an easy man to help, was he? When he was alive? Maybe now he's dead we'll have more luck.'

*　　*　　*

Human beings think of the tip of the Antarctic Peninsula as cold, wet and windswept: one of the most Godforsaken

255

places on earth. Yet for tens of millions of penguins, seals and seabirds it is the womb in which they are conceived and the cradle in which they are nurtured: a place not Godforsaken but Godsent. So perhaps it is fitting that human beings never set eyes on Lockwood's grave. Only his friends the creatures of the Antarctic see, close to the site of his *behouden huis*, the simple slab of granite, with its inscription:

JAMES CALDER LOCKWOOD

1920–1991

A lover of Antarctica

'Here he lies where he longed to be;
Home is the sailor, home from sea,
And the hunter home from the hill.'